PRAISE FOR A SATCHEL OF RICHARDS

"An engaging lust-to-love comedy of errors with two charming leads."

KIRKUS REVIEWS

"Impressively original, deftly crafted, and a fun read from cover to cover, *A Satchel of Richards* by Lee Taylor is a perfect pick for the legions of Rom-Com fans who like their characters memorable and their plot lines presented with many an unexpected twist and turn... [I]t is especially and unreservedly recommended for community library Contemporary Romance collections."

MIDWEST BOOK REVIEW

"Compulsively readable romance. [P]layfulness dot her breezy-and, in a handful of scenes, genuinely sexy-prose... *A Satchel of Richards* may poke light fun at the romance genre, but it fulfills its requirements with infectious gusto."

PUBLISHERS WEEKLY BOOKLIFE

A SATCHEL OF RICHARDS

A Satchel of Richards

LEE TAYLOR

PERIWINK PRESS

Paperback edition, January 2026

Interior Design Allison Capps & Author Photo by Olivia Eades

Manufactured in the United States of America

1-14971045791

Library of Congress Control Number: 1-14971045791

ISBN 979-8-9929604-0-2 (pbk)

ISBN 979-8-9929604-1-9 (ebook)

For The Lovers

We that are true lovers run into strange capers.

— Touchstone, the fool

Act 2 Scene 4

As You Like It

William Shakespeare

PART 1

BRIDGET

ONE

HUNTER'S MOON

I pick my way across what could best be described as a moor. Aren't moors boggy? Shrubs pull at my long dress. Heather, I think, but honestly I haven't a clue, having never been on a moor before. My gown—not the sleeping but the dancing kind— is soaked to the knees, and clings uncomfortably to my calves. From the empire waistline, I'm thinking Jane Austenish times.

Looking up to get my bearings, I stumble over a mound of grayish-purple grass to find everything languishing in varied shades of gray. I'm alone except for a giant moon that peeks in and out of wispy clouds that drift lazily past its sallow light.

I trudge on, as there is nothing else to do. A wolf calls mournfully in the distance.

The whole thing is *Wuthering Heights* meets *The Hound of the Baskervilles,* which is okay, I guess. I do love Brontë, but I'm on the fence about Doyle—great book, but didn't he steal the manuscript and murder someone over it? No, thank you. If anyone's going to join me on this boggy jaunt, I'll take a dark, broody hero, not a bloodthirsty hound. I'm in no mood for a nightmare.

Wait.

A figure appears in the distance.

It's coming closer.

And closer.

Closer still.

Shit!

I jerk back and almost fall into the mire, but he catches me. His hand is warm, and strong, and kinda beautiful, and definitely attached to a he. Unfortunately, a hoodie obscures his face, not really period appropriate, but what the hell, I like the shape of him—like an hourglass but sharply defined—two triangles meeting in the middle. There's something so compelling about it.

Wait, I *know* this shape.

Oh my god.

It's Beach Runner.

Closer than he's ever been before. So close I can smell the sweat on his skin, and it's not a bad thing, not a bad thing at all. It's a *may I please lick it off you* kind of thing.

Whew, pheromones in a dream. Pretty cool.

Now, if only my lucid dreaming came with agency, because I want to see what's hidden in the dark—his face, likely chiseled— his eyes dark—his hair, darker. I want so bad to push back his hood because I've spent so many mornings imagining him as he runs the beach, but somehow I know he'll outshine even my imagination. And still my impotent-ass hands remain stubbornly by my side.

Hold up.

Something's happening.

He drops to one knee.

In a bog?

Slowly pushing up the sleeve of my dress his soft manicured

fingers send a tingle dancing down my skin all the way to my ruined slippers. The moment is charged.

Will he lean in, kiss my hand, pull me into the mire, lick my elbow?

Wait. What?

He's licking my elbow. This is a new kink.

EARTH TO BRIDGET.

Like a voice-over, it breaks in to let me know something's happening in the real. And with that realization, the dream dissipates like a fog, and Beach Runner disappears, even as my actual hand reaches out for him.

Damn!

So close.

"Sally Girl," I moan, opening my eyes to see my Irish wolfhound dancing by the edge of the bed, her tongue lapping at my arm. "It was just about to get good!"

Which is probably a lie, as even in my sexiest dreams, I never get to actually *have* sex. A true shame, as I bet the dream version would be much better than anything I've had in real life. Reality rarely lives up to my imagination.

And to think, my extended dry spell could have been sated by Beach Runner, of all men. Beach Runner who moves so steadily and strong, setting a brutal pace in sand I can barely walk in. I bet he has the endurance to take me where no man has ever taken me before.

"Ow-ooooooooo!"

"Shhhh," I admonish her.

I can't believe it slipped my mind that tonight is a full moon. If I'd remembered, I would not have stayed up too late watching the best half of *Sixteen Candles*, most of *Ferris Bueller*, and all of *Real Genius*. Unable to turn it off, despite the time, not only because Val Kilmer was hot back in the day, but because the popcorn-destroys-the-house scene is so outrageous it always makes me taste butter.

Now I'll be comatose at work tomorrow, the day after fall break, when the kids will be bonkers on Halloween candy. But there's nothing to do. I will not be angry at my sweet pup, who is wagging her tail so hard I don't know how it stays attached. It's instinct, I tell myself. She can't help it. And she nudges me with her long nose, as *HUNT* rattles around in my brain.

Yes, I know, it's absurd, but for some reason, I can hear my dog think.

"Okay. Okay," I say.

I scratch her chin, tilting her head out of the way to see my kitty-cat clock, the only pet my mother permitted me as a child, with its big blinking eyes and wagging tail, happily telling me it's 4:45 a.m.

Fuck.

Rolling over I sit up with as little effort as possible, like at the end of a yoga class, to find Sally Girl's wolfish grin an inch from my face. This smile makes me love her all the more but tends to make others think she's about to eat them for lunch.

HUNT!

"Give me a minute," I beg, and she relents with yet another nudge on my shoulder, practically knocking me back to bed. Then she pads across the floor and uses her mouth to turn the doorknob that is at her eye height.

They told me she would be big. Her paws as a pup were almost as large as my hands, but I still marvel at her size. And yet, no one told me when I adopted her I would be a zombie from lack of sleep after every full moon. No one told me she would eat her weight in the most expensive shipped-in-by-the-pound raw food in the world, and yet it wouldn't have mattered. The moment I saw her slate-gray eyes, the exact same shade as mine, I knew we were meant to be. Well, that and the fact that the word *HOME* assaulted my brain.

That was the first time it happened, her speaking directly into my mind. Now it happens all the time. That first time, I dismissed it as my imagination—I have an active one, being a writer and all.

Are you a writer?

Oh, shut up. It's too early for that line of questioning, I tell my inner critic, who always sounds exactly like Mother.

HUNT.

Damn, it's getting crowded in here.

I roll out of bed, happy that Sally Girl's voice is so simple—so carpe diem. I wish my inner voice were so sure of what it wants and less snarky for one. But once Mother has a bone, she can't stop chewing, so while brushing my teeth, I try to remember the last creative thing I wrote. All I can come up with is a seating chart. It *was* color coded.

And while we're talking about the last time …

No. Just no!

I spit.

It's *way* early for this shit. Seems like I need the peace of the beach as much as my dog, and thanks to my brand-new freshly painted butter-yellow St. Pete beach house, all I have to do is cross the street. That puts a smile on my face even career disappointments and a perpetually unsatisfactory sex life cannot diminish.

Best of all, I did it myself. No help from boring glad-you're-gone Gill. No help from Mother or her husband number four. With what Sweetie left me, I managed to buy a home all by myself. And as small as it is, seven hundred and forty-nine square feet, it's mine.

I dig yesterday's clothes—the ones I rarely wear to yoga—

from the hamper, already in a better mood, and rush to pull them on before—

"Ow-oooooooo!"

—she wakes the neighbors. So far, they don't hate me. They don't like me or even know me, but that's much better than how my last apartment neighbors felt about me, thanks to Miss Howls-A-Lot who got me evicted, forcing me back into my teenage bedroom while my loan closed. Fun times.

Grabbing a canned coffee and Sally Girl's pink reflective leash on my way out, I open the door and WOW.

The moon cuts a line of light across the ocean to my front door. A golden carpet.

And I get to live here.

On cloud nine, I ignore the lime-green plastic monstrosity that is my front yard. At least the flamingos no longer line the walk. What *were* the snowbirds who sold me this place thinking? Is it so hard to mow thirty square feet of grass? So much for ignoring, but I mean, who puts astroturf in their front yard?!

Floridiots.

Don't be mean. You're one of them.

But I do wish I still had some of the nest egg Sweetie left me in the pickle jar she kept under the sink. Thankfully, it was industrial-sized, stuffed to the brim with Benjamins. She probably got it at the Cuban café where she worked until the day she left us. But I'd give it all back—the house, the beach, all of it —to have Sweetie back again.

I have no idea how she managed to save so much, and I feel guilty my grandmother might have kept herself from some treat in life in order to leave it to me. But using the pickle stash, that still smelled like dill the day I delivered it for counting, to get my home seemed fitting, as wherever Sweetie was always felt like home.

But after a down payment, closing costs, and new paint, I'm left with an anemic savings account, so the sod will have to wait. And even though I have a bit of retirement, having taught for ten years, I can't touch it.

Hopefully, my Christmas bonus will be enough to pay for grass. Oh, and a new bed. I desperately need one of those. Then everything will be perfect.

Like this morning.

I look both ways and cross the single street that separates me from the beach. The tide is low, the wind soft. I glance left and right, not really expecting company, and release Sally Girl to lope, run, paw, and play on the deserted beach. Her shadow looming large and small as she frolics under the moon that so calls to her.

It's not quite warm, but close enough for the first of November. I do so love the winters here. Love everything about my life here.

Everything?

Okay, not everything. I plop down on the sand, suddenly exhausted by the mere suggestion of my job.

When did every Monday become a chore? Every Friday— every holiday—a reprieve, every summer a lifesaver? Sometimes I look at my life, at myself, and wonder, Who are you? Like I'm an anime avatar of myself with those too-big eyes and tiny feet. And who I am seems like something I should know by the age of thirty-three.

Baby girl, you'll know when you're ready to know.

Hey, Sweetie.

Her warm, croaky voice is my favorite in the world. Or not *in* the world anymore, but it's still my favorite. And after how many hours we spent on this beach together while I was growing up, it makes sense this is the only place where I can reliably hear her. When she comes to me like this, if I close my eyes, it's almost as if she's still with me.

Couldn't get rid of me if you tried.

I miss you so much.

Me too, baby girl, and not to parrot your mother—heaven actually forbids—but Red, when was the last time ...

I laugh. Those two can say the exact same thing, but it always hits differently.

Been busy, Sweetie.

Never too busy to get busy.

You're incorrigible.

I wait for her response, moving my fingers through the soft sand, making letters, hoping she'll come back. Our little interludes never last long enough.

Like she can sense my sadness, Sally Girl runs back to me, screeching to a halt so fast she sprays sand. Tilting her head, like she's asking a question, her eyes level with mine.

HURT

I scratch behind her shaggy ears. "Everything's fine. Go have fun."

She takes me at my word and digs a hole I'll have to fill in later to make sure no one breaks a leg. Then a gull squawks, and she's off again.

I look down into the hole.

With those big paws, she made it to the waterline in no time. Grabbing a handful of wet sand, I squeeze, and drip by drip, make a tower, like Mom and I used to back in the day. Before husbands two through four. Before she had money for much else to entertain me. Before my mother was so appropriate, so proper. When she had to leave me with Sweetie, even on the weekends, so she could work. Of course, that was fine by me because the only thing more fun than building a drip castle complete with shell guards and feather flags with Mom was watching the moat fill and yelling *Fe Fi Fo Fum!* while trampling it with Sweetie. That unbridled destruction gave me such glee.

You're so careful these days, Red, Sweetie's voice admonishes me.

"Adulting. I'm adulting," I say to the light breeze coming off the Gulf.

You're never too old to be young.

If Sweetie had a motto, that was it. The day she died, she was younger than me in so many ways. When did I get so jaded, so unsatisfied? When did I settle? I'm so much more like my mother than I ever wanted to be.

I notice gray light marking the sky, signaling it's time to go. I push sand into the hole with my feet and call out to Sally Girl against the wind, but she doesn't hear me. So I stand, stiff from what must have been more than an hour of staring off into space, and walk toward her. That's when I see him. Running in the distance.

I can't believe I missed him. This of all mornings. He must have passed right by. Always gray sweats, always hood up.

I've lived at the beach for only a few months, but if I'm on the beach in the mornings, which, thanks to Sally Girl, I often am, it seems like I see him going one way or the other. Lately, I've been hoping for a big breeze to knock off his hood—show me Beach Runner—but this being the west coast of Florida, we rarely get those kinds of winds without a hurricane and I certainly do not want to see one of those!

Oh well, maybe I'll figure out a way to pull down that blasted hood when I see him next in my dreams.

———

Eight exhausting hours later, my favorite student, Elizabeth Lee, pounds erasers outside my classroom window while I wait, even more impatiently than my students, for the final bell. So when Karen, the school secretary, comes over the PA system, I barely pay attention. That is, until I hear my name.

"Bridget Stanton. Report to the principal's office."

There is a sharpness to it, which is hard to pull off as the PA system makes everyone sound like they have a head cold. And it's strange. Karen and I are, if not friends, at least friendly.

The tenor of the request is not lost on the twenty-six wide-eyed eight-year-olds looking up at me. Thomas, a preppy brat I secretly hate, whose shirts are never without the Brooks Brothers logo, singsongs, "Miss Stanton is in trouble." I scratch my neck to hide the bird I'm shooting him and his ludicrous lamb-that-looks-like-a-pig swinging from a ribbon.

"It's probably a parent issue," my teacher's assistant says.

I roll my eyes as if to say, It's always a parent issue.

She nods and adds, "Go on. I've got this."

On the way out, I pass Elizabeth Lee juggling erasers in the hall, and the way she looks at me, you would think I was headed for the block.

TWO

RUG BURN

Sixteen hours later, I'm mopping up the turbulence-spilled Bloody Mary soaking into my crisp white button-down thinking what the hell am I doing on this plane?

"Miss."

The pity-filled face of the flight attendant regards me while her hand holds out a can of LaCroix.

"Thank you," I say. "I'd like to try to save it. It's my favorite." I pour the lime-flavored water on a little square napkin, but most of it rolls off to soak my skirt.

"Sorry. Those aren't very absorptive, but I hope it helps."

"Me too," I reply. "I like the black stitching on the collar and the double cuffs. It's my adult shirt." My seatmate groans. "I wear it to all my book launches," I follow up with a groan of my own. "But I bet it's pretty pissed I pulled it out of the closet after six years to do this to it." I dab at the shirt with another wet napkin. "But I guess shirts don't get pissed. And I'm not either, I swear. It was my first drink."

A touch of turbulence has the two empty bottles rolling into my lap.

"I mean, it was a double, but it was my first double. Five o'clock somewhere," I say cheerily, and my seatmate groans louder. "Sorry, nervous. Going to see my agent today. Richard Piner, have you heard of him? Very successful." She doesn't even register my presence. She is polished and put together and all in black—a New York person. I should have worn pants.

"That's nice," the flight attendant says. "Can I get you anything else?"

"A job. Just kidding. Not really. I kinda got fired yesterday for teaching *A Wrinkle in Time*. You know it? Ms. Who, Ms. Which, Ms. Whatsit? Ms. Whatsit is my favorite. You know she used to be a star, like a real one. But my kids will never know that. They'll never get to see Meg fight for the ones she loves, assert her individuality in the face of power—be courageous. Anyway." And with that, Ms. Put Together slides on her noise-canceling headphones.

Oh my god, what am I doing?

And I realize I've become one of those people. The ones who tell their stories to strangers on planes.

"Miss, would you like me to take those?"

The poor woman has been standing here only to haul away the carnage, not hear about the carnage of my life. I pass her a mass of tomato-soaked napkins so she can escape while my seatmate leans away, grimacing like humiliation is catching.

I look down. "Maybe I can save it," I say morosely, mostly to myself.

But nothing can save this shirt, this day, this life—least of all this trip. What was I thinking?

An hour and a half later, we touch down in a city as gray as the Beach Runner dream. My shirt looks like a period accident. My skirt is wet from seltzer—so what, now I peed?

As I get out of the cab at Stone Street Literary, I honestly think I survived the most mortifying moment of the day.

How wrong I was.

Turns out wearing that murder scene of a shirt while kneeling in supplication before the most uncompromising receptionist to ever grace a literary agency will take the cake.

If only I had known when I booked my flight where I would end up, I might have made better choices, because I smell like a distillery and look like a bar fight. I would love to blame the vodka for my present circumstances, but hardly any of it made it to my mouth. And I'm certainly rethinking the whole falling-to-my-knees of two minutes ago. Not only because it hurt, but because I'm still making no headway. I thought it would make my point that I'm committed—like a conservationist chained to a tree; I'm not leaving until I see my agent. But I'm afraid the only point I'm making is that someone should call security.

"Ms. Stanton, please get up," the receptionist begs. "You don't have an appointment. And Mr. Piner has a full schedule. A meeting with Random House at ten and an editorial meeting just after, and then a lunch out—"

"I'm Richard Piner's new author, and I need to see him," I say too loudly. I take a deep breath and remember my inside voice. "I understand your reluctance. You don't know me. I used to be with Murial Coventon at the Flatiron Agency. Before … well she was lovely, Murial. Did you know her? Anyway, Mr. Piner agreed to take me on after …" I stop there, thinking if I go on I might cry. And I cannot cry. There is no more room on the humiliation cake—the cherry already squarely on top.

"Please just tell him I'm here."

On the carpet.

But it would be even worse to get up and go sit in a chair like a rational human being. I have to follow through with this "protest" plan. Too bad there isn't actually a plan, or a protest, or even a tree. There is a ficus in the corner, but it would likely just drop all its leaves. Certainly, the one in the corner of my classroom does if you so much as breathe on it.

Not your classroom.

Not your ficus.

I wonder if the sub will water it without touching even a single branch or feed Karma Chameleon, the class iguana. What if she's squeamish and won't touch the crickets? Oh well, Preppy Thomas is good for something.

The office phone rings, which takes her attention from me. I admire her professional, pleasant voice, and she sits serenely behind her chrome-and-glass desk, legs primly crossed at the ankles. My mother would approve. While she's distracted, I spy a beautiful silver clicker pen on the edge of her desk and realize I've never needed one more. It's etched with STONE STREET LITERARY in Times New Roman—the font's a nice touch.

I inch closer, giving myself the most unsatisfying rug burn. Then quick as a snake, I swipe it from the desk. I hold it tight but can't help myself from clicking. Just once, I think.

Click.

I breathe out, feeling better already.

Okay twice.

Click. Click.

Hiding it in my hand, I ignore my mother's voice in my head telling me she raised me better.

The call the receptionist answered is taking longer than I expected, so I sit back on my heels, wondering how to extricate myself from this untenable and uncomfortable position, when my cell rings. It's Kimberly, my critique partner and best friend, who wrote the most amazing middle-grade series based on Jamaican folklore that she is still trying to get published. I wish I had thought to bring a copy, to I don't know, leave on a desk as Stone Street reps everything. Next time. I know it's her because Beyoncé's "Run The World (Girls)" ringtone blares from my bag, which is comfortably seated in a chair about four feet away. And since she's feeding Sally Girl, because I forgot—I can't believe I forgot—I scoot over and pull my purse onto my lap about the time the phone stops ringing.

Immediately she texts.

> Kimberly: Sorry! But she won't eat, and I don't have time to come back later.

I quickly pound out a response.

> Me: No, I'm sorry! She does this when I'm away. Do you have time to scramble an egg? If so, mix it into the food or she will just eat the egg on top. So sorry! Pup baggage.

> Kimberly: She needs a shrink.

She's not the only one.

Shiny black shoes enter my view. Security looms over me.

"Miss," the rent-a-cop says while looking down at me, clearly perplexed.

"Holy hell, I'm thirty-three. If one more person calls me Miss, I swear I'm going to—"

"Bite their knees?" The words issue sardonically from behind my head.

I know that voice. That's my agent. That's Richard Piner.

Moving my neck like an owl, I try to face him—my cool, collected, brand-new agent in a pale blue linen shirt, blond linen pants, and driving shoes that probably cost more than my car.

Can you wear linen after Labor Day?

He looks down on me with a hint of a smile.

17

Shuffling around and taking my rug burn to the third degree, I reach up to shake his hand. I'm nothing if not polite.

"Bridget Stanton. Pleasure to meet you."

"Charmed," he says as he pulls me to my feet.

"Yvonne"—he gestures to the mess that is me—"assist."

To me, he says, "Give me but a moment and we'll retire to my office." But the shake of his head tells me he wonders what he did to deserve this at 9:45 on a Tuesday.

Following her, I click the pen all the way to the restroom. If she notices, she doesn't say a thing.

THREE

SCOTCH BONNET

Thanks to Yvonne, the wonder receptionist, in short course I'm seated in Richard Piner's expansive, Scandinavian-styled office, complete with original brick walls, arched windows, and soft-as-a-baby's-bottom leather chairs with whitewashed wood accents. I'm wearing one of Yvonne's spare *designer* button-downs and sipping a cup of calming chamomile tea.

Like they were prepared for me.

Richard sweeps in with a smile on his face and sits in the matching chair across from me. "Bridget, so good to finally meet."

Like the last thirty minutes never happened.

He looks at my shirt, not my cleavage, and nods like all is right with the world. I guess turbulence-spilled Bloody Marys mar his aesthetic.

"And you popped over because …?"

The euphemism hits.

Why did *you max your credit card to get here?*

Holding the swiped silver pen to my chest like a binky,

straining not to click it, I try to think of something to say, but I've got zilch. What exactly did I hope to accomplish by this ill-considered trip?

After an interminable sixty seconds, he looks at his watch and begins.

"So, Bridget, as I said, nice to finally meet, but speaking of meetings, I find it best if they are scheduled. There's email for that, and the miracle of Zoom. Imagine we could meet while you're comfortably kneeling on your *own* floor."

"Richard. I am ... mortified, humiliated, chastened."

"Let's go with chastened. But now that you're here, let's skip to the chase as I have *meetings*." He says the word like I've never met it.

I click the sleek silver pen. Once, then once again.

He narrows his eyes. "Are we going to converse through correspondence? There is a postal service for such needs."

It takes all of my restraint to keep my worst nervous habit from exploding. Sometimes, I click so hard that pens do explode. And I can't explode this pen on Yvonne's shirt. I just can't. So I set it in my lap and let the last twenty-four hours spill out of my mouth in a classic info dump.

When I'm finished, he's pensive. Giving him time to process, I look out his window onto a Manhattan I didn't even know existed. I could be in Europe with the cobblestone streets and narrow storefronts.

"Might I recap?" he says after a moment, and not even waiting for a response, continues, "Your day job is in jeopardy due to an authoritarian regime that has taken over the state of Florida who believes teaching *A Wrinkle in Time* is an abomination."

I nod.

"Therefore you are in my office since I agreed to take you on for Murial, god rest her soul, because you need a large, quick advance to help cover the expenses of your beach cottage. Oh, and you have no new book for me to sell. Does that about sum it up?"

I nod again, afraid to open my mouth. I mean, when he puts it that way ...

"Well, can I be frank?" He uncrosses and recrosses his long linen-clad legs, and I know what's coming. He's dropping me. I have no idea why he agreed to take me on in the first place. He's the hottest agent in town at the oldest literary agency. And he's *hotter* than me. Looks just like Rupert Everett in *My Best Friend's Wedding*. He's also kind for letting me in his office in the first place after the scene I pulled. So I recross my legs at the ankle, making my mother proud, square my shoulders, and prepare not to behave like a doofus when he lets me down hard.

"Please do," I say, ready for whatever is coming.

"What you need is some sex."

Not ready.

Click in, click out, click in, click out, click in —

The point moves in and out—like a metronome.

"Preferably spicy sex."

*Click, click, click, click, click, click—*my fingers a blur.

"You've got the idea," he says with a sly smile, looking directly at the pen.

What's happening?

"Blushing? Seriously, Bridget? You do realize you're an adult."

I feel the heat on my skin and know I look ridiculous. When I blush, it's not a sweet blushing bride—more like Tickle Me Elmo.

"So maybe we should get this out of the way. Not something I normally have to do." He lets out a sigh. "Are you comfortable talking about the ins ..."

He looks directly at the pen, waiting. I click it.

"… and outs …"

I click again. I'm nothing if not a quick study.

" … of sex in publishing?"

The deer-in-the-headlights look I give him answers for me.

"Then listen and learn," he says, leaning back. "I realize this is not a genre you have written in before, but don't look so terrified, I'm talking romance, rom-com, rom-dram, romantasy, not BDSM." He lifts a finger to his lips and taps them gently. "Come to think of it, has anyone done a BDSM rom-com? Can floggers be funny?"

"I don't …"

"Not asking you," he says with a dismissive wave, then scribbles something on a robin's-egg-blue sticky note the same color as his tastefully wrinkled shirt. The one he shouldn't be wearing after Labor Day.

"Let me guess, you don't think about floggers. Didn't imagine you did," he says with a chuckle. "But I might have just the author who could pull it off." He has actual dollar signs in his eyes. "But back to you …" And the way he says it lets me know he has no hope of making money off me—ever.

"Can I ask you a question?" He looks at me appraisingly and doesn't speak, so I go on. "Why did you agree to take me on?"

"Simple. Murial was my mentor. She let me stay in her guest room while I interned at her agency not that many years ago. I owe my career to her. So when she asked me to take on her favorite author—"

"Really?" I'm so touched.

"Did you know I was working with her when you published *Red Bridge*?"

"I don't remember you."

"Well, I was. And I loved it. Still love it. You have a gift. Your stories come to life in a way that is hard to make happen. When I read *Red Bridge*, it was like I *was* the protagonist. And making a six-foot gay man feel like a twelve-year-old girl is no small feat. But Bridget, I looked while you got settled. You have yet to earn out on two of your three objectively beautiful novels. So if you're here to try to make a living at writing, might I suggest a slight pivot?"

"A pivot?

"Well, maybe a one-eighty. Might I suggest sex."

I swallow. "So what you're saying is if I want to make money —real live-on-my-writing kind of money—quick, I need to write books with, you know, sex."

"Do you know?"

I don't move, hoping it's a rhetorical question, not wanting to even hint at my nonexistent sex life. And just when I'm about to answer that I once dated an accountant for eight months, he thankfully moves on.

"Bridget, many authors make good money selling all kinds of books, but I'm what you would call a niche agent. I sell romance. Specifically, spicy romance. A good bit of it. For lots of authors who make very good money for me and for themselves. This is what I do. I never intended to nudge your career in this direction. Honestly, I don't know what I intended when I took you on, and there it is. So having said that, now you have two choices: continue to write what you will and I promise I will help you find an agent who can try and sell it, or come over to the dark and profitable side of publishing." He says it so seductively, like I'm about to sell my soul to the devil. "Your choice."

I don't even think.

"You! I want you!"

"Well, it's not every day a cis woman says that to me, but we've already established it's been a surprising start to a

Tuesday. And as thrilling as your confidence is, all of my authors have one thing in common. They write great sex."

"Then I'll write great sex. How hard can it be?"

He smiles a little smile that says *harder than you think.*

"If that's what it takes, I'll do it. Do you have any idea how much an Irish wolfhound eats?"

"Given that non sequitur, I assume you have one."

"Yes, and a mortgage, property taxes, hurricane insurance, and after a down payment and a same-day ticket to New York— pretty much nothing."

"Well, that *is* a problem."

"And don't forget the totalitarian regime that banned my favorite childhood book and is about to fire me for teaching it. So no, I don't have a problem—I have a disaster."

"But you said you are suspended *with* pay?"

"Ninety days at most, until SCAB—"

"Scab?" he asks incredulously.

"School Content Advisory Board."

"Well, if the acronym fits."

"Exactly."

"Anyway. SCAB," I say with as much venom as I can muster, "will advise the local school board with their recommendation within thirty days, and I'm not even guaranteed a hearing. How equitable is that? But I won the first round; they have to pay me until they decide."

"Hooray," he says, clapping his hands like he's at Wimbledon. "May it be the first of many victories against oppression."

"So I need help." I say sincerely. "Serious help, like, George-to-Julianne help. You really do look like him, you know. Has anyone ever told you that? Rupert Everett, from that movie."

"*My Best Friend's Wedding.* A classic." And with that smile, it's like he just sang the lobster place song. How does he keep his teeth that white? He can't possibly drink coffee. But despite that character flaw, he's my best shot.

"Richard, will you be my George?"

At that point, I thought I had seen all of Richard's sardonic looks, but the way his eyes narrow lets me know there are more.

"Let me ask you something. Do you *like* romance novels?"

"Of course I do. Who doesn't? But write them?"

"That is the question. Whether 'tis nobler in the mind to suffer the slings and arrows of *outrageous* fortune—cue the romance books— or," he says, falling out of the accent, "write lit fic."

I take a deep breath.

"And you already write romance. All of your books have a love story embedded. I would argue all stories do, be they between people or ideas or things. Just make it between people this time, and make it spicy and make some real money for once."

"I like it. A manifesto. All stories are love stories. I can work with this. And you're right, I haven't seen a royalty check in years."

"Bridget, honey, you're out of print."

I open my mouth. Nothing comes out.

"Murial should have told you."

"Murial was dying."

He sits back, sadness evident on his face. "I will assume you have been on your own, in reference to your career, for a while now."

I look around the office, anywhere but at him. If I see the hurt in his eyes that mirrors mine, I will cry, I know I will. So I look at the beautiful bottles displayed on individually lighted shelves on the far wall of his office. Dozens of them—tall, short, porcelain, glass, even a rainbow splatter one—next to a black glass skull that looks at me through dead eyes. Eyes as dead as my career. One I need to resuscitate.

"What happened to me?" I ask that skull. "I was going to be a writer."

"You are a writer," Richard answers softly.

I face him.

"Your plots are devastating, your internal dialogue brutal, and you could wring tears from Scrooge, but to make a career of it, to be able to count on it, you need to either be a King, Christie, or Patterson, or ..." He stands and walks to his desk. Picks up a book. On the back cover is an author smiling, like all-the-way-to-the-bank. "Write romance—preferably spicy." He hands me the book like it's homework.

"How spicy?" I ask, terrified I'm even considering this.

"Let's shoot for cayenne?" he says as he gracefully folds himself back into the chair.

"How spicy is that?"

He just stares at me.

"Sorry, I'm allergic to capsaicin."

"Mother Mary and Josephine," he says under his breath.

Traitorous blood infiltrates my neck, but I square my shoulders and say, "And my situation—living alone—it's not conducive ..."

He leans forward, his elbows on his knees, tenting his fingers in front of him, like I'm holding out a juicy morsel. I immediately stop my train of thought. But he's on to me.

"Let me guess, you've yet to have yourself some spicy?"

I don't move. I don't breathe. I clench my neck to keep my head from nodding. Shaking his head, he adds under his breath, "I'll never understand the hetero crowd."

"I've had good," I say. "*Really* good."

"Bridget, if you use the word 'good,' you have not. And I'm sorry for you, but it seems fairly irrelevant, don't you think?"

"Irrelevant? If I haven't had it, how am I supposed to write it?"

"Use your *imagination*?"

"That's just not my process."

"*As a fiction writer.*"

"I, well, I write things I know, things I've learned. Things I've researched." I gesture at the sky. "Not things out of thin air. I mean, I write fiction, but not really. For *Red Bridge*, I lived in that little town in Maine for three summers in a row. For *Vision Quest* the boy was my childhood neighbor—his father already behind bars. My imagination can bind things together but not make them up completely. That's just not my process." I look him in the eye. "I'm fucked, aren't I?"

"Actually you're not, darling. And given your 'process'," he air quotes,"that is the problem, right?"

I stand up. I have to move. I pace past, clicking the pen violently.

"Make yourself at home."

Yvonne pokes her head in, causing Richard to glance down at the bold Roman numerals on his sleek watch.

"Put them in the conference room. Offer Fred tea, green; he's on a health kick."

And with those words I realize my time is up. But I can't leave without knowing about those bottles and if I can't or won't write smut I doubt I'll be asked back.

"What are those anyway?" I say, pointing my pen at the beautiful individually illuminated bottles behind his desk.

"Memories," he says wistfully and moves to join me.

"Of what?" I ask angrily, my hope almost gone.

Richard picks a rustic-looking bottle made of green glass

from the wall and reads the handwritten tag attached.

"December 2019. Montego Bay. Skinny dipping is never cold."

Then he puts it back and says, almost to himself, "A perfect night."

The look on his face, what he is remembering, the brightness in his eyes—I'm astonished. And he has *dozens* of these?

Have I ever had such a night?

"What was in it?"

"Tequila—La Gritona. Hmm. Speaking of the screamer," and taps his lips. "I know what you need."

Then he reaches back for another bottle—a crystal skull—holds it out in front of himself, his other hand theatrically across his chest, and with great fanfare says, "Thou shalt ingest a satchel of Richards," in a quite passable Shakespearean accent.

"A what? Good accent by the way. Theater kid?"

"You're too kind. Shakespeare in the Park—amateur. Now *that's* a veritable satchel of Richards."

"Wait, which one? The third? I didn't think Shakespeare did more than one Richard."

He chuckles. "My guess is Shakespeare did more than his fair share."

"I'm confused."

He tilts his head. "You don't know what a Richard is?"

I move my head left. Then right.

"Where have you been?"

"Elementary School."

"I can't even," he says while massaging his temples. "Dicks. Richards are dicks, my dear."

"Dicks? I'm talking dicks with my agent," I say, pacing.

"No, you're talking *lack* of dicks with your agent. And, well, that is where I would begin my research if I had your 'process' issue. But, I'm an enlightened queer."

He sits back in his chair, and I join opposite him, sinking into the leather.

"I guess some new experiences could be … helpful?"

"Bridget, think hard on this." Another chuckle. "If you want me to rep you—"

"I do!"

"Then, dare I say, a satchel of Richards is your *must-have* accessory for spring."

"Fuck," I mutter under my breath.

"That's the idea," he says blithely. "It could be fun. But now that I think of it, spring will be too late, although it's a better word, for the context. Evokes accessories—even satchels—just better. But you? Should get right on it." More laughter.

"Spring *is* better. And word choice is everything."

"Touché."

"And I see your point." I switch the cross at my ankles. "I've always done meticulous research for my books. I actually rode the unicycle over the Red Bridge and that one got me nominated for a Booker Prize, for all the good it did my bank account. So, research. Like a professional," I say seriously.

"That might work. Vegas?"

"No! I mean *be* professional, not *hire* one!"

"It's not a half-bad idea. Research," he says with a twinkle in his eye. How does he do that—a trick of the light?

"Pay for sex? I don't think so."

"Don't knock it till you try it. Sex work is work."

"Not ready for that. Will *never* be ready for that."

"But seriously, Bridget, if you can write it, I will sell the shit out of it because that crap with the school board scabbies—god, it makes me itch just to think on it—is beyond the pale."

He looks at his watch, for the second time.

"Okay," I say and move to leave. "I've taken up too much of your time already."

"So you have your marching orders?"

"Yes. But Richard"—I point to the picture of the author on the back of the book he gave me—"it won't be me they see. No pictures, and a pen name. I will do this for the money, but only for the money."

"Your choice."

"And thank you. Thank you for seeing me—thank you for taking me on. I know I am not what you're looking for and that you're a hot-shot agent and have no need for a hand-me-down author, but I won't let you down. I can't let you down. I'll stop at nothing—*short of Vegas*—from making us both some kiss-ass-level money."

"Perfect. I love a good ass."

"You really can sell the shit out of this stuff, can't you?"

"You have no idea."

On my way out, with the word *cayenne* floating around my brain, I turn and say, "How hot?"

"If you want it to sell like hot pants in the '70s, Scotch bonnet. Give me Scotch bonnet."

FOUR

PRIDE AND PORNJUDICE

I step out of the building and immediately FaceTime Kimberly. She picks up on the third buzz. I see the soundstage behind her, so I wait until she closes a door.

"Are you okay?" she asks.

"He wants Scotch bonnet," I say, powerwalking for no other reason than I am in New York and that's what people do. "Like, I can write that! I had to look it up. I thought it was some kind of Outlander fetish porn. Turns out it's a pepper."

"Wait, there's Outlander fetish porn? What do I google?"

"Let's stay on point."

"I bet there are lots of points in Outlander fetish porn."

"God, you're worse than him!"

"Who?"

"Richard. Like dick. Didn't know that. Did you?"

"Your agent's a dick?"

"No. But he's lost his marbles." Now I'm walking circles around the corner pole, waiting for the light to change. "He wants me to write smut. When I told him I don't know smut, he suggested research. Like hire a professional!"

"Interesting idea. You should do it."

"Have you met me?"

"Sounds perfect. Write what your agent wants and end your epic dry spell. Two birds, one stone. Listen, we're live. I've got to go. When do you come back?"

"In like three hours. I didn't have the money to stay."

"But you had the money for a same-day flight?"

"I didn't say I was rational at three this morning!"

"Well, it's for the best. Your dog misses you, even with the scrambled eggs. Speaking of food, meet me at the Shack later?"

"Sure, why not? I don't have a job or anything else of import —sorry," I say after almost accidentally kicking a rat terrier off the curb. Realizing I'm a danger to the general public, I sit down on some brick stairs. "Kimberly, what am I going to do? He only reps smut. Can you imagine me writing smut?"

"I can."

"What would my mother say?"

"Bridget, you're a grown-ass woman, why the fuck do you care what your mother thinks?" She's shaking her head at me, and the tears I have not let fall all day drip down my face.

"Sorry."

"Don't be. I needed to hear that."

"Hey, you know what? Wipe your eyes and get on a plane. I have an idea. A brilliant idea. And a craving for carnitas. Taco Shack at three? Can you do that?"

I check my app. "My plane lands at three."

"Then make it four."

Someone opens the door behind her, and she whispers, "Got to go." And the screen goes blank.

I wipe my tears on Yvonne's shirt along with some mascara. Curse. And then put 'a brilliant idea' on repeat. Because Kimberly is the ultimate fixer. Seriously like Mafia level. That's why one day she will be writing for *GMA*. She can turn anything around.

By the time I Uber home from the airport, I barely have time to change out of Yvonne's button-down and hop in the shower. I can't even take Sally Girl as I have no idea what's on tap. The poor thing has been cooped up all day, so I take her out back on a leash to do her business and promise her an extra-long walk tomorrow.

When I arrive at the Shack, hair still dripping, Kimberly is not there, so I grab a top-shelf margarita that goes down like water. The next one I try to sip. When she finally shows, she's all business.

"I got hung up at the studio. The fucking prima donna," she spits out. Needless to say, Kimberly is not a fan of the female host of *Tampa Today*. Then she kicks off her heels by the outdoor shower at the Shack, grabs my free hand, and marches us down the beach.

"What now? And where are we going?"

"She didn't like tomorrow's opening. So we had to rewrite. And someplace."

"What was the issue? And helpful."

"Her hedgehog. Seriously, we are opening the show tomorrow with a hedgehog."

"Slow news week?"

"Not at all. We had a piece about elementary school funding for the top of the hour, but she wanted to introduce her fans to her hedgehog because it was more 'upbeat.'"

"More creepy. Never trust a pet smaller than your hand. Speaking of, I almost killed a rat dog in New York."

"Give me that drink."

"We're breaking the law by having it on the beach."

She rolls her eyes, but sucks it down in one pull.

"Are we eating? After we walk *somewhere*?"

"Maybe. We have a limited window." She looks at her watch and picks up the pace. I hurry to keep up with her much longer legs.

"Window for what, exactly?"

She points ahead.

"Why are we going to the gym of scary men?"

"Why do you call it that?"

"The last time I walked south, there was like an entire motorcycle gang there. That's why I always walk north. Even with Sally Girl, one must be careful."

"Well that's where we're going. Look closer."

She continues to set a brutal pace.

"Hey! Little legs here. And what am I looking for?"

Then I see him. And there is no unseeing him. I will never be able to unsee him again. "Oh," falls out of my mouth.

"Oh, indeed," she adds. "Sable told me to be prepared, but whew, romance cover model indeed."

"My. Oh my."

"So, my aunt reps him. Since basically forever, even before she moved out west. Says he's *very* popular."

"I bet he is. But what does this have to do with me?"

He's moving up and down on the pull-up bars, slowly, methodically. And I wonder if he does everything with so much precision. He's wearing only bike shorts, his assets on full display—arms, abs, ass.

"*Damn,*" I breathe out.

Kimberly fans herself.

When he sees us watching, he drops down and walks to a nearby picnic table. Pulls a water bottle out of his backpack and stuffs in a pair of sweatpants. Then shrugs on a zippered hoodie leaving it open. There is an hourglass design on the back advertising something called Rapid Screen.

An hourglass?

Oh my god. It's Beach Runner.

Kimberly is talking, so I try to focus, but the hood is down. The. Hood. Is. Down.

"… so the word on the street is he helps writers with their sex scenes. It's very much on the *way* down low, but Suzanne used him and her book hit the teens on Amazon for shapeshifting romance." She turns to me, and I perform the herculean task of transposing my gaze from him to her. "Meet him. That's all I ask."

"Wait, what?"

"Have you been listening? This is what you need. He helps writers with their *sex scenes*," she whispers angrily, doing that weird thing with her mouth and hands like the old uncle in *Christmas Vacation*.

Then, like in my dream, before I can blink he's in front of me.

"Josh …" Kimberly holds out her hand.

"Josh?" I question. "You look more like a *Royce* or a Daemon."

Kimberly looks at me like I've lost my mind.

But Josh says, "Thank you, I guess." Then he smiles. And my panties drop into the sand.

No one can be this sexy.

I want to climb him like a pole.

I try to write him in my head, but I just can't. It's like I can't take him all in at once. So much tan, glistening, tantalizing skin. So many ridges, so many bulges. So much. Too much.

There aren't words. I could never do him justice.

You could, Bridget. You could do him justice, Richard, the devil on my right shoulder says, and I tingle just thinking about being able to touch so virile a man.

Prostitute. That's what's standing in front of you, my mother intones.

I take it back. My mother's the evil one.

He glances down, and I notice his hand is out. For shaking. So I do. I focus on his hand, trying very hard to not look at his abs, which are right in my line of sight.

Why doesn't he zip up? Does he want to cause an accident?

"Nice to meet you," he says. "Sable tells me you're a writer."

I look up into powder-blue eyes that seem to fade away and take me with them. And can eyelashes be that black, that long? It hurts. So bad. But I can't stop.

"I've got to take this," Kimberly says before walking away with her phone to her ear when it didn't even ring. Leaving me alone with this man.

What does one say to god's gift to humanity? In an unintended flash the answer pops into my head: *How much would a night with you cost?*

At least I didn't say it out loud.

FIVE

A PROFESSIONAL RICHARD

H is lips move, forming words, which makes it hard to think. So I don't. I just look up at him, tilt my head, and smile. He's very tall.

"So, Sable tells me you're writing romance and might need some help."

"Sable?" My voice is monotone like a robot. A sexually frustrated robot.

"My agent," he says, smiling wider.

How can a person look so sincere and so sinful at the same time? And those blues. So light they seem to shine from the inside out.

I tear my gaze away from his eyes, but nowhere is safe. Certainly not his cheeks—that dimple—his dark hair cut tight against his tan neck, the perfect waves on top.

Did he have someone fix it? It couldn't be more enticing. It pulls at my fingers like in the dream so I stuff my hands into my shorts to keep from reaching out. Because that would be weird, right?

Shit, he's talking again. I stare at my feet so I can listen,

focusing on the kick-ass red color of my toes. Not candy apple
red, not orangey like the sun red—no, kick-ass-likely-to-spray-
paint-a-bridge red.

Right!

What are we talking about?

His agent, my kick-ass toes remind me.

"So you have an agent for this?" I look up with a smile and
then down again. How does anyone talk to someone this
attractive?

"Helps me to get jobs," he says.

Like *that's* not shocking.

"I'm pretty well-known on the East Coast, but it helps with
out-of-town work like LA. I've even done some work
overseas."

"Wow," I reply. "I had no idea there was such a market."

Where have I been?

Elementary school, Richard quips.

"That's nice," I say politely, looking anywhere but at him. "I
mean, to have a steady stream of business."

Do you hear yourself?

"I have no trouble keeping busy."

And just like that my eyes are rising, up his tan, toned legs,
narrow waist … fuck. I skip the abs to find he has the most
compelling collarbone. Then the face. Smiling. I hope the
"SexyBack" montage didn't take as long as it felt it did because
now I'm locked in place, on his face, and I can't help imagining
'getting busy' with this man.

My face burns, and I know I must look like I'm on the verge
of a heat stroke. Then he blinks, and time stands still. I want to
look away. I want to do anything. I want to say something
poignant or funny or impressive.

I just want.

He must see my embarrassment, because he says, "I'm always happy to help out a writer."

"Why?" I ask honestly, kicking my toes in the sand.

"Because I'm good at it."

Bet you are.

Shut up, Richard!

"So let me get this straight: Your agent helps hook you up with writers so you can help them with …"

"Anything they need."

Mother Mary and Josephine.

Finally Richard and I agree.

I cover my mouth with my hand to keep everything I don't want to say inside.

I wonder if Kimberly knows about this, that her aunt is involved—pimping him! Of course she doesn't! How will I tell her? I won't. Kimberly loves her aunt, idolizes her, and she's in Hollywood. Who knows what goes on there? It might even be legal.

I look over, but she's far enough away not to hear us, yet I'm hoping she'll come back soon and extricate me from this, my second untenable situation of the day or reveal she's actually Dr. Strange and can stop time so I can stare at this work of art.

Then he shrugs. "I mean, people *say* I'm good at it." And this man being self-deprecating about his sexual skills is so disarming I almost say, "I'll be the judge of that."

I'm so completely out of my comfort zone, just easy-breezy discussing sex for money, or work, or something. So I step back as if to distance myself from the very possibility and almost trip, and like in the dream—he touches me.

Holy. Hell.

His hand *is* warm *and* soft *and* strong *and* beautiful. His cuticles look better than mine. I want that hand all over me.

I audibly swallow. He lets go.

"Sorry, day drunk," I say. Like that's better than I'm tripping on my lust. He looks nonplussed.

Must be used to bitches in heat.

Mother!

I shake my head. "And you were saying ..."

"I like to work with authors. And the more I work with them, the more experience and exposure I get. Helps keep me 'a hot commodity,' as Sable would say. Well, that and the scar."

I make the mistake of following his gaze to his hand on his hip. His hip bone. Ripples of lean muscle with their own ripples. Abs. Side abs. Low abs. A jutting muscle heading south, a slash of skin that looks like it would taste like mangos—and low to the left, a lightning-shaped scar pointing directly at his—my mouth dries—Richard.

I cough. I cough again.

"I've never let anyone photograph it. But Sable says it's time, so I'm thinking about giving in."

Holy fuck! Full frontal! On a book!

Where would they sell it?

Dark web, Richard answers with what I picture is a wicked smile.

I shake my head, trying to clear the vision. But it's like a movie in reverse, and when I get to the place where he is doing pull-ups, I am looking nowhere else, imagining how they would pose him. I've never wanted to jump anyone's Richard before, but at this moment I'm ready to offer just about anything.

I cough again.

"Are you okay?" he asks.

"I am so out of my depth."

"Depth?"

Oh fuck. Stop talking.

40

But he said depth and now the picture is pornographic and I'm in it. I continue to cough, like I'm choking.

"Do you need some water?" He holds out his bottle. "No cooties, I swear."

I take it. I need it. It tastes like cold, clear water but with a hint of mint—on my lips, like ChapStick. I lick to confirm.

Then *he* clears *his* throat, and the sound draws my attention to his face. His eyes are half lidded, darker than before. And there's something there. A pull. This could happen. This could be amazing. This is totally out of control.

I look over to Kimberly, who is still ostensibly on the phone. I have to get out of here before I do something reckless.

As always, I fall back on my polite gene.

"So, how long have you been doing this kind of work?"

Did I just say that?

"Since about sixteen."

"Sixteen!" I'm horrified.

"Well, modeling. Helping authors didn't come until later. I had to get good at it. I actually minored in it in college."

That *must* be a euphemism.

"And they were paying me for the cover anyway. But I wanted what was in the pages to be good—better than good."

Don't we all? Richard adds.

"Great, actually. I want the books I help sell to be great, so I thought, what the hell?"

What the hell?

Thankfully, at that moment, when even the polite gene knows not what to do, a little white convertible MG pulls up to the outdoor gym and a woman steps out. No, a bombshell steps out. Sleek curves on a tall frame, platinum-blond hair that actually looks real, clear skin, dark eyes. She is what AI would give you if you said "hot white blond."

He glances her way. "Sorry, Bridget. I have to run. I have a client waiting."

"Do you always meet your clients at the gym?" I ask snarkily.

"No, but I always go to the gym before meeting with a potential client."

I look at the woman by the car, and he sees my mistake. "No, Kayla's not the client; she's working with me on this one."

Well, I never!

"Are you ready, Josh?" the Kayla person calls out.

"Always," he adds with a smile, and against my will the panties that fell to the sand melt like Velveeta.

That face, those eyes, that scar, that Richard—of course people pay for it. Even at four thirty in the afternoon, people pay for it. Like a blue plate special I wonder if there's an early bird discount.

"Just let me know if I can help. And very nice to meet you," he says.

I think I shake his hand. As he walks away, he takes off the hoodie to shrug on a T-shirt and shows me the dimples at the base of his spine, and I realize I will never have it that good, never have a man half that fine in my bed. Never. Because I will *never* pay for sex.

Kimberly, the traitor, comes back and asks, all innocently, "How did it go?"

I look at her like she's insane. Because *she's insane!*

And that is when I short-circuit. I don't know if it is my mother's voice registering my shock, the surreal conversation, day drinking or heat stroke, or maybe just my entire life imploding, but stick a fork in me, I'm done.

"I. Am. Not. Paying. For. Sex!"

Kimberly's looking past me now. I turn.

He heard me. At the car. He heard me. And he looks

beautiful because it is literally impossible for him to look any other way, but sad, almost hurt. Is that what I see in those crystal-clear eyes, hurt? A knot forms in my throat.

Sex workers have feelings too, Richard scolds me.

But then Bombshell says something across the car, and he waves and laughs and gets in while she glares at me like she could spit fire. They drive away. I feel like crying.

So I do.

Kimberly brushes her hand against mine to console me, but I'm inconsolable.

"You're more drunk than I thought you were," she says.

I should not have been let out today. I should not be teaching children. I am an absolute disaster area. A cautionary tale. And all I really want is to reverse the last two minutes and take him up on his offer because I know I'll never have another chance to have a man like that in my bed, which makes me cry even harder.

Kimberly pats my back and orders an Uber.

SIX

ON A JAG

In the Uber, Kimberly tries to engage me in conversation, but I can't find the will to stop crying. It doesn't seem like anything else is left in the whole world but crying.

Mere days ago my life was so staid, so boring, so safe I couldn't imagine anything making me cry. As a matter of fact, I haven't cried in years except for when I lost Sweetie. And this is the second time today. And odds are there is a third time coming when I'm safe in my bed with my covers pulled up and Sally Girl cuddling me. Which makes me cry harder. I mean, why stop only to start again? When you've got a good jag going, just let them roll. But if I don't get it together, I'm going to shrivel up like a prune, which makes me think of water, which makes me think of water flavored like mint, which makes me think of those lips and what it would be like to taste the mint *on* them. I cry harder, thinking of Richard's bottles that held not water but memories. Memories of a kind I don't have. A kind I'll never have. Which makes me think of the closest I ever had—Saturday nights at Sweetie's.

She moved all the furniture against the walls. Her friends

gathered, all suave and sexy and well coiffed like they were at a club rather than her tiny living room. And they knew all the moves. Samba and swing. Loud laughter and half-empty cocktails filled the room. Cigar smoke drifted, surprisingly pleasant, as loud music blasted from a ceiling-hung record player—a setup her boss devised to avoid skips.

She was so vibrant, and they were all so alive. And Juliet—I remember Juliet, her boss's niece. She was twenty to my seventeen, taught me to dance, and I was a little bit in love with her. And Mateo, who visited the next summer and for one perfect month of Saturdays, threw me around that room with abandon. Mateo, who I literally attacked in the carport one wild night after sneaking half glasses of everything only to find my head in my mother's toilet the next morning. Her *tsk*ing over me.

She hadn't let me go back to Sweetie's Saturdays after that. And I missed saying goodbye to Mateo. It was my first heartbreak, and I swore off them at the ripe old age of nineteen. Because look at me.

"We're here," Kimberly says, and pats my back. "Get some rest. I'll call you in the morning."

As soon as I'm through the door, I drop to the floor to be enveloped in soft scratchiness. She's sniffing me like she's looking for something.

HURT.

"No, honey, I'm not hurt. Not on the outside."

But on the inside, I feel like I've been pulped. Ground up till everything is mixed up and nothing solid remains. It's only five, but I get into bed exhausted without even brushing my teeth.

I wake up to a slew of texts from Kimberly and a mouth that tastes like dog food. I remedy the mouth first, then text back, telling her I'm fine. But I need to hibernate for a while.

And since then, I've been avoiding her calls. And her texts

make no sense. What does she not understand? I will not pay for sex. As if I had any money anyway.

The idea is ludicrous. After the trip to New York, I'll be eating ramen to get by, and yet I'm waiting for Uber Eats to arrive with Thai, which I can't afford. But after doing nothing but crying with Meg Ryan all day, I don't have the energy to cook even ramen.

That's when I see the pile of mail on the corner of my kitchen counter. If I go through it, I will have accomplished something today.

It's mostly junk. Oh, but lookee here, a Garnet Hill coupon for $50 off $200.

What kind of a coupon is that anyway? Who has two hundred dollars for white button-downs and cropped jeans? I toss it into the open recycle bin, now full of obnoxious flyers.

But wait.

I go to pull out the grocery one, but last night's fizzy water has dripped all over it and I doubt I can salvage the buy-one-get-two-free Wonder Bread coupons.

You don't eat Wonder Bread.

I consider starting.

If Sweetie were still alive, I would call her. She would listen, take me to the diner for the skillet special, and then probably wiggle her eyebrows and horse laugh at me for not jumping on that man when I had the chance. She used to say there was never enough time for all the men she wanted to love. I swear, it was like she didn't even care when they didn't love her back. Like my grandfather, whoever he was. But after making me feel better, she would have emptied her bank account to get me what I needed.

But what I really need is some self-respect. And what self-respecting thirty-three-year-old runs to their grandmother for money? Probably a lot, but I'm sick of feeling so helpless.

I should have saved more, waited longer to buy the house, made sure I would be able to handle the responsibility before purchasing.

I can't believe I'm even thinking it, but I should have listened to my mother.

But since I didn't, she is the very last person on planet Earth I want to talk to.

Back to sorting through the stack.

Jeez, have I gone through the mail this month at all?

I wiggle my finger under the flap of one that looks important. But you can't really tell anymore; sometimes the hearing aid ads come in an open-or-face-the-consequences type of envelope. But no, this one's official. From the City of St. Petersburg, with its seal complete with pelican, palm tree, and poinsettia.

It informs me the reassessment of my property taxes has been completed.

I scan the rest. But when I see the number, I release the letter like a hot pan, and it floats to the floor.

Lovely. I can't afford my mortgage, and now this. I calculate in my head, only to find that reality is weirder than fiction because my escrow fee is about to go up to $666.66.

You should've married the accountant.

I slump onto the sofa. I wondering if it's possible to have your inner voice removed, if there's medication for that, because if I have to hear my mother berate me one more time from the inside I might just lose my shit. She's always there, always happy to help me feel horrible for each and every mistake I've ever made. If she'd had her way, I would have walked down the aisle with Mr. Boring—like put-me-to-sleep-at-climax boring. Who am I kidding? Gill never brought me to climax.

But safe, she quips.

And boring.

Perfect. No one will steal him.

I shake my mother out of my head while my phone vibrates on the counter.

It wiggles across the granite.

It's my mom. I know it is. She has trouble radar.

But there is no way I am talking to her today. She would know in an instant that something is wrong. The wiggles stop and then immediately start again. At this time of day, she'll wonder why I'm not answering. It takes all my will to stand and walk to the kitchen.

I text her *spin class*.

Not "in spin class" because I've never been able to lie.

But the truth hurts sometimes.

And what I said, yelled, yesterday comes back in full color. I still cannot believe I let it out of my mouth, as true as it was. I stare out my window, watching hummingbirds fight at the feeder, until my phone rings; an unknown but not spam pops up. It must be the Thai.

"It's yellow. You can't miss it," I say as I answer.

"What's yellow?"

"Richard?"

Shit!

"Sorry, how are you today?" I say.

"So, now we're doing polite. Fine. Very fine day here. But enough of that. How is it coming, with the love and the people and the Richards?"

"I'm getting right on it."

He laughs.

Is it even possible to avoid sexual innuendo with this man?

"I called to check on you. Make sure you are all right, after, you know ..."

Don't romance writers freak out all the time? Maybe not. Maybe they are all business. Yes. This is a business. But it's my writing too, and I love it, so I ask the question I've been afraid to ask since I left New York.

"Once I've done this, and done it well, that will be it, right? Once a Scotch bonnet, always a Scotch bonnet. I mean I'll have to keep writing ..."

"Romance. If you can't say it, you can't write it."

"Romance. I'm not ashamed. Sells like hot pants."

I pace, then pull a pen from the coffee cup on the counter.

"Indeed it does. Keeps me in vintage tequila bottles. And no. Well, no and yes. We'll put your romance under a pen name if you want; you can keep writing whatever you want under your own." And strangely, it comes to me—my name has never been my own. My mother changing it with each new husband.

"I don't promise I can sell it, but we can find someone who can. What do you say we get you some money and then we talk?"

"I can live with that."

"Excellent. And Bridget, try to have some fun. It will help the writing—well, probably with more than that. I bet I know what would be fun. Some Richards. Oops, did I say that out loud?"

"It's okay. It's the kind of thing George would say. Fun. Got it."

"I'm not convinced. Fun is not a job; it's just fun. Have some and get me some pages. Soon. I know you can plot—your characters are flesh and blood—so really, I just need the hot stuff. And if it doesn't work out, there are many other ways to make money. You'll be fine."

I don't know if he's trying to convince me or himself.

I find myself in front of the bookcase that holds multiple copies of my three books.

"I wanted to be a writer," I say, then rephrase. "I *want* to be a writer. I know it's not time to give up my day job ..." And then I laugh. Maniacally.

"All will be well, Bridget. Must run. Remember, fun." I hear a click before I can even say bye.

Fun.

When was the last time I had fun?

Then an idea comes to me from out of the blue. I search "dance lessons," and on the second page is a group at the community center just up the beach at Treasure Island that has free Salsa lessons on Tuesdays and Thursdays. I promise myself I'll go tomorrow. I mean, why not? I've got nothing else to lose.

SEVEN

I'VE GOT THIS

I stride toward the white stucco building with Treasure Island's logo on the side featuring a Purple pirate peering into his chest of treasures perched right above the entrance. Perfect.

Assuming I'm going to be greeted by folks five or six decades my senior, I am surprised to find the community center day room full of women about my age.

Hmm.

I notice a few seniors in the back, but they are also women.

"Have I been lucky enough to find a women-only dance class?" I ask the young woman sitting at the entrance with the Treasure Island Community Center badge on her shirt.

"Yes, you have. And they won't mind that you're not gay."

"How do you know I'm not gay?"

"Takes one to know one, and one would know walking into this room if one was one."

That was a lot of ones, but I get her. Just.

"So how does it work? If I'm not gay and didn't bring a partner?"

"Most are here looking for a partner, but let's see," she says while looking around the room. "Celeste," she calls out, and a tall woman with spiky blond hair walks my way. She looks kinda like a pirate or a Viking.

Celeste looks down on the sheet I just signed up on and says, "Bridget. Care to dance?"

"It's been a while," I say.

"Since you've had a partner."

"Yes, that, and since I've danced."

"Good thing I wore the Doc Martens," she says as the music starts. "Top or bottom?"

"She's not one of us," the community center employee informs her.

"No shit, Sherlock. Lead or follow?"

"I better start with follow."

Everyone else is pairing off, and they all look so comfortable with each other. Talking and laughing and spinning.

"Don't worry. It's like riding a bike."

But it's not. And I'm so bad. Tight. Uptight.

"Trust your body," she says more than once. And thank goodness Celeste has on the boots or else I might have broken something. When it's clear I can't get into the swing of it, she takes me to a corner and starts with the basic moves. And once she has slowed it all down, I'm a quick study.

By the end of the hour I'm sweating and smiling, and for the first time in a long time I feel like I can do this.

I've got this.

I've totally got this.

EIGHT

I SO DON'T HAVE THIS

R ichard is right. The sex scenes will be the hardest, all puns intended. The romance? No worries. Cozy to romance, sister love to romantic love—I've got this. But Scotch bonnet? Well, it's time to put pen to page.

I set the stage.

First, I need two glasses of rosé in me and a dark candle lit. Ken and Barbie, from my childhood toy box, ready on their Barbie bed because Kimberly once told me in film school people sometimes use them for blocking. They bend *pretty* well, so I think this is going to work. I wonder if they make Barbie-size ropes? I shake it off. No need for the BMSD—or is it BSMD? No, BDDS.

Like a dentist?

Anyway, no need for bondage. Just hot sex.

By midnight, Ken and Barbie are a tangled mess. I have seven hundred and eighty words of sex, and I'm so pleased with myself and a bottle in that I send it right out to Richard with the subject line Hot Stuff.

The next morning, I wake to an annoying *ding* in a bed with sheets so rumpled you would think I'd done all I wrote about yesterday. I pat around, looking for my phone, and find it under a pillow.

He's seen it. A response already. Must be a good sign.

I sit up in bed, ignore my pounding head and rumbling stomach, and open his email.

Dear Bridget,

It's hard to know where to begin. If this came from any of my other authors, I would assume a practical joke.

First, dicks don't bend, not that way, not if you want them to keep "working" and working is a word you actually used. And FYI, women don't just hang from walls like pictures. They have to be held up by something when their intimate partner "crosses the room like a tiger for two fingers of scotch." Capiche?

Oh. And No. No to throbbing. Hard limit—engorged. You made him sound like he had elephantiasis. What kind of research have you been doing? And WTF with "giddy-up"? I'm speechless. For future reference, that only works in cowboy romances, and not even then. And why, oh why, would your guy, who is an accountant, ever say that? And the counting thing … it's creepy, really creepy, just no.

Honestly, I don't think this is going to work. Have you thought about transitioning to another career: tutoring, piano lessons, dog walking, or rocket science, which all seem to be more within your grasp than romance. Sorry, but there it is.

Warm regards,

Richard

P.S. Bridget, honey, do you know where your clitoris is?

I scramble out of bed, knocking my thigh on the footboard while making too tight of a turn and leaving what will surely be a purple bruise, and get to the bathroom in time to expel all of last night's liquid in heaving gasps. When I'm done, I plop onto the floor and lay my head against the cool porcelain tub.

I failed. Failed miserably. And I don't fail. I'm the little engine who could. Everything I set my mind to, even if I'm beginning to wonder why I set my mind to certain things, I succeed at. But this time, I failed.

Using the sink, I pull myself to my feet, then brush my teeth. Drink some water. Take a Tylenol and sit down at my kitchen table. Coffee on and laptop open. I brace myself and read what he found so offensive. When I finish, I sigh, and open up my email account.

Dear Richard,
You're right.
Please look on it as a practical joke. Haha, funny. But don't give up on me. I once wrote a shitty first draft that became Red Bridge.
Have a nice day,
Bridget

I have done this before, and I can do this again. The first draft of *Red Bridge* was disjointed and rambling and had no sense of place, but it had heart, so I fixed it. I found an actual red covered-bridge, lived near it for three summers, and talked to sisters—lots of sisters. Learned how they worked. I did it. I fixed it. Better than that, I am proud of that book, out of print or not.

I can do this. I know I can. And it wasn't *that* bad. I mean, the positions? Okay, I get they need some work. And the talk? I definitely need to look into that. But some of it—the beginning? That was good, I think.

If you use the word good, *it wasn't*, Richard parlays.

But it's a start.

I reply again.

Richard,

This was only my first try. I mean, sure, I need to look into the mechanics, but it was somewhat hot, right? In the beginning?

Have a nice day,

Bridget

I push Send. At the unreasonable hour of 6:50 a.m., but he started it.

After ten minutes, when I'm working on my second cup of coffee, I hear the ding. He's switched to text. I picture him powerwalking somewhere.

> Richard: Hot? Put me off my breakfast.

Me: So not hot?

> Richard: On a scale between Bell and Scorpion peppers I rank this submission at skim milk.

Then he returns to email.

Curdled skim milk.

Warm Regards,

Richard

Shit.

I take my cup to the sink, wondering what in the world I'm going to do with my day, with my life, my mortgage, and then I hear another *ding* and shout, "What more can you have to say?"

But it's not him. It's SCAB, or their lawyer, offering me a meeting Monday before they make their decision. And given the shit show of the last twenty-four hours, I quickly agree.

NINE

JUST THE RICHARD FOR THE JOB

R*UN* Sally Girl screams at me the moment I open the door. I've only been gone for two hours but she clearly misses me. I guess it's because lately I take her almost everywhere and I'm no longer gone for eight-hour days at school. But I couldn't take her to Saturday's 'spin class' brunch as she might have eaten everything on the table. I brought a selection of pastries from Café Soleil minus the guava and cheese one I devoured in the car on the way over. And Celeste is right. It is like riding a bike, if relearning to ride a bike is like falling down a lot. At least that's how I remember it. I actually did fall down today. Ended up on my ass after a petite septuagenarian swung me so hard I couldn't hold on, knocked me into Doris, the oldest regular, and as graceful as a drunk moose, I fell to the floor. But I was laughing again, and that was something.

It's too busy on the beach to let Sally Girl go and she's chomping at the bit to be off this leash, so I resolve to come out here again tonight with her so she can run free.

Being on the beach, of course, makes me think of Josh—how could it not?—but I haven't seen hide or hood of him since the fateful I'll-never-pay-for-sex day. Of course I'm not getting up before dawn anymore. What's the point now that I don't teach?

And since I have been avoiding the subject for a week, I might as well have the conversation. With myself.

So, I've done some research. I have to be delinquent two payments before they can file for eviction, and they will. I got the house at a steal, as the snowbirds sold by-owner. The bank looks to make a pretty penny if I default. I'm sure that's how I got the loan to begin with. No risk on their part. But if they foreclose, I will never get another house again. At least not until I'm forty. And renting for the next seven years is not an option.

I could grovel. I have an appointment with SCAB, and I might get my job back. I'm sure they'll want some kind of statement, some kind of written apology for my file, but whatever, it would solve the problem.

But would it?

That's another problem, the job, but house first.

I could borrow from Mom. I could. I *really* don't want to. Her "told you so" will cost almost more than foreclosure in terms of my mental well-being. So, that's a last resort.

I could swipe right and get some experience, which sounds about as enticing as a root canal.

Or you could take up a nice man on his extraordinary offer.

But how would I pay for that?

I'd take out an equity loan for the privilege.

Richard, I'm not paying for sex!

I look up to see I've taken a Freudian walk. I'm standing five feet from the picnic table at the outdoor gym. Sally Girl has curled up underneath in the shade.

I'm alone. But looking at the equipment, it's impossible not to picture his long, lean torso as he hung from the bars. And his eyes—so light blue they were almost colorless.

And he was nice, polite, professional, if a bit shocking. I bet I could climax just running a finger down that scar.

And he said he wanted the books to be the best they could be. Something we have in common.

And regardless of what I said to my inner Richard, my subconscious brought me here for a reason. Before I chicken out, I text Kimberly.

> Sorry. I've been incommunicado. Can I have Josh's number?

> > Kimberly: Sure. Are you okay? You were a mess. Made no sense.

> Me: I'm fine. Really. But I could use Josh's number. Just, please don't ask me why.

Like she doesn't know. Soon thereafter, his contact card comes through.

> > Kimberly: Take care of yourself. And remember you're a badass. Fuck SCAB. They don't deserve you.

> Me: Thanks. Talk soon.

Now that I have his number, I can't think of what to say.
You could start with sorry!
No one is working out, so I walk over to the equipment and sit at the bench press. Then I picture him using the bench press. In the sun. Hot, glistening.
Stop.

Apologize, *then* fantasize.

I guess I could go with "Sorry I judged your chosen profession."

Or "Sorry, sex work is work."

Or maybe, "I've changed my mind and am happy to pay for you-know-what." Because I can't type "sex," right? It's a crime in Florida to pay for sex, and that's the last thing I need.

You could take him to Vegas.

On whose dime?

Nothing seems appropriate. I guess there is no polite way to ask to pay for sex.

And if I am being truthful with myself, I'm humiliated by my reaction. As Richard said, I am an adult; this is sex. Sex does not have to be about love. Sex can be about sex. Actually, wouldn't it be great if sex were just about sex? No responsibilities like attending office functions and meeting potential mothers-in-law. I still can't believe I wasted eight months of my life with that wet rag. What was I thinking?

You were thinking you like a roof over your head, Mother's voice provides.

I got a roof fine without him.

But can you keep it?

I hate you. Didn't mean that.

Maybe it would help to work out. Let off some steam.

The gym equipment is pretty: white-painted metal, clean curved lines, and many weird-looking things I don't know how to work. But the pull-up bars I've seen in action. I grab ahold, and there are rough edges to help me hang on. I pull and get almost two inches off the ground. Do it again, and then lift my legs and cross them behind me like Josh. After no time, I'm incapable of holding on a second longer and drop before I hurt myself.

When did I get so weak?

I used to run cross-country and even swim—intramural, of course---but I want to be strong again. Fearless. Like I was when I published my debut. That day it seemed nothing could stop me from having everything I ever wanted.

Maybe you wanted the wrong things?

I lie down on the sit-up bench, which thankfully is only slightly sloping, loop my legs through the leg rests, and do a pretty convincing crunch. I continue until I'm sure I will not be able to breathe without pain for the rest of the day. Then lie back, staring at the world upside-down, seagulls flying through clear blue skies, when out of my fantasies the most beautiful sight comes into view.

I don't even startle.

"Bridget?"

This is real.

I sit up, with difficulty, finding I have crunched too much to see Josh, all covered up and dripping sweat from his brow. And it is like I'm suddenly sitting on top of a volcano.

"Working out?" he says as he unzips his hoodie.

"Don't do that," I say worried what an unencumbered view of his abs might do to me.

"Do what?"

"Nothing."

That's when Sally Girl notices a big man near me and charges between us. Josh jumps back like he's seen a snake.

"She's sweet," I say as I try to untangle my feet from the equipment.

"She's *huge*."

I swing my legs around and land ungracefully in a slanted sitting position. Josh reaches out to touch my shoulder, to keep me from tipping, and his finger is like a hot poker on my skin. I burn.

Sally Girl rushes in again, extracting his hand with an upward nudge. He looks startled and I can't help but laugh.

"What is that?" he asks.

"An Irish Wolfhound. They get big."

Now she's sniffing him and he's staying very still. She uses her head to bump his hand.

PLAY.

"She wants to play."

He pats her head hesitantly. "What do you feed her, smaller dogs?"

"No, silly. Raw meat."

"Really?" His face. Priceless.

"Do you live here?" I'm looking at the abs—I mean, why not? They're on display.

"Seems that way sometimes," he says.

What the hell. No time like the present.

"Hey, so I think I came here looking for you."

"Then I'm glad you came," he replies, pushing off the hood and wiping sweat off his face with a towel from his backpack.

"How do you stand the sweats?"

"The point is to sweat. Keeps water retention down."

He doesn't look like he's retaining a teardrop to me. He's all tight, lean, loveliness.

"Sure, makes sense," I say, even though it doesn't. "I was thinking. Can we talk? Get a cup of coffee or something?"

"Sure."

"I mean if you don't have a … job." I realize I say it like it's a bad word. "I mean work or something."

"No, just my normal routine. Run. Work out. Run. Do it every day. Sometimes twice."

"I know. I've seen you running. I've seen you a lot. Oh shit!" I turn to run myself because Sally Girl is licking the face of a child on the beach.

Josh whistles, fingers in his mouth. Loud.

Sally Girl turns, and like a soldier, comes directly back to his feet. Sits. Waits. *What the fuck. You've known him five seconds. What am I, chopped liver?* But I don't think she hears me the way I hear her.

"Thanks," I say reluctantly, a little pissed.

"I had dogs growing up. Just not bear-sized dogs. There's a nice teahouse a few blocks away, shall we?" he offers as I clip on the leash.

"Green Leaves?"

"You know it?"

"I live just down the beach."

"Nice," he says, taking off his small backpack and then his hoodie and replacing the hoodie with a light gray V-neck.

"I go just about every day after my workout. Caffeine affects me strongly, so I prefer tea."

This strapping six-feet-plus man can't handle coffee?

"Shall we?" he asks.

And polite.

We walk in silence while my head psyches me up.

No one will ever know.

It's on the way down low.

Live for once.

Have some fun.

When we arrive at Green Leaves there is a line out of the door as the place is popular. Josh gestures to an outside table under an umbrella that was just vacated.

"Jasmine okay?"

"Love it," I reply with a hardly suppressed smile.

"Be right back."

I can't help but notice the attention he garners as he stands in line, but he seems to have this way about him that is friendly without inviting further interest. Once he makes it inside I know I am running out of time and try and figure out how I'm going to say what I have to say. Too soon he returns with a medium white pot and two cups, I decide it's now or never.

"First, I'm sorry," I say as I pour for both of us. "For offending you. It was … Well, I am mortified at my behavior." I shake my head at the memory. Close my eyes and take a deep breath.

"Bridget, I—"

I put my hand up. "Let me get this out." I open my eyes and look into his clear, kind ones. I see no judgment. "I need your help. I would like to hire you to help me. With …"

You can do it, Richard says in my ear.

"Sex. The sex scenes in my book."

Once it's out, I talk fast, like if I stop I'll never be able to finish.

"I need to know how much it will cost—the sex. I'm not very flush right now."

He chokes while sipping from the small handleless mug, which looks like a sake glass in his big hand.

"I would be happy to help you with your scenes. But normally I only offer those services to authors who are paying me for the cover."

"I don't get to choose the cover. The publisher will. I mean, I can make recommendations—"

"Trad? Interesting."

"Yeah. My agent works almost exclusively with the big five."

"About to do a cover for a big five—the scar, giving them the goods."

Wow.

What does one say to that?

"Congratulations?"

"No big deal. Just had been holding out to get the most money. Sable, my agent, is a whiz at that. And it worked. This time they seem to be writing the book around the art. But for your cover? Would you like me as a model? Would it work for your book?"

"I don't care."

His eyes narrow. I've offended him. I backtrack.

"I mean, I've never been allowed to care, to choose. They do that—the big publishers—take care of all of that, but yes, you would be great. Wonderful, even. You're beautiful." Okay maybe a tad too far.

"I have been told." But he says it like it's a bad thing.

"It is not up for discussion. It's an objective fact." I set my cup down. "You're the most beautiful man I have ever seen in or out of person. I find it hard to look at you and yet I don't want to look away."

What the fuck is in this tea?

"I mean, for a book cover, that is, one wants that, you know? The not-being-able-to-look-away part."

He's smiling while obviously trying not to, and it makes me want to jump his … Richard.

You can do this. This could be fun.

I pour more tea for each of us. Business meeting, I remind myself.

"I'll need you to agree to only work with me during the project," I say directly.

"That's fine. I'm between jobs."

"And I'll need to know when you were last tested."

"Tested?"

"You know, STDs. I'm on the pill and can never feel anything with a condom. And I need to feel something. So, I'll get a test as well, and we'll exchange—"

He laughs. It starts slow and then builds. "Jesus," he says, laughing harder. It's a deep rumbling sound I never want him to stop making.

Wow. So this is chemistry.

Sally Girl, likely sensing the swirling pheromones, wiggles under the table between us. I pet her head. He's still laughing.

I didn't expect laughing.

"I don't know what's so funny."

"It makes so much sense now," he says, rubbing his eyes. "Kayla said so, but I didn't, couldn't ..." but he can't get out any more. And his laughing is a sound I already miss. "Bridget."

The sound of my name on his lips, and just like that, my toes curl into the sand.

I have read about toe curling and have been fucking annoyed, because what in the world kind of sexual reaction is curling one's toes, and yet, my feet betray me.

He wipes his hand across his blue-ocean eyes, finally getting himself under control.

"Honestly, I don't think it's funny," I say. "Sexual health is important and—"

He shakes his head, his face contorting as he tries to keep from laughing.

"Bridget, that's not how I help."

"What do you mean, that's not how you help?"

Trying hard to keep a smile off his face he swallows.

"When I work with authors"—he presses his lips together before resuming—"I describe scenes for them. They write them. I inspire them, maybe help plot them out. I'm an actor as well, but in this case," he looks away, his cheeks pinking, "there is no actual acting *it out*, so to speak."

Oh my god.

He's not a sex worker.

He's like a developmental editor.

"Oh, Josh. Oh, oh my … I-I … I can't think of a single thing. To say. I should stop saying things entirely. For good. I'm leaving now."

"No, it's fine, really. I'm strangely flattered." But he looks even more embarrassed than me. And Josh with pinkish cheeks should be illegal. Now he can't seem to hold *my* gaze and reaches below the table to give Sally Girl a bit of his egg white bite.

"Don't. Give her mine. I can't get it down now anyway." I hand him my scone.

"If you're sure. Afraid she might eat me if I don't give her something," and he chuckles embarrassingly.

I'm suddenly so uncomfortable. Where do we go from here? I mean I asked him if he had STDs. A person I have known for all of—I look at my watch—twenty-seven minutes.

It's so not fine. It's horrible. I'm screwed, or not to be, which is the same thing. I stand.

"Did I say something to offend you?" His sincerity makes me wince.

"Did *you* say something to offend *me*?" I shake my head. "It's me who's been offensive from the moment I met you. I have to go." I'm mortified and defeated. I had put too many hopes on this plan. And it's crumbling like my scone that Sally Girl is eating from his large, strong hands. I move to stand.

"You don't want to work with me?" He looks crestfallen.

Be honest; he deserves that at least after your behavior.

I sit back down. "I would love to work with you, but that's just not my process. I need more ..."

God, I can't believe I have to say this.

"Hands on. To say, when I do research for a book." His eyes get wide. "This is my first spicy romance, and I need to have the experience myself. You see, that is *my* process. Now I'm going to let Sally Girl dig me a hole so I can crawl into it." A thought comes to me. "Can't you just write the scenes for me? I'll pay you."

"I wish I could," he says. "But that's not *my* process. I think in pictures, scenes, movies. I can never get the words right, except for dialogue. That's why I don't write fiction. I can paint the scene, but the writers have to get it all down."

"Well, then we are well and truly screwed," I say.

"Or not." He blinks. When did I start noticing blinking?

I shake my head. What was I thinking? This level of beauty is not for me. And it's certainly not safe. But what a good-natured person to find all this funny.

I hold my hand out across the table as an offering. "Thank you for your time, and the tea. You're wonderful." And somehow I mean it.

He looks at my hand but doesn't shake it.

"What if we tried? You know ..." he says quietly. "Your way." He doesn't look at me when he says it, but then those clear blue eyes meet mine and I want to fall into them, swim around in them. Live inside them.

This has disaster written all over it. This is so not safe. I am losing my mind, have been since the day I was kicked out of school.

"Thanks, really. But I'm not sure this is going to work. It's all so muddled and I can't even look you in the eye. I mean, you know that, right? You're actually hard to look at. This whole idea is bonkers. And it's going to be fine. I have a meeting later today that is going to fix everything." I stand. "I have to go."

I pull on her leash, but Sally Girl won't budge.

He pats her head and says, "Okay, beast, see you on the beach." And she relents.

TRAITOR! I push out of my brain.

I hope she heard.

I'm going to have to change where I walk.

TEN

SCABIES

I spend Sunday watching old movies, nothing strange there, but the fact that I picked *Pretty Woman* and *Risky Business*, arguably two of my favorites, is not lost on me.

By Monday morning I am resolved. I need to get my job back. So, I put on Yvonne's newly pressed white button-down my new favorite that I should have already sent back—what is the world coming to?—and arrive early, hoping I can check on Karma Chameleon before having to face the SCAB attorney.

I park around back in my favorite space under the live oak— well my favorite except in the spring when it drops all its semen —but when I try to use my keycard, the light flashes red, so I walk to the front on the way waving at Frank the groundskeeper who keeps the palms nice and tidy.

It really is a beautiful school—older, with character, something I never appreciated when I was coming here every day.

The front door is open, but it turns out my keycard doesn't work for my room either, so I go to the main office. The principal is coaching Little League out back, so I ask the school secretary, Karen, to give me the master key so I can get in my room.

"I'm sorry, Ms. Stanton. I'll have to accompany you."

"*Ms. Stanton?* Karen, I've known you for ten years. I've been to all your baby showers."

"Again, if you need anything from your room I can escort you to retrieve more personal items after your meeting with the representative of the state School Content Advisory Board." The way she says it, it's like she is about to break into the Pledge of Allegiance or something.

I shake my head, but she is showing me into the little conference room off the principal's office where a man who looks like a mite sits.

It's his eyes. Small. Beady.

"Miss Stanton, please have a seat."

"Bridget is fine, Mr. Sikes. Thank you for meeting with me."

He has a folder in front of him, and he opens it ominously. It's full of paper. What the fuck is in there? He clears his throat and passes me a document.

"You have the right to have an attorney present," he says.

I look at it. Read it, and sign the waiver. I can't afford an attorney.

"So this is your opportunity to explain, but please know that all you say can and will be used against you."

"I read a children's book ... to children. It's not like I committed a crime."

"But you knew it had been removed from the library."

"I thought it was checked out."

"Ignorance of the law is no excuse."

"If the law's ignorant, is that an excuse?"

Do you want your job back or not?

"The book in question has been reported to SCAB under the

76

terms of the newly enacted House Bill 1549, which says that if a book is reported to be harmful to children it will be removed within five days."

"And how exactly is *A Wrinkle in Time* harmful to children?"

"That is not for me to say."

"Then who's to say?"

"The person who reported it."

"So if I were a vegetarian and thought that all farm books were about murder I could have *Old McDonald* removed?"

"Yes. If you were a parent."

"That's the most absurd thing I've ever heard. There has to be *some* rationality. I mean, I would understand if I were reading *The Giver* or *The Diary of Anne Frank*. When teaching upper grades I've actually sent home letters to parents about books I wish to teach that have difficult subject matter. But *A Wrinkle in Time* is fantasy, a heroine's journey, a deep dive into imagination."

"Well, the reporter thinks it's dangerous. But since the book was removed after you started reading it, that in and of itself would not be enough to suspend you."

"Great. I can come back to work?"

He shakes his little beady mite head.

I take a deep breath. "What do you want to hear? That I wish I hadn't read a children's classic to my enraptured third-grade class? Sorry I can't find it in me to apologize for *A Wrinkle in Time*."

"Miss Stanton—"

"I'm thirty-three. Call me Bridget."

"Mizzz Stanton, it's not just the book. That was only the beginning of the report."

"By whom? Did one of my children call SCAB? Was it Preppy Thomas? He's the only eight-year-old I know with an iPhone."

"No, but one of your children's parents did."

"Which one?"

"Confidential. But they also reported your *Alice in Wonderland* tarot cards."

I snort. I can't help it.

"It's not just that the book has occult leanings, it's that you exposed a young lady to the occult arts."

"The occult arts? I wouldn't know a pentagram if it hit me in the face." And then something hits me in the face. Elizabeth Lee, dusting my desk, opening my drawers, finding the cards that were a gag gift from another teacher because we both love Lewis Carroll who's also banned. Elizabeth Lee and I looked through them together. They have the original drawings—the tea party, the Mad Hatter, the Cheshire cat—her favorite. I think I even made a photocopy for her.

"It was Elizabeth Lee's mother, wasn't it?"

"I can't tell you that."

"Rich coming from a woman who doesn't work except on her tennis game and yet drops off her children early and picks them up late every single day."

"Regardless. What do you say to this?"

Elizabeth Lee has colored the Cheshire Cat. "She did a great job. The cat is purple and pink."

"Not to mention the violation of the Drugs on Campus Act."

"You must be high!"

He huffs at me and points at the paper.

"It is a violation to display any paraphernalia on school campus."

And sure enough, the cat's hookah is Exhibit B.

I'm speechless.

"And as if that was not enough, we've found the emailed receipts from the Pagan Supply Store."

"The what?" Now I'm laughing and looking around. Is he for real? This must be a gag.

"Candles on the Corner, it says here." He passes me a stack of emails.

"You searched my emails? Ten years of them?"

"As is our prerogative."

As is my prerogative to shoot you a bird under this table.

"Don't they have bigger fish to fry?"

"Bigger than our children's hearts and minds?"

Oh my god!

I roll my eyes. You've got to be kidding me. This is so much worse than I thought it would be.

"Yes, this receipt is from my favorite candle store. I like the lilac ones. And sure, this Shop.com receipt certainly does say *Pagan* Supply Store at the top, which I never noticed because *who* reads Shop.com receipts? And what the fuck difference does it make anyway? What country am I living in!"

He leans back like I slapped him. I wish I had.

"SCAB is recommending termination effective immediately."

I stand. "Then why invite me? Clearly nothing I can say will change your mind. What is the point?"

He looks at me with pursed lips but smiling beady eyes. He's enjoying this. The fucker!

"There is no point, is there? Never was," I say.

"You can make a statement. I'm required to add it to the report. That's the point."

"Required?"

"Yes, by law."

"Then please take this down *verbatim*."

He pulls out a yellow legal pad and stares up at me expectantly.

"Tell the members of SCAB."

79

He's writing; I wait for him to catch up.

"To please ingest, with my compliments, I might add"—he writes the words and then looks up at me quizzically—"an entire fucking satchel of Richards. All caps."

"I don't even know what that means."

But I'm already out the door, breezing by Karen, saying, "Keep it. Keep it all. But feed the fucking iguana."

Her gasp gives me a small sense of accomplishment. I wish I could take back every onesie.

All right, Bridget, you've burned your bridges. Now what?

I'm so mad. Slamming the door, stalking down the covered hallway. I bet steam is coming from my ears. So when someone says my name, I bark, "What now?"

Until I see who it is. Elizabeth Lee. She's snuck out of after-school again. She hates after-school—her sister's a bully.

"Miss Bridget, where have you been?"

I walk back to her and sit down on the concrete stairs to the auditorium. Pat the spot next to me.

"I've been ... working."

"But you work here."

"I also have another job."

"What job?"

"I'm a writer."

"Like Madeleine L'Engle?"

I sigh. "Just like her."

And big fat tears form at the corners of her eyes. She bites her lip to keep them in. I pull her close.

"I'm sorry I didn't say goodbye. But I need to do stories for a while."

"So you're not coming back."

I shake my head, and as much as I will miss this little girl—so like me at this age—I want to thank her. Thank her for telling her mother whatever she did to put this all in motion because I forgot. I'm a writer.

"I have to go. Be good."

I stand and walk her up the stairs, as she has no business walking around here alone.

She opens the door but pauses to ask, "What happened? To Meg and her father? To all of them?"

"You're a great reader, and the public library is sure to have a copy. Find out. Oh, and stand up to your sister. The sooner the better." I wouldn't say it if her sister had ever hurt her body, but her words have hurt this child, so I add, "Meg would."

She smiles.

And it was worth it all.

That one smile is worth everything.

ELEVEN

NEVER SAY NEVER

s soon as I'm in the car, I text Josh, because not only have I burned bridges, I've decided to build some too.

Me: This is Bridget Stanton. Are you busy? I'd like to talk. I'd apologize again but I bet that's getting old.

> Josh: No need to apologize and I'm standing next to Kimberly as we speak. PS I think we should be on a first name basis after the whole STI convo;) BTW I'm all good in that department. Results in the car.

Me: SDI?

> Josh: Sexually transmitted infections. They're not a disease.

Me: What are you a doctor.

> Josh: Not quite and yet regardless SDI is the proper term.

Me: Fine. Properly scolded but you didn't have to do that. I didn't.

Josh: It was no trouble.

Me: And I realize I don't even know your last name. And why are you with Kimberly?

Josh: Joshua Anjo Silva, and I have an audition in twenty minutes at her studio.

Josh: Oh and Kim says "for Bridget to have an STI it would have to be an immaculate infection."

Me: Tell Kimberly har de har har *middle finger emoji*

Josh: Want to come watch?

Me: The audition? You sure?

Josh: I'm sure.

Then a text comes in from Kimberly.

Kimberly: Get your ass down here. He's in a kilt! A kilt I say! It's all Outlander fetish porn up in here!!!

I try not to speed and fail miserably. Kimberly meets me at the door of the station.

"They've just started," she says and *click-clack*s toward the studio.

"Why is he auditioning for *Tampa Today* in a kilt?" I ask, while trying to keep up.

"He's auditioning for a movie, like one you'd see in a theater."

"Really? Cool."

She holds her fingers to her lips, and we walk through the door with the green light on top.

The scene is surreal. Josh is on stage, right in front of the desk with the big orange sun. The one that the prima donna, the female host, is actually sitting at like a spectator. Meanwhile Josh is dying in a kilt. He's been gored through the scar, it seems. And when he says to his invisible foe, "I will meet thee in hell," not only do I believe he's Scottish, but it's like those words alone can pull his enemy down into the deep with him. I want to clap.

"He's good," Kimberly whispers.

Meanwhile, prima donna has rolled her chair around and I swear is trying to peek up his skirt.

Kimberly must see it too because she shakes her head and mouths, "That woman!"

The camera operator moves in for a closer shot while he writhes. Then from somewhere, a disembodied voice calls, "Cut."

She whispers in my ear, "It's a live feed. That's the casting director you hear."

"Okay, Joshua, nice. Can you stand? I'll need a close-up."

He gets up gracefully, somehow not flashing the bitch at the end of the table his goods.

"Just stand. Face forward. Fine, closer." The camera operator moves. "Fine, right side. Chin up. Fine. Left. Fine. Rear. That's a wrap."

"You said there were lines, as in plural," another voice says.

"That's Aunt Sable," Kimberly whispers. "She's on the call as well."

"There are, but we don't need to hear them all," the casting director says. "This is a quick look and proof—you know the drill."

"Let us know," Sable says on a sigh.

"I'll be in touch."

The camera operator drops the camera and the host, in *The*

Devil wears Prada heels, stalks over to Josh and purrs, "I'd be happy to be in touch."

Gross.

Kimberly turns to me. "Oh god, let me go save him from The Thing."

She walks right up to shirtless Josh—doesn't he ever get cold?—tells him Sable is on the phone, and hands hers to him. He takes the bait and walks away from the female host of *Tampa Today*, much to her chagrin.

I don't deserve the smile he gives me once he clears the lights.

"Hi," I say. "That was weird."

"Always is."

"I expected something different, like a scene, like Josh as Hamlet or something."

"To be or not to be—"

"Why do people keep quoting Shakespeare to me?"

"What about," he says in an overly gravelly voice, "I think this is the beginning of a beautiful friendship."

"Play it again, Sam. But you need a trench coat and a hat."

"I look great in a hat."

"You'd look great in a lunch bag."

"Hmm. If couture."

I laugh.

Kimberly comes over to shoo us out. "We've got to wrap it up. Time for *Cooking with Kim*."

"You have a cooking show?" he asks.

She and I snort.

"Kimberly can't cook cereal. But speaking of, can I buy you lunch?"

"Join us," he says to Kim.

"Sorry. Must file my nails."

"Ooo-kay. Bridget, give me a sec to change."

"No need. To change." Then I look down at his muscular thighs. "No. Yes. I take that back. Change. Wouldn't want a pileup. And put on a shirt."

"Planning to."

As soon as he turns, Kimberly gives me the villain eyebrows and I mouth, "It's business. Just business." But I feel like a villain as I watch him pull on jeans under the kilt, flashing tight black briefs. At least he turned to the wall to zip up.

We end up just a few blocks away at a place he knows called Goddess Green. It looks like healthy fast food. He holds the door for me. Then we stand next to each other in line, and it feels weird. Too much like a date. I study the colorful menu on the board above the counter to keep me from staring at his profile because coins should be minted just to display that sexy silhouette.

"Go ahead," he says, when it's our turn to order.

"I'll have a large order of sweet potato fries with garlic aioli and a buffalo chicken salad, extra blue cheese, double ranch."

"And you?" she asks Josh.

"I'll have the miso-glazed salmon bowl. Double the salmon, hold the rice, hold the miso, hold the pickled onions—add protein greens, avocado, two eggs, and nutritional yeast."

"Any dressing?"

"Do you have lemons?"

She nods.

"Perfect."

"Anything to drink?"

"Water for me," he says.

"I'll have the kombucha," I say, proud of myself until I taste it on the way to the table and it might as well be weird fizzy Kool-Aid with an amoeba floating around in it. I go back for some water and scoot into the booth across from him. An order marker with the letter D on it stands between us. Seems a bit on the nose for the conversation I'm about to start, but I didn't know I needed to let someone jump in line to avoid it.

"So," we say at the same time.

I point to him and keep my mouth shut.

"So, Bridget. I've been thinking. It goes without saying that helping you would be my honor. And pleasure."

Wow. That's unexpected.

"And as I have said, I like to work with writers. You are very talented. I read *Vision Quest*."

"In the last two days?"

"Last night. You're good at what you do."

"I don't really do it anymore, but I want to. I want to give my agent what he needs to get me what I need, which is an advance, quickly."

"I know about the suspension. Kimberly told me. I think she was trying to make excuses for you, but there was no need."

"There was and is. But I've been thinking, and good writing is just good writing. I just want to write a really good story with some spice. Well, a lot of spice."

And my traitor cheeks go hot.

"And I would like to help," he says, and pulls on his straw. I swallow.

But he is deadly serious. And clearly not mesmerized by puckered lips.

"Why?" I ask. Honestly astonished. I thought it would be a hard sell.

"I can learn from you."

I shake my head. "You cannot."

His mouth does that thing where he tries not to smile, but

one escapes anyway. A signature look, I'm learning. "Not about that, but I bet I will learn plenty."

"I'll pay you."

He leans back, looking horrified.

"A percentage. A percentage of the royalties. Not the advance —sorry, I'm going to need every penny but of the sales."

His eyes go soft.

"Bridget, that's … I don't know what to say. No one, not even authors who used my likeness on a seven-book series ever offered me a percentage. Thank you."

Just then a guy takes the big letter D and leaves our food.

"Don't get too excited," I say. "No guarantee I will earn out."

"Earn out?"

"Make enough on the book to pay back the publisher for the advance so I can get royalties. I've only ever done it once, with my debut, and barely then."

"So that's how it works with trad. No one ever told me. I never get to meet the authors when I do covers for the large publishing houses."

"I looked up your covers. Did you know you have a fan club?"

"I do."

But something about the response lets me know he doesn't want to talk about it. I tuck into my salad. Pensive. Somehow talking to him at the gym was easier, like in his native habitat. This is too normal. Too much like a lunch date. An uncomfortable lunch date. We eat quietly. Too quietly, which makes me think.

"Do you talk? You know, in bed?"

He chokes on some protein.

"Is it necessary for the project?"

"Maybe. I'm horrible at it. You?'

"I'm the strong silent type, normally."

"Good. I wouldn't want you to lie."

He wipes his mouth and puts down his napkin.

"What do you mean by that?"

"Well, you know, you are you and I am me, and I wouldn't want you to say anything that wasn't true."

"Oh. I know what this is." He's shaking his head. "And to quote a friend of mine, 'Bridget, you're objectively stunning.'"

Wow.

"I've thought so from our very first meeting. I could wax poetic for ten minutes just on the color of your lips, never mind your cheeks when they pink, or ..." His eyes drop. Just for a second, but I know where they went and get a little zing out of it. "Let's just say there is plenty to inspire dirty talk if you want it. Just let me know. Happy to oblige."

I think I've stopped breathing.

This isn't going to work if I can't even handle the illusion of sex talk.

What would I say to Kimberly after such a speech?

"Purple."

He puts his fork down and laughs. "I'm sorry, did you just say purple?"

"You know. It's a writing thing. When you use over-the-top linguistics or overtly, almost uncomfortable, sexual phrasing— just anything over the top—they call it purple. It's what my editor used to put in the margins."

"She'd just write 'purple'?"

"Yep. And then I would kill my darlings."

He points his finger at me. "I know that one." And yes, even one finger can be tan and long and sexy. "We do that in screenplays too. The perfect line that is not perfect for that script. But we save our darlings. You?"

"Sometimes. Mostly they go to that virtual trash pile in the sky."

"Hmm."

I dip a fry in aioli. "They're really good, want one?"

"I'm good," he says, cutting up a boiled egg he didn't even salt. Just sprayed lemon juice across the whole bowl. This guy is dedicated.

"Too good, I'd say. But I get it. It takes dedication to look like you, doesn't it? Speaking of, that was the strangest audition. Is it always like that, and what was that bit at the end—what's proof?"

"In my case, proof of abs, like proof of life—you know, with AI, no one trusts pictures anymore."

"That's … offensive. Now that I think about it, it was all kinda offensive. Except the part where you died. That was great. Horrible line, but you made it work."

"Thanks. The star has better ones, but just barely."

"The star?"

"The one who gets the movie made. Names are trivial when you're the star. Kinda like singers with only one name, being the star."

"Bowie?"

"Exactly."

"Chakakhan?"

"Technically two, but points for going deep."

"Prince?"

"The reason for the rule."

"Beyoncé?"

"Only just behind the symbol no one can pronounce, but only because he's ridden that big black bike into the sky."

I laugh.

"I am perceiving that I am not the only one who likes some

classic MTV."

"Hungry like the wolf." He takes a bite of salmon while looking me right in the eye and how, oh how, can that be a turn-on? Chewing. Who can chew sexily?

Rhetorical.

"Well, it was weird," I say.

"That was pretty mild. Hell, I've had snakes draped across my shoulders. Like multiples."

Don't have to tell you where my mind went then.

"I've had fake tattoos painted on every scrap of skin. I've even been green-screened and told to talk to a giant cherry to sell condoms."

"No!"

"It was *so* purple."

I laugh at the proper use of the term.

"But I'm glad you think I pulled off the line and the dying part. I'm basically a body, go figure, that talks twice and dies once, but it *is* a major film with an Oscar-winning director and big names attached. The lines are shit, though. *I will meet thee in hellllll,*" he says like the Grim Reaper, if the Grim Reaper was Scottish.

"Well, you pulled it off. I didn't even notice how bad the line was when you said it. I'm getting a to-go box. You?"

I come back with a cookie and a box. Pack up the rest of my salad for dinner while he finishes his protein, protein, protein bowl. He eats like it's a job. Like there's no pleasure. And it makes me want to stuff a cookie in his face. But then three twenty-somethings walk in the door, chatting … until they spot Josh. Their gazes feral. He's aware, but I can't tell if it bothers him.

"Is it a curse?" I whisper.

He laughs a low rumble that has them looking his way again.

"Not a curse."

"If you say so."

"When you're a *New York Times* bestselling author and people stop you on the street, you tell me if it's a curse."

"That's different, and you know it. And you're—I hate to be cliché—but more than just a pretty face. I saw that in the three minutes you lay dying. And I don't think I like the way your business treats you. I'm not sure I like the way the world treats you."

He tilts his head and looks at me, eyes narrowing.

"I know. Ironic. Kettle black and all that, but I'm going to try and stop doing it," I say.

"Doing what?"

"Objectifying you."

He nods thoughtfully. "I'm not sure I mind *you* doing it." He pushes his empty bowl away. "When would you like to get started? Bridget, tell me what you need?"

Whew. That was a hit of something strong.

But time to come clean.

"So. In the interest of the project I'm going to say this once, and you are never going to repeat it to any person dead or alive."

He crosses his heart. "I rarely speak to the dead."

"Speak for yourself."

"So, what do you need?"

I put both hands on the table, take a deep breath, and let it out like a cleansing. Then tell the truth.

"Everything."

His eyes go wide.

"Oh, god, I'm not a virgin. I've had six sexual partners—the last one I thought I might marry—and implements too, but it's like … it's like I'm broken. I honestly don't know what the fuss is all about."

He smiles the trying-to-tamp-it-down smile. I love this smile. Licks his lips, considering his response to my truth vomit.

"Bridget, I've had countless partners—alas, no implements—and I can say beyond a shadow of a doubt"—he moves his finger back and forth between us—"This. This is going to be … well, more than fuss. Much more."

He says one F word, but I can't help but hear the other.

"When would you like to start?" he asks.

I look across at him—the whole of him—and I see something more. It pulls to me. Like there is a deep pool of want in him that has nothing to do with sex, but I think it might be one of the reasons he is so sexy. Maybe I'll be lucky enough to get to know him not just in the biblical sense. Only time will tell.

I push across the macadamia-and-dark-chocolate cookie like an offering. He takes a huge bite, eyes never leaving mine. Moans. *Fuck me.* Then a sip of his water.

So patient.

Not me.

"Tonight."

TWELVE

BRIDGET MEET CLIT

I put on the only piece of lingerie I own, the one bought that very day after leaving Josh. It was from a downtown boutique I really couldn't afford, but I thought, live a little. I also thought I could write it off. Like the three books I got yesterday to begin my research: *Come as You Are*, *She Comes First*, and *More Orgasms Please*. The last title I wholly agree with. It's polite. And I do love polite.

What the salesperson showed me was anything but polite. All kinds of crotchless and nipple-baring shreds of fabric, but I went with the short babydoll nightie she called the Purple Rain.

It's satin. And a purple so deep it's almost black, with lace at the breast and little teardrops of lace at the hem that reach not quite to the middle of my thigh. And given how pale I am, even I have to admit it's striking.

I slide it on over skin softened from a sugar scrub and shaved and plucked in every way I could think of realizing to do this, I'll need to get out of my body, become my protagonist. I decided she would have already had many of those bottle nights. Many with the hero of the story, it being a second chance romance. Which inspired my choice of libation.

I pour a shot of vodka from the crystal skull sitting next to the white shell I picked up on the beach this morning while getting a pep talk from Sweetie. Like a talisman, it gives me courage.

On the advice from the man at the liquor store, I chilled the vodka in the freezer first. I know Richard's skull contained tequila, but I'm more of a vodka kind of girl and was happy to see they had one in a skull—for a price I should not have paid as broke as I am.

I know I should eat, and look at the cheese-and-fruit tray I put out for my guest, but I can't quite stomach it. It's six p.m. and barely dark. I feel somewhat silly in lingerie, but I need to set the tone—keep this what it is—and get down to business.

Expecting Josh any minute, I take another shot and it goes down clean, like drinking a glacier.

Everything might have gone to plan had Josh not gotten stuck on the bridge. But stuck he was, behind a pileup they were trying to clear. I almost called it off. I actually tried to, while continuing to sip from the skull, but he said he was almost here.

The vodka is cold, and it is making me warm and brave. I sip away as I wait. And wait. And wait.

A soft knock on the door.

Another.

I must have fallen asleep.

A little unsteady, I get up to peer through the peephole. He stands under the porch light, looking dark and dangerous in black from head to toe. He takes my breath away. His ten-o'clock shadow as dark as his hair. Eyes so bright against his tanned face, and lips the prettiest pale bubble gum pink you have ever seen. And like he can read my mind, he chooses that moment to lick them.

Right.

I swing the door open a little hard, and it hits the wall.

Oops.

He actually looks nervous. But all I can think about is how those lips will taste.

I move to join him on the porch to find out, and my fuzzy slippers catch on the doorjamb.

Not sexy.

I kick them off high into the house. Then I rise up on my tiptoes, and kiss those bubble gum-colored lips.

"Well hello to you too. But Bridge, the lights are on, and you—"

"You gave me a nickname?" I kiss him again, this time running my fingers over the stubble, and he gently backs me into the doorway. I lick my lips—mint.

"You taste like your water bottle."

"Let's get you inside."

"Let's get *you* inside," I say, giggling at my own joke, and pull him into the living room. For some reason, I stumble again, this time backward until I fall, pretty gracefully I think onto the couch. My mother's voice chooses that moment to break in.

Maybe you should have had something to eat with your liquor bottle?

But I couldn't care less. He is mouthwatering, and I am ready to do this. I pat the seat next to me, suggestively, and he sits. I'm straddling him before he can say lickety-split. And even though he's slim, there's quite a lot to straddle. But maybe I moved too fast. Things are not right. Things are spinning.

He reaches around me and picks up the now quarter-gone skull.

"A bit of liquid courage?" he asks.

I shake off the spins and wiggle in his lap to find he is *very* ready to go to work.

This is going to work.

"I don't think I can have it without one."

"Have what? And it seems like you had more than one."

"No, you know—the big O."

"Oh," he says, and a breath of mint brushes over my face. But something is wrong.

"What time is it? I'm tired. I don't want to be tired."

I take the bottle from him, uncork it, take a swig, and offer it.

"Richard thinks I don't even know where it is. I bet you know where it is."

"No, thank you," he responds to the offered bottle, but he takes it from me anyway.

"So polite," I muse.

"Wondering who Richard is, but maybe not the time to ask, and even though I'm not really following you, I think I get the gist."

"Oh, you know." I tuck my head into his shoulder, suddenly shy. "You smell like apples."

"My grandmother's crumble. It's in the car. She tries to feed me sweets."

I'm pressing up against all of him and he's talking about his grandmother? What am I doing wrong? But he runs his hand down my hair, onto my back. It's large and warm and he's doing circles. Around and around.

The next thing I know, I'm prying my tongue off the roof of my mouth. Reaching for the water that is miraculously on my bedside table. I drink it to the bottom. What a dream! Needing to pee, I get up to use the bathroom, but when I get there, I must still be dreaming because I'm not wearing the purple lingerie I had on when I fell asleep last night. I'm in my Mr. Magoo nightshirt. But, when I sit to pee, my undies are the ones that match the purple nightie.

Wait … what's going on? Purple Rain is hanging on the shower curtain. Drying?

I continue to sit on the toilet long after I finish, trying to piece together the night, until my stomach rolls like a sea of acid and I know if I don't get something into it I'll be sick, but not before I brush my teeth. The little clock on the bathroom vanity tells me it is 5:05 a.m.

My head is a fog. I walk into the kitchen and click on one of the electric candles scattered around my main living space because I hate bright lights in the morning. By that flickering yellow glow, I reach up into the tall cabinet above the fridge and pull down my special occasion cereal. Take out the milk, squinting against the brightness of the fridge light, to find Cap'n Crunch smiling back at me.

Then there's a noise.

Soft, like a scratch on fabric.

You're not alone.

Fear spikes my blood. I stand completely still. Don't even breathe.

There it is again.

I peer past the kitchen island and like a balloon that's been popped, release the breath I'm holding. Because it's Josh. He's asleep on my couch, a throw crocheted by Sweetie over his hips. Sally Girl stands up from her perch next to him and I think *traitor* but whisper, "It's all right," so she lays back down.

How did she even get in here? She was in her room at the back of the house.

Then it all comes rushing back to me like snapshots from hell. Letting him in, attacking him, being put to bed, spilling

99

orange juice all over myself … being a complete and total jackass.

Trying to take his clothes off—against his will.

Oh my god.

I drop my spoon, too loudly, on the counter and put my hand over my mouth to keep my exclamation inside.

He changed my sheets, took care of my dog, wiped my face, *changed my clothes.*

Oh my god, oh my god, oh my god.

I look up to the ceiling mortified and think I'm no good at being bad. I sneak another glance, and his hip bone peeks out from under the multicolor throw covering him, and it's almost obscene how hot he looks. Even in his sleep he's camera ready. Then I see on the coffee table my books.

No.

No, no, no, no, no.

He's been reading my research!

She Comes First is tossed aside, but *More Orgasms Please* is open to the middle.

I want to slink away in shame, but this is my house.

Why is he still here? Why didn't he leave?

I retrieve my spoon and eat my cereal as quietly as possible because if I don't get something into my stomach, I'm going to be sick—chewing slowly, trying not to wake him. But if Cap'n Crunch with Crunch Berries is anything, it's crunchy.

"Good Morning, Bridge," he says, running a hand through his hair, looking like a dream.

I sigh and smile back. With a mouthful of cereal, I probably look like a chipmunk. Then remembering all I did last night, I choke it down.

What can one say after such a debacle? Particularly after

what I promised at lunch. I fall back on my training. *Always apologize when you're wrong.*

"Josh, I am so sorry. For every—"

He breaks me off with a hand. In black form-fitting boxers. And stretches.

Holy hell. It's like Christmas morning, watching him unwrap himself from sleep.

You deserve coal!

"It's all good," he says with a yawn.

"If you say it's good, it's not."

"What?"

"Sorry, something my agent says."

"Okay, well then, everything's fine. Better?" Then he looks at his watch. "And perfect timing."

Like being woken up by a woman in a Mr. Magoo nightshirt at five in the morning is somehow a good thing?

"Coffee?" he asks and then matter-of-factly walks by me to press the Start button on *my* coffee maker.

Last night he set up coffee?

Who's hosting whom?

"Why are you still here?" I ask, as I can't imagine why he would stay, why he would ever speak to me again after the way I behaved around him. It's like I'm at my worst whenever he's in the room. But he seems perfectly comfortable, and strangely, I'm glad he is. Glad he's in my home. I shake that line of thought right out of my head.

"I can leave if you want me to. But I was worried. You were … Well, I was worried."

"You washed my negligee."

"I didn't want it to be ruined. It was …" He faces me, looking like he walked off a billboard with his light eyes almost glowing.

"Bridget, you were—you are—lovely. Thank you for wearing it for me."

He's thanking me.

What kind of topsy-turvy world is this? This inordinately beautiful man, waiting patiently by my coffee maker, is a *good* person. A great person. A very great person. Who at this moment, with food in my stomach, eight hours of sleep, and the long, sleek curve of his body in view—the scar pointing the way —is a temptation I refuse to resist for one more minute.

"Come here," I say quietly. "Please." I will not make the same mistakes. "That is, if you want to …"

He seems hesitant, but when he is close enough, I take his hand. I remember the feel of it on my back.

"I'm so very sorry. For everything. For all of it." I kiss the back of his hand. "I'm so glad you stayed. So glad you're here. Right now. So glad it is still dark, because I don't know if I'll ever have the courage to do this again."

I lift my nightshirt, but only to the tops of my thighs, all the while looking him in the eyes. "Is this okay?"

He nods.

I slip off the shirt and toss it into the sink to join one of my fuzzy slippers. Ignoring the humiliating snapshot that brings up, I return to his exceptional face. His lashes are low, his eyes lower.

He couldn't help but look at my body last night when he put on the Mr. Magoo, so I'm not showing him anything he hasn't already seen. But he is looking at me like he's never seen a woman before. When he speaks, it's quiet.

"There is nothing to be sorry for. This situation is … unprecedented." He swallows. "And if I didn't have to drive last night, I'm sure I would have taken some liquid courage. But Bridge"—That nickname. What it does to me—"You're wrong about it helping with, you know …"

I suck in a long breath.

He looks at his watch. 5:16.

"Just enough time, I think," he says almost to himself. "May I show you? How it can be. Without it."

I nod, and then when he continues to wait, I say, "Please."

He lifts me like I weigh less than a sack of sugar and sets me on the countertop. I shiver, not from the granite but the hand he runs down my neck, past the indentation between my collarbones, between my bare breasts—somehow without touching them—and along my stomach, all the while pressing me softly to the counter. Across my hip, around my thigh—his hand so large his fingers send tingles down my leg until he reaches my ankle, lifts it, and places my foot on the granite next to my hip. Then without a word, he pulls aside the purple panties with one hand; the other presses against my knee.

I gasp.

He starts off soft. Light touches of his lips, then his tongue. Then presses my knee all the way to the counter, and my head falls back.

He goes to work.

I last all of twelve seconds before I'm writhing against his face, my other foot in the crease of his hip, pushing, arching, pressing into his tongue, his mouth. He murmurs against me. I have no idea what he's saying, but the vibration of his words lights me on fire. And without knowing what I'm doing, I press his head down. Hold it. I can't stop myself from moving against him, from whimpering, from crying out. His tongue, pressing, pressing, pressing. And I'm pressing too. Making sounds. I think I'm begging. But slipping away from him on the counter.

Then he slots his hand under my ass and pulls me toward him by the pussy. His tongue never leaving my lips.

So. Fucking. Hot.

But when he slides his thumb through my wet lips, pressing inside, I shatter on a scream.

I wake with tears pricking my eyes.

What. Was. That?

I let go of his hair. Shaking mine, I look down at him, astonished. My mouth is stuck in the shape of the first letter of the word I *finally* understand. His thumb still inside me. His body arching over me in the flickering light. His watch glows 5:19.

"How." I ask. "How?" Unable to believe he proved beyond a shadow of a doubt—in three minutes—I have never had an orgasm before.

He looks down at me like the cat that got the cream. Stands up slowly. Stands to his full, extraordinary height, and I cannot help but notice what those three minutes did to him. But he just licks his lips.

Fuck.

"I find a consistent pressure, applied to the appropriate point, of course, usually does the trick. I think most men piddle around too much. Of course I adjusted pressure and place based on your sounds, your movements. You actually showed me what you wanted; I only had to pay attention. I'm impressed. Didn't even need a finger. Only a thumb." Which he holds up like an Exhibit glistening with me.

"Again!"

"With pleasure," he says, as his gaze moves from my face down my body like a caress. "Bridget," he says as his focus lands just where I want him, "meet clit." And as he licks his lips and moves in for another go, he says so that his breath hits right against that point, "Clit, meet Bridget."

This time I watch.

THIRTEEN

BRASS TACKS

I'm scarfing down a hunk of his grandmother's apple crumble after warming it up in the microwave. He brought it in with a change of clothes, the fork still stuck in it and somehow untouched. All that buttery cinnamon sweetness, warm from her oven, sitting right next to him in the car last night—for hours! How did he not take even one little bite?

He's found a sticky note and is placing it in *More Orgasms Please*.

"Didn't like the other one?" I say around.

"*She Comes First*? That's a given."

God's gift indeed. And that book has a lot of oral in it and he needs no help there. This man has a PhD in cunnilingus.

Where do you think he got all that talent, *Bridget?*

You're not welcome here. Leave.

And because she's my mother I say, *Please.*

And she does. Just like that. Miracle.

Have I never asked nicely before?

Finishing my second piece of his grandmother's crumble, I decide I want to see what job could possibly be worth missing out on all this appley goodness. So I'm going to the shoot this morning. He admits he hadn't planned on staying the night as his call is at 5:45 a.m., and that only endears me to him more.

This man saved the cat last night and made her purr this morning. A sure sign of a promising hero. Yep, this one's a keeper.

Rudely, my mind flashes back to how we got here. What this is. This is not the end of a date. This is not a meet-cute. This is business.

And he has more of it this morning. When is this man not working? He leaves before me as the shoot is to happen at daybreak on the beach across from the gym, allowing him to "get defined" first—as if he could become any more defined than he was while leaning over me on the kitchen counter this morning. But that's just what he does before a shoot.

I miss the workout by taking a quick shower, but I'm there in time to see the sky lighten. See the photographer place and direct them. I must admit, Kayla is objectively stunning—a match made in heaven, those two. However, as I watch him work, I can't help but remember what that now-brooding mouth did to me—not once, but twice—less than an hour ago.

Does he smell like me? Can Kayla tell? The cavewoman in me hopes so; the polite me is convinced he washed off my scent when he visited the bathroom before leaving the house. And some other part of me wonders what else occurred in my bathroom, since I never heard the shower. Breathing exercises, visions of old people naked, or something much sexier? Because he went in rock-hard and came out ready to face the world. The thought makes me squirm.

They work quickly, racing sunrise. Adjusting, posing, even changing clothes right on the beach. Pink clouds streak across the horizon.

He lifts Kayla in his arms and spins her around, the bright orange ball of the sun flashing in and out behind them, the white wedding gown floating in the wind. They are good together. The way they look at each other—it's intoxicating.

This is acting, I tell myself. They're professionals. As are we.

But it was to the taste of me this morning when he likely got himself off. And I no longer have to wonder what I taste like. When he kissed me through the second shuddering orgasm, his abs doing the work his tongue had been doing, which was, fuck all, the best thing ever, I learned the taste of me. Salty as the sea.

The photographer calls out, "That's a wrap," and Josh swings Kayla around once more, her laughter floating on the breeze.

And I wonder, for which one of us is Josh just business?

Me. Don't forget it.

And it's working. The scene already percolating in my head, the subtle tap of inspiration that, in this instance, feels more like lightning needing to escape. Words running around. Pictures. This is going to work, if I let it. If I don't get confused. If I keep my head.

So when he jogs over, shirtless of course, it's the perfect time to clarify what we are—business partners. And yet hopefully keep the kindness, almost playfulness, we found this morning.

"What did you think?" He seems almost high from the endeavor.

"I think you are going to have one hell of a cover."

"Three, actually. We just shot the trilogy."

"No wonder there were so many costume changes. I liked the last one best."

"The wedding pics. Yeah they're going to be sweet."

"She's—"

She has a name, Bridget.

"Kayla is lovely."

"A very good friend."

I will not decipher this comment. It's none of my business.

"An old friend," he adds.

"Not my business as long as we agree to be monogamous for the duration of our working arrangement."

"Of course."

Good. I'm getting back some of the business manner from our meeting over tea. I decide to press on. Time for brass tacks. Well, after my curiosity is sated.

Curiosity will put the cat in a big ugly mess, Bridget Stanton.

I slam the door on *that* voice for what I tell myself is the final time.

"So, since this is just business," I say, "we can be honest, right? Like, you know, maybe you can't always be honest with someone you are with in other ways. Capiche?"

"Fine by me," he says, still moving—almost dancing—on the sand. This work really lights him up.

"So in that vein, just wondering," I continue, determined to know, "did you, you know, take care of yourself before you left this morning?"

He barks out a laugh. "Hell, yes, I took care of myself. If not, I would have been obscene."

"I like that, that I did that to you." True, but ... I pull it back. "It bodes well for the process."

"Indeed it does," he says like a promise.

Go for levity.

"I have a pretty good idea how well it bodes," I say as I look at the promise of the premise. And I swear he's blushing. Good, this is working. Getting my feet under me. "But back to brass tacks. About consent. I do."

"What do you mean?" he asks.

I lower my voice as the photographer walks by with his

equipment. And squirm a little in the sand. But after the debacle of last night, I feel we need to have this conversation.

"I could tell you were concerned this morning, and last night … well, I'm not sure we need anal in this book, but otherwise I consent."

"Surely *some* anal play?" he counters impishly.

"'Light petting' so to speak in the anal department is fine, I guess."

Did you just say that?

Indeed you did, Richard croons.

Go suck an egg; I'm in a business meeting.

"But in the moment, Josh, I'll tell you if I don't want anything, if I'm uncomfortable, if I want to stop. You do the same."

"You damn well better!"

"You damn well better."

We stare at each other, neither backing down.

"Okay," he says first.

"Okay."

His doubtful gaze has me adding, "I promise."

He's nodding like he's trying to convince himself this is okay. Advance consent. Then he seems to shake it off and says, "But there is this one thing—"

Kayla chooses that moment to call his name against the rising wind. I pull my cardigan closer around me, and he waves to her. She holds her hand to her ear in the universal sign for "call me." He gives a thumbs-up. I watch the entire thing with forced detachment, knowing there is something more between them. Something intimate.

But of course there is. Look at them.

When he turns back to me, I force myself to not care.

"So one thing?" I prompt.

He puts his hand on my back as if to guide me, and we walk toward the house, where his car is parked.

"You see, Bridget, I'm strong—"

"Quite the update, Captain Obvious." His biceps could crush walnuts.

"It's just, I've been known to position my lovers assertively, sometimes swiftly." I can't help but remember the way he held Kayla like a doll and swung her around. "Described by some as 'throwing them around,'" he continues. "But I don't have to. I can control it."

What a strange way to put it. He seems all control to me. Certainly, he was this morning. And that untouched apple crumble!

I ask honestly, "Do they like it?" wondering what it would be like.

"Never had a complaint." His voice is unemotional.

"Don't change what works. It sounds hot, and I need Scotch bonnet."

"About that. You said that last night."

He takes a long pull off a water bottle, and mint ghosts across my taste buds. Which sends me on a little fantasy montage trip. Pulling his hair, biting his lip, rubbing against him, locking him against me.

"Scotch bonnet?" he reminds.

"My agent wants this book to be sexy, like Scotch bonnet sexy, versus, say, only cayenne."

"Good to know. I'll ponder that. Actually, I'm Scottish, on my mother's side."

"No shit?"

"Aye."

"Well, spread me on toast and have me for breakfast." Then I realize what I've said. "Okay, that might be too close to the bone." I shake my head, laughing. "Fuck me."

"That's the plan," he says, smiling so big I can't help myself. Business or not, I laugh. Out loud. We both do, and the hilarity cuts right through the tension. His laugh is deep and throaty, and if a laugh can be a flavor, his is a double-dark-chocolate cake. And wonder when was the last time I had so much fun?

"How can you be Scottish? You tan like a—"

"Brazilian. My father."

"We are going to make one hell of a book."

"Indeed we are." And it's all promise. From a man secure in his body and his skill.

Can't wait to see the pages! Richard quips.

Enough of you, Richard. I've got enough people in my head already. Too many. I round them all up—my mother, Richard, even Sweetie—and put them out the door. Shut and lock it.

I've got this. I've *really* got this.

"One other thing," he says. "Do you have a character sketch, an outline, the tent posts?"

And that might be the sexiest thing he has ever said to me, because this man knows his way around a story.

"You'd like to see?"

"If you don't mind. It would help."

"Not at all. I should have shared it with you already. If you have any suggestions, please send them my way. But soon. This morning's scene, once I've written it, and the outline of Act I, are going to Richard tomorrow."

"Another mystery solved. Richard's your agent."

"Yep."

"The one who thinks you don't know where your clit is?"

"Well, if I didn't before, I certainly do now, thank you very much."

"My pleasure."

"That was rhetorical!"

But he's laughing again, that deep laugh of his. I shuffle my feet.

"So whatcha doin' today?" I go for casual and get seventh-grade dance.

"Thought I would finish my workout and then maybe later this afternoon we could go get some business supplies."

My mind immediately goes to dildos, butt plugs, ropes, and maybe the size of my eyes gives him an indication of where my mind is taking me because he adds, "You know, something to help you see better. Help you write the scenes."

"See better?"

"I was thinking a mirror."

"Oh. Oh, sure."

Oh. My.

"I need to stop by the home and see Nana, but say, three?"

I am so in trouble. I'm a sucker for a man who loves his grandmother. And even though I think I could stand here all day with a barefoot Josh, I have a sex scene that's not going to write itself.

And yet, that is exactly what it does when I get back to the house.

It's effortless. I close my eyes and let my fingers fly. See the whole thing from inside my body and outside of it. The way he almost-reverently slid my panties down for round two. The way I leaned out my other knee in anticipation. How wet I was when I came.

And I remembered things about Josh too. The way his hand held onto the counter, his knuckles white. His breathing at the end that almost mimicked my shuddering, like he too could feel what was rocking through me. His bright eyes in the low light.

The candlelight flickering across his skin. The way his hips rocked, subtly in time with his tongue.

Damn.

Remembering that did it to me, and for the first time in a long time, I decide to try to take care of myself.

But it's not the same. It is, ironically, anticlimactic. It's supposed to take the edge off—keep me from texting him—because after writing that scene, all I want to do is see him again. And that feels more dangerous than anything else in this unconventional, free fall of a situation.

So I go get *She Comes First* because it starts with an exercise in self-pleasure.

To survive this, I need to learn to get myself off.

FOURTEEN

THROUGH THE LOOKING GLASS

"Y ou're introspective this afternoon," he says.

"Hmm" is all I say because my mind is racing with things I'm never going to admit to Josh, like how blown away I was when he suggested we find a mirror for my bedroom to let me watch. He understood how important seeing what is happening from the outside, as a voyeur, while feeling from the inside was for my process. And there is no way I'm going to verbalize what I can't wait to see in this mirror.

If you can't say it, you can't ride it.

Ha. Ha. Punny.

Fine. Cock. I can't wait to get a look at his cock.

Nope, I like Richard better.

I wonder if he's neat down there; I've never been with a man who scapes. Bet he is, being a model. Damn, can we just find a mirror and get the hell out of here?

"What about that one?" I point to a small round one hanging on the wall.

"Not much of me would fit inside it," he says, and it's all I can do to not say *Prove it.*

"We need one you can lean up against the wall,"

"Maybe we should ask someone?" I ask impatiently.

"Don't you like to browse?"

And that's when I see it reflected in the too-small mirror in front of me. A little uptick at the corner of his lips. He knows perfectly well what this is doing to me and is pleased as punch to watch me suffer. But I don't look like I'm suffering. I look alive —color on my skin, pupils blown wide. He leans in, his breath warm on my neck. His pale blue eyes lock my reflection in place. I feel bold, so I say, "I can't wait to see all of you."

"Me too. If all of me is in all of you."

Damn.

His hand is touching my waist. Pressing into my hip bone in little pulses. I push back against him—

"Can I help you?"

Behind us is a salesperson. And she's checking out *my* Richard.

I flash my best fuck-you smile. "Please, we're looking for a large mirror. For the bedroom. *You know* ..." I raise one shoulder coyly. Josh tries not to laugh, turns it into a cough.

Does she ever.

But it works. I've staked my claim, and she helpfully takes us to the back of the warehouse to look at dozens of mirrors tilted up against the wall. At the end of the row, Josh nods toward a huge gilt-framed one.

"A bit decorative for me," I say. "But the size is ... appropriate?"

"We'll take it. Can you deliver?" Josh says and hands a card to the woman.

"No, I'll get it."

"Bridge, I've got this. I'll write it off. Business expense," he adds, smiling the can-barely-tamp-it-down smile of his. The salesperson looks shocked but takes the card to run it.

We spend the few minutes until she returns looking at each other in the reflection. I don't know what he's thinking, but I can't wait to find out.

"If you're local, we could deliver next Thursday," she says.

His eyes stay locked with mine.

"I have a truck. I'll get it today."

And suddenly I'm nervous. I squeak out, "Saturday?"

"As in four days from now?" he asks, incredulously.

"I need to make revisions on the first chapters. Get a feel for the characters. You know, before …"

"Of course." He licks his lips. "Saturday."

And never before has a day of the week held such promise.

As the salesperson writes his name across the mirror with the word SOLD, I realize I have set myself up for the longest few days of my life.

FIFTEEN

COMING LIKE MEG RYAN

I try to write all day, but it's like I have ants in my pants. I get up and don't even know why. I've peed like ten times when I don't even need to. I've made four snacks and three cups of tea. Finally, I decide a walk on the beach may help me, and Sally Girl and I go north for like three miles.

No help.

By Thursday I'm losing my mind, so I attend spin class. Now it's not just Mom I'm using the euphemism with. Kimberly too. I can't explain why. I'm not embarrassed, but for some reason I want to keep it to myself. There's something mysterious about going somewhere three times a week in secret. It seems, I don't know, out of character.

I've decided that my heroine will know how to dance and I'm writing off the small donation I make every class to the center.

"Hey, Bridget. Back so soon?"

I like that they know.

"Can't get enough, and it's research for a book."

"Cool. What do you write?"

"Romance." It rolls right off my tongue.

I dance with Sara, Celeste's partner, and it is different, as she likes to follow, so I try to lead. We end up laughing a lot.

After class I'm feeling almost giddy. I clean house, as it has been a while. My thoughts wander when I get to the kitchen island.

I take the book back to the bedroom to practice and end up falling asleep frustrated, only to have the best dream where I not only get to pull down Beach Runner's hood but his pants too. And holy hell, I gave oral in a dream, and it was hot as fuck.

I wake to a notification and wonder if I'm still dreaming.

> Richard: Yes, yes, yes, yes, yes, YES! (picture Meg Ryan fake-coming over coffee). Needless to say, I am orgasmic about your scene. You do have it in you! I'm shocked and delighted.

Oh my god he liked it!!

> Me: Really?? It's good?

> Richard: Don't be coy. You know it is. So good I think someone snatched your body when you wrote that last horrid thing or has a Richard who knows what they're about entered the picture?

I chew on my lip. I can't decide what to tell him. When he's this happy with me I'm certainly not going to text *I promised that Richard some royalties.*

Richard: Never the mind—your work, your process—but it works. As you might imagine, I have never, quelle horreur, nor will I ever, partake in the joys of cunnilingus, but even I was turned on. (Although that might have to do with the specific descriptors regarding the partner;)

Me: Yeah. He's ...

I can't think of a single word that could describe the package that is Joshua Anjo Silva, so I send it as-is, figuring Richard will get it.

Richard: A gay man's wet dream? Speaking of descriptors, I have no idea what your protagonist looks like. And a name would be nice. Can't keep writing her as "her." Remedy that, please. And let me know when you can get me more pages. If you can get me to midpoint I'll put it out on proposal.

Me: Wow that's amazing news. How long will it take? And I didn't even realize.

Richard: You've been distracted. And as long as it takes. You've been on submission before, no more than a month if we're lucky. if not, threeish.

Me: Okay. The faster the better.

Richard: I know. Well, carry on! Seems like someone is finding her fun.

I'm so excited that before I know what I'm doing, I've called Josh. Without so much as a text, a true violation of modern-day etiquette. But he answers on the second ring, also a departure from, at least, dating norms.

"What's up?" he asks.

I wait for Richard to quip something Richard like but my mind is blissfully blank.

"Bridget?"

"My agent, he loved the pages. He wants more as soon as possible." Then because that sounds desperate, I add, "You know, whenever."

"That's great. I knew you could do it."

"He's going to try and sell it on proposal."

"Before you even finish?"

"Yep."

"That happens sometimes in screenwriting—selling on the pitch—but only for the greats."

"Then you make me great."

I'm blushing. At least he can't see.

"So, I know it's last minute and all, but can we start tonight?"

"Be there in twenty." He hangs up without even letting me thank him. I head to the bathroom to get ready, or as ready as I can.

About seven minutes later I get a text.

> Josh: OMW have the mirror.

In the mirror before me I see heat bloom on my skin. My cheeks pink. My lips suddenly look more rosy.

The purple rain.

I need the purple rain.

SIXTEEN

PURPLE RAIN

J osh hurries up the walk, carrying the mirror slanted away
so the raindrops miss the surface. I open the door wide for
him. He leans it against the couch and pins me with a look
of wanting so base, so savage, I'm glad I pulled out the purple
rain.

"No liquid courage this time?" he asks.

"No need. For that or the panties."

He swallows. His Adam's apple lifts and drops. His stunning
face is dripping, and as I walk to him, he slowly moves his head
back and forth. Like *I'm* the dream. I lean into him and take a
lick of cold rain off the hollow at the base of his throat.

Then I'm in his arms, legs around his waist, and he's pulling
off his shirt, my labia slipping along his ridges. I ignite. Teeth,
tongue—I want to devour every fucking inch of him. I kiss, suck,
nip. All the while, he is rhythmically pressing me against the
hard ridges of his pelvis, and it lights me on fucking fire. Burns
across my skin. I can't get close enough, can't press hard enough.
It's almost painful.

The bedroom is too far, so we move down to the cold tile. He pulls over the white shag entry rug and lays me on it. I watch in the mirror as he strips and lowers to move over me. Then he turns, our eyes locking in the reflection. Bare skin beneath the lingerie, sliding against the most beautiful cock I have ever seen. I still, and nod, and he pushes in slow and steady. I grimace. It's been so long. He stops. But I push up, off the ground, taking him in as he holds himself steady. His right arm is banded around my back, holding me against him.

"Now," I say, when he is fully seated. "Show me what all the fuss is about."

He comes down on one elbow, still holding me against himself. In the mirror I marvel at our contrasts entwined. He takes a peaked nipple between his lip and teeth and presses to the edge of pain. Not until I cry out does he start to move. Wave after wave of undulation. Slow and steady, against me, tilting me to push against my mound. I watch the effort flow through him. Again and again. A work of art in movement. And it's like I'm observing someone else, voyeuristic. So turned on by his control of himself, of his body. Of his beauty, his motion. Then he hits a spot and I cry out.

"Gotcha," he says softly.

And oh god.

In the mirror, my back arches, my breasts lift. I watch the slow, controlled movement that I push against with the help of his arm beneath me.

Fuck.

He is hitting that part of me didn't know existed—the one I've only read about in books.

Oh god.

"More," I cry out. "More. Josh, more." I'm begging.

In a flash, the soft rug is bunched under my hips, and he's planking over me. Moving with short, fast flexing of his abs.

"Unfucking. Unfucking believable," I hear him say as I push up into him.

He's hitting that place again and again. I cry out. He's relentless, giving me no room to breathe to catch up. I close my eyes and go inside. To a dark place I have never been, and hear my scream. I keep screaming, and he doesn't stop. I'm crying, and I can't stop. I don't know if I exist outside that spot. Then I explode, and every single part of me, every cell, says yes all at once, and I am calling out yes over and over again. And I'm floating, coming down from a height I didn't know I could reach.

He stops. Presses hard against me, his hand cupping my head to hold me in place, shuddering. I open my eyes. His are blown, barely blue, and his semen slips out between us.

"Wow," I mouth up at this man and take a picture with my mind. I never want to forget the look of him at this moment. Forget the place I took him to. Because he is looking at me—stunned—awestruck.

Then he falls on me, breathing hard, and whispers, "Wow doesn't even …"

He trails off, and I realize he can't stop shuddering. As am I. Tears continue to stream from my eyes. I don't know why they are there or when they will stop as I try to catch my breath.

"Josh. I didn't know. I didn't know."

He rolls over onto his back, on the cold tiles. Stares at the ceiling.

"Bridge. Believe me. Neither did I."

SEVENTEEN

LABEL-ON-A-BOTTLE KIND OF NIGHT

Maybe one day when I am old and wrinkled, someone is going to ask me what was the best night of my life. I won't even have to think. And I suspect for a little while it might be the same for him. A night of firsts for both of us. His first time skin-on-skin and my first time climaxing from the inside.

After that, we were pretty insatiable. We may have used the book as an excuse, but there was a tacit understanding neither of us wanted to stop.

We plotted between "scenes"—that's what we called it when a look or an accidental touch sent us back into a whirlwind of lust.

And that mirror.

He moved it into the bedroom after we managed to leave the cold, hard tiles of the entrance.

And I watched him in that mirror touch me, move against me, study me, over and over and over again. Until I lost myself completely. Became someone different in that reflection. Someone who wasn't scared of their body, what it felt, what it wanted. What it could do to him. Wasn't scared of anything.

And I could see how this thing between us, this chemistry, could make it so easy for my characters to fall in love. And they did that night, those characters. They fell hard and fast as we plotted between scenes, discussing their motivations. Jessica—she finally got a name from Josh's first-grade crush—and Royce—originally a joke name based on that first thing I said to him about not looking like a Josh that stuck. I voted for Daemon. So Josh took to calling himself Daemon in the third person for at least an hour. *Daemon would like to soap you. Daemon needs some water. Daemon is not done with you.* It was funny as shit when he said it and usually broke the scene, but I didn't care, as we only had to start over. In the end I lost a bet on who could hold out the longest and, lost, Royce it was.

We dove into their past. Scened their tentative first time when they were seventeen, their make-up time at a closed bar where she worked at twenty. That scene happened on the bar stool where I eat the Cap'n. It will never taste the same.

And a quiet and tender encounter in Jessica's childhood bedroom down the hall from her parents when she was hours from leaving for overseas. For that one, we wrote it first. Spoke the lines quietly like we might be overheard. Painful hurtful things that they both knew were lies meant to make it easier. Until they gave in and let their bodies tell each other the truth. I was not the only one who cried during that scene.

My god, it was a night. One beyond expectations. Not of what sex could be but also what collaboration could be. In that short, yet long span—thank god I'd had a nap—we became what I promised myself we would be. We became writing partners, *and* lovers—although that word did not seem large enough for the intimacy we shared that night.

And he was so damn charming. Like when I was reading back a passage where Royce was holding onto Jessica's thigh and Josh said, "Don't forget the cellulite." I asked what he was talking about, and he explained how much he liked it. My cellulite, my thigh. How he had been with—well, let's face it—more than a few models. He even said that with charm and chagrin, and then he took one of my "tiny meaty thighs" in hand, saying, "This, this is something a man wants to hold on to." Of course, not all models were thin, he said, but he was too much of a gentleman to further elaborate.

And the whole time I kept wondering, what's his fatal flaw?

Every romantic lead has to have one. In the end, I decided it must be that he really liked sex and would continue to have it with varied partners, and why wouldn't he? I mean, he clearly enjoyed it—took my pleasure seriously. Josh did tell me for him it was only women, he was straight, and I told him I wished I was bi. He laughed and agreed.

He obviously had had sex with a lot of women to acquire such skills. And rather than being jealous, I was thankful for every woman who taught him.

If the world was our oyster that night, I was the pearl.

I could no more lie to myself and say it was just business. We passed that on the floor by the door. But I could say it was fun, because it was the most fun I remember ever having.

We finally collapsed around four in the morning.

I woke to a room in shambles. Towels littered the floor, the comforter catty-corner on the bed, pillows from the living room strewn about. Josh was rustling in the kitchen, and for a few moments all was right in my world.

Sitting up, rotating my neck, hearing it crack to find a bottle of refined coconut oil spilled across my bedside table. Josh had found it at some point after I admitted I didn't have lube.

The bottle wasn't fancy, but it was glass, and I planned to put a tag around that bottle's lip and place it on my shelf. I would write, "Learned what all the fuss is about."

I might never have a collection like Richard, but this bottle of coconut oil I would keep forever.

I went to stand it up on the table and found my arms didn't feel like working. I was sore—*very* sore. Needed a hot bath.

We took that bath together with coffee, mine sweet and light, his black as midnight. We barely fit. Josh's long legs poked out of the water at sharp angles. It couldn't have been comfortable for him, but it sure was comfortable for me. He asked after me, made sure I was only sore and not hurt. Added some Epsom salts halfway through when he realized I had some.

After the bath, we stayed away from the mirror. Worked at the kitchen table, back-and-forth typing, speaking out loud as we took turns.

We didn't talk to anyone else, no matter who called or texted that day, because everything seemed gossamer like blown glass. We were racing to midpoint.

But by dinner, with the chapters I had written before, we had thirty-eight thousand words and were ready to turn the corner, to pass through the middle. Beginning, middle, end—the simple recipe of all great stories. And this one was lining up to be surprisingly, remarkably, great.

"Josh, this is really good," I said staring at my screen. "I'm actually proud of it."

"Of course you are."

"And hungry." His eyes shot to mine. "You?"

"Ravenous. Something quick."

"Something easy," I agreed.

Double entendre aside, I heated up Campbell's tomato. He made grilled cheese and moaned as he ate. Like a simple slice of American cheese was a treat. Afterwards, we quietly we put the dishes in the sink. It was dark again, and by some unspoken rule, we went back into the bedroom.

I was sore, so he used his mouth, as did I. And I knew this wasn't a scene, would not make it into the book. This was for us, a further exploration of the details of each other's sex, each other's preferences. Josh liked when I talked to him around his cock. I found that a bit surprising. I liked it when he was almost still, pressing firmly against my clit. I knew its exact location by this point, and any tiny movement, change in pressure, undid me.

There was nothing between our bodies. No artifice, no resistance—our bodies spoke only the truth. And as I rolled him over to explore the planes of his back, I realized I had never known a body like I now knew his.

And we were just getting started.

EIGHTEEN

ABS OF PAIN

"Can I stay the night?"

It came from the bottom of the bed. With all the strength left me, I push up to find Josh gone.

"I can't move," a voice says at my feet.

"Where are you?"

"On the floor, using Sally Girl's tail as a massage roller. I have such a cramp. Hey, and what happened to her nose? I never noticed before, but it's literally in my face."

I scramble to the end of the bed. Sally Girl is smiling so widely that her big back teeth show, and her nose is like a centimeter from his.

"The day I brought her home, she had stitches. They went from ear to nose and her head was in a cone the size of a steering wheel." Now she's nudging his nose. He looks terrified, his eyes not leaving hers, but manages, "How did that happen?"

"They said she knocked over a bookshelf and broke a plate glass window, after tearing up her new family's living room."

He's looking up at her open mouth, which is big enough to eat his neck. And he is definitely afraid.

I can't imagine being afraid of her, although a lot of people are. Which is convenient as no one bothers me when I have Sally Girl, regardless of the fact that they are only in danger of being nudged to death.

He speaks again, but it's like he's trying not to move his mouth. "Does that happen a lot?"

"Sometimes. She needs her person. Me. And exercise. She gets anxious sometimes and gets a kind of oral fixation. It's hard. I can't blame her. But it's expensive. Hard to be away from her for too long, which is sometimes hard. Life and all. And she always seems to feel so bad after. Even if I don't scold her. I'm glad I don't have school days anymore."

"Oral fixation, like a smoker." He's scooting out from underneath her head.

"Yes. But she eats the thing. Eats everything. Can't stop chewing. That's why they gave her back, that family. It's not as bad as when she was a puppy, but it still strikes. She's banned from my Mom's house."

"Really?" he turns to me and starts laughing. Laughing and pointing.

"Come here, girl," I say. "What?"

"Please, no. Have mercy, Bridge," he says.

"*What?*"

"Your hair, my god. Your hair." He rolls to his side with his hand on his stomach like it's killing him.

In the mirror still propped against the wall, I see the meerkat nest that tops my head. I comb through it with my fingers but get stuck, and he laughs again.

"Please," he says through pained laughing. "Lie down, please."

"What's wrong with you?" I try to tuck my hair behind my ears, which makes him laugh even harder.

"Abs, hurt. Stop," he says between bouts.

"Really?"

"So bad."

"All sixteen of them?"

He sits up from the end of the bed, groaning.

"You counted?"

"Only a hundred times. Research," I add cheekily.

"Well, if it's for research, my dick hurts too. It all hurts. But the hair, please. No more."

I lie down, strangely shy. "I hurt you?"

"I hurt me, but in a good way, but so tight—"

"Don't say tight."

"Right. Not tight, but I need a massage after a night with you."

"That was more than a night."

"You can say that again."

I roll over and smile into my pillow and kick my feet. Then the other side of the bed dips and an arm flops over my head. Such a wingspan he has.

"Give me a minute. I'll get dressed," he says.

At the very last second, I stop myself from screaming No! Because it sure is nice to sleep with someone with such a wingspan. Would be hard to avoid ending up in the crook of his shoulder, and holy hell, Jessica loves the crook of Royce's shoulder. Maybe they will turn the corner, Jessica and Royce, in the morning.

What happens in the morning?

I need some tension. Maybe she burns the toast—no, Royce wouldn't give two shits about burnt toast. He'd scrape it off and fuck her over—

Throat clearing.

"Sorry, in a scene."

"Am I there?"

"Royce is scraping burnt toast and about to fuck her over a counter."

"They made toast? Bridge, I don't have it in me to butter bread."

You unbuttered him!

"It's the next morning," I say, softer than I mean to.

"Thank god. So can I stay?"

I look at the crook. "Of course. You know how much Jessica loves it."

"Well, for Jessica, but please for the love of god, don't touch my abs or tickle me or do anything that could remotely turn me on like put on Mr. Magoo. Royce needs to rest his dick."

"Maybe we do need to call him Payne," I say, as it was another of the name possibilities.

"And Bridge, what's the deal with this bed?"

"What do you mean?" But I know what he means.

"It's child-sized."

And sure enough, his wingspan reaches from one side to the other, hands falling off either edge.

"It's kinda my childhood bed. I brought it from home."

"How is that even possible? I have to replace my mattress at least every five years."

"Yours gets more use."

"Well, you need a new one."

He never takes the bait. Such a gentleman. But I secretly like how he takes up so much space in my full-size bed.

"I know I need a new one. It's on the list." I move my head into the Joshplace between his shoulder and clavicle; it's such a nice crook. He uses one long arm to pinch the wick on the candle on his bedside table, then rolls over to clasp my hip. Right before I fade to black, he says, "I take jelly on Sundays."

NINETEEN

JUST MY JAM

I find Josh still in bed, looking like he's reenacting my favorite of his covers, and I feel like pinching myself. He's lying on his side, tousled hair, blue eyes serene, white sheet pulled over a hip, that delicious Adonis belt of his, and ripple upon ripple of sleek firmness above that I trace with my eyes, remembering the feel—I am well and truly obsessed with his abdominal muscles. And to see them at work while he is in me is not just hot, it's primal—makes me bloodthirsty. And I know it is ingrained deep inside me, in the history of my DNA. To have one so strong in my bed—it's heady stuff.

"Like what you see?"

His head on his hand, his barely blues tempting me back to bed.

"You know I do."

I have my phone in my robe pocket, so I snap a shot. He pulls the sheet down a couple of inches to put the scar on display— and turns up the wattage with a smile that promises pleasure and, wow. I mean WOW. I snap another and another. Knowing this shot is something I can get off to. I shake my head, wondering how I can consider another orgasm. Shouldn't we get over them at some point?

I crawl back into bed and lean up against the headboard on top of the covers that barely cover him.

"Don't usually let people take a picture of the scar," he kids.

"Can't give away the goods for free. Particularly after someone's about to pay a mint for them. But with you. Well for you, it seems I always have more to give."

"Sorta assume from your, how should I put this, talent, that it is always that way with you."

"Far from it. Last night was a lightyear away from. Well, you and I. We are ..."

He doesn't finish the sentence. Like he suddenly remembered we are not in a scene but are ourselves. It is so easy to be our characters, but I wonder as an actor, if is it harder for him to stop? Which we must. He must have something else to do, other than me?

Well, if anything will put him off such thoughts, it's my Invisalign machine. I open my bedside drawer to get it.

I spent too much money to straighten those four pesky bottom teeth to avoid using it just because I have the hottest man on the planet in my bed. Actually, because I have said man in my bed for reasons that are not romantic, it is a good idea to use it right now; I haven't used the device in days.

You've been distracted.

Richard, welcome to my bed. Now go away.

It is well past sunrise and yet still early. I grab my phone and open my message app.

"Mighty early for texting," Josh says, and I note something in his tone I can't decipher.

"Richard wants to meet."

"That's good, right?"

"I hope so."

Then he points at the book on my bedside table, the one Richard gave me for research. "Have you read it? It's okay. Not as good as ours."

I put the phone on the bedside table beside it. "Have you been doing homework?"

"Bridget, I've read more romance than you ever will," he says as he sits up in bed next to me. "Thanks for inviting me to stay."

"Thanks for staying. And I promise not to share your scar picture, if you promise not to take mine in about five seconds." I pull the dental tool, a small blue half-moon-shaped piece of plastic with a handle, out of the bedside drawer.

"What the hell is that?" he asks.

"My vibrator," I say.

"No wonder you were having trouble. Where do you even put that thing?"

"In my mouth."

"Does that work?"

"It's for my braces, Mr. One-Track."

"You don't have braces, and you like the tracks of my mind."

"I do, and the invisible kind."

Then I lie back against the pillow and put the device in my mouth so it can vibrate my teeth straight.

Josh reaches out to touch it tentatively. I swat his hand away.

"It's vibrating, all right."

"Just kneed ten min nuts," I say from around the contraption.

"If you need ten minutes, I don't think you're doing it right."

"Bunny."

"No, really. Happy to help. I mean, ten minutes is a lot to work with. Of course, an albatross could raise young in your hair, your mascara is on the goth side—"

"Ha ha. Bunny."

"But your freckles are showing, and you know what that does to me."

"I boo?"

"Oh, yes, you do. That was the first thing I noticed when I walked in the door with—" He tilts his head toward the mirror. "Even before that decadent slip of silk and lace you were wearing. Bridge, seeing your freckles, seeing under the mask, under the makeup you wear. It makes me ..."

I have to know.

"Bes?" I ask around the vibrator.

"Ravenous."

Later I burn the toast.

On purpose.

And the ever-helpful Josh fucks me wide-legged over the counter, and it is fast and furious and fucking amazing. He is still holding me off the ground, which helped him at this angle to find the spot that is my new best friend forever.

"Did I hurt you?" He's breathing heavily. Massaging hip bones that I'm pretty sure are bruised from the granite countertop.

My feet touch the ground. I stand up and lean back against his chest, smiling up at him.

"Couldn't care less. And if they bruise, it will make for a good mirror-musing later. Jessica asked Royce to not let go in that scene in the shower. Could very well have left some marks."

"Committed," he says, as he pulls up his briefs and lifts Mr. Magoo to see the damage.

"Yes, we both seem to be very committed," I say.

A strange second stretches out before us. That word between us. *Commitment.*

Neither of us speak. The toaster dings, helping me to recover.

And to break the tension, I blurt out something I've been thinking about since our conversation this morning.

"You want a byline?"

He turns me to face him.

"On the book?"

"It's as much yours as mine at this point."

He just silently stares at me.

"If you don't want to, it's—"

"I would be honored."

Now the moment is even more charged.

"Like I said, it's pretty much yours as much as mine at this point, and it's been really good."

His eyes narrow.

"Extraordinary. Fun. I've never done this before—written with someone. I like it."

"Bridget, I'm speechless."

"Don't lose your words; we need them."

"And my mouth, my Richard, my abs—"

"I think I've had enough of all of the above for a full series. I feel like a glutton."

"Speaking of …" He takes two perfectly toasted white bread slices and slathers butter on them.

"Have any grape?"

"Only strawberry," I say, and move to the fridge to get it.

"I know where I'd like to put some strawberry—would fit right in." He's looking at the apex of my legs. "About that? The bodywork doesn't exactly match what's under the hood, so to speak."

"Purple. And weird. But at least you didn't say carpet. That would have been an invitation to my front porch."

He holds up his hands in a non-threatening way.

"No offense meant. I like strawberry. Very much."

I reach for the jar and add jelly to my already-melted-on-the-hot-bread peanut butter toast.

"And Bridget ..."

"Yes?"

"I would love to co-author this book with you. I cannot think of anything—okay, well, maybe a few things—that I would love to do more, more of."

"Tongue-tied?"

"I'm serious. It's not just that I'm learning from you—I am, so much—but it might help others take my screenwriting seriously. Being published. Something I have never managed to accomplish. Hell, acting is only a way to get into the business. I want to write movies. Good ones. Great ones."

"I have no doubt after only a weekend of being directed by you that you could make beautiful movies. Your mind is a joy to work with."

He stares at me. For a good long time.

"I like you," he says.

"I like you too."

He takes a bite of his toast and moans, and the noise makes me tingle all the way to my toes. If only I could feed this man sugar all day every day. And yet he makes that sound at other times as well and is beyond willing, if this weekend is any indication, to decadently indulge in those pleasures as much as his abs can handle. And damn Sam, he has quite the core, which he's showcasing at my kitchen counter. We may need to have a rule about when he can let it all hang out or I'm never going to get any writing done.

"But I don't agree?" He says.

"With what?"

"If it's real. If it's how they feel, sexually or otherwise, it should never be considered over-the-top, never out of bounds. People are too afraid to feel."

"They are a little afraid of sex too."

"Well that *is* sad."

"Indeed it is." Until him, I had been afraid. Holding back. Never letting go. Always holding back some part of me that was too real even for me.

"So," he mumbles around his toast, "if I was to write 'I would love to smear this jelly'"—he holds up the jar—"'between your legs to see if the *artificial* color of this jelly matches the *natural* color I find there,' would that be purple?"

"That might be a run-on sentence, but yes."

"So, about that natural color. Why would you color hair the color of a sunset?"

Awww.

But I don't want to talk about all that so I say, "I'll tell you when you tell me the story of the scar."

He takes another big bite, almost finishing the bread, and moans again like he has never had sugar before, shaking his head, and I don't know if it is to my question or the marvel of sweetness on his tongue.

Since I don't anymore want to talk about my red hair than he his scar, I change the subject.

"What's your schedule this week? I mean, I have plenty of material to last a few days if you need a break, but I thought we could do some editing."

"All work and no play." He winks, which makes me want to do anything but work. Then he looks up at the microwave. "Is that right?"

"Yep, it's 9:45 a.m. Do you have somewhere to be?"

"Oh, shit. Fuck. Yes. Shit. Fuck."

He runs around the room, looking for something. Looks at

the last bite of jelly toast like it's a traitor and drops it on the counter as he passes by.

To help, I say, "Pants behind the couch; shirt in the bathroom." He runs to fetch them. "It's a Sunday?" I call out.

"It's my turn to take Nana and the Golden Girls to church."

"I didn't know you went to church."

"I'm not sure I do, but every other Sunday I drive Nana and her four best friends to their churches. They take turns. This week it's Mount Zion Calgary, one of my favorites. Have you seen my shoes?"

"Why a favorite? And behind the door."

"The way they move when they sing, it's almost like dancing. I also love the quiet of Nana's Catholic chapels, but I could use some evangelical fire this morning. Good for the soul."

"But you can't confess?"

"Nothing to confess."

"Fornication?" I laugh.

"Bridget. What you and I do together is no sin. Can't be a sin. It's too good. Not good ... nope, still don't have the word, but it's ... it's something else entirely. And of course I'll shower. Have to change too, that's why I'm so late." He grabs his keys from the counter he just had me on, and it looks like he's debating something, then pops the last bite of toast into his mouth.

"So good," he says, with his eyes closed like he's eating manna from heaven. Opens them, looks right at me, and adds, "This is harder than it should be. I feel like a teenager. Everything in my body is telling me not to leave."

"Because everything in my body wants you to stay. But Nana."

"Come with me."

That shocks me, and what shocks me more is I want to.

"Can't, I have a Zoom with Richard this afternoon and pages to get to him before the meeting."

"On a Sunday?"

"New York people."

He lets out a sigh, kisses my cheek, and is out the door before we can change our minds.

The moment he leaves, a smile breaks across my face—breaks my face. No matter what I do I can't erase it. I walk around my house, tidying up the complete mess we made, and shaking my head.

What all the fuss is about, indeed!

And as if that's not enough, the scenes, the characterization, the plot. We're building toward something monumental. Jessica and Royce are never going to be the same.

TWENTY

SAVED

The editing comes easy for once. By lunch I have the entire first half, minus the all-important midpoint.

It's extraordinary—I've never written this fast. It's so much easier when you have someone to brainstorm with, bounce ideas off. Someone to point out your plot potholes before they become black holes. But it's not yet paying the bills.

Next week I will miss a mortgage payment. I've considered getting another day job. I could tutor, but who would hire a suspended, surely soon-to-be-terminated-the-next-time-the-school-board-meets teacher. Waiting tables? It's been a decade since I was in the service industry, and I pretty much suck at it. The environment of a restaurant, the white noise of murmuring voices, clacking cutlery, and background music, puts me into a state where my mind wanders, most often to my current novel in progress, so I mess up orders, forget checks. But then when I get home I'm too tired to get the words on the page. So I end up sucking at both.

That's why I got my teaching certificate. And for the first

three years of teaching, I wrote a lot, but then Murial, my biggest cheerleader, was no longer checking up on me; instead, I was checking up on her and certainly not bothering her with my writing for those four years she fought ovarian cancer.

But someone believes in me again—Richard. I want to finish this book. I think it can be good. Maybe great. A love story with the kind of sex most people would kill for. Because I know that's how it is for me, with Josh, and I don't want to give that up either. Not yet.

When will I have the opportunity to have this kind of sex again? No, I need to go all in. Not distract myself. Write day and night. I need Richard to come through for me, and hopefully in about three minutes he will tell me he can.

He signs on to the Zoom from his phone.

"Hello, Bridget."

Horns blare in the background, pigeons fly past his head, people are everywhere.

"Hey, Richard. Whatcha doing on what looks to be a lovely Sunday afternoon?"

"Headed to brunch, and I'm late."

"Brunch? It's three."

"It's New York. So I have news."

I bounce on the exercise ball I sometimes use for an office chair. I'm so excited.

"Are you on a trampoline?"

"No."

"Then stop. And listen. I have half a block."

I nod. Not daring to interrupt again.

"Since you don't care whose name is on the book. It is almost as if the stars have aligned. I have an author experiencing difficulties, and she will not be able to perform under her contract. I need a ghostwriter and thought of you."

"Why?"

"Because, to my complete surprise, the book is great. So far. I will need more to convince the publisher. At least through midpoint. Can you get that to me by tomorrow?"

I open my mouth to talk, but he says, "I have one hundred feet." I zip my lips.

"She is willing to give her advance to another author to maintain her reputation with the publisher, if the ghostwriter can perform under her deadline, which she has already passed three times. It would be hush-hush but pay—" He's drowned out by a siren.

"Wait, what? Can you repeat?"

I pick up my calming chamomile tea, having gotten a taste for it, and then spit it across the kitchen.

"Did I hear you correctly?" I ask, wiping my mouth with my hand.

"Ninety thousand," Richard repeats.

I'm speechless. I'm saved.

"Bridget? I know it's good news, but don't have an aneurysm. Any questions?"

"But it would be her name on the book?"

"Yes, you would be ghostwriting it."

"So I will get no royalties."

"Yes. And you'll sign a contract that says you will never tell a soul."

I can't believe I'm about to say this.

"I'll think about it."

"What? What is there to think about?" He sounds angry, something so out of character for my George that I'm taken aback.

"Um—"

"I'm sorry. I didn't mean to snap. It's been a week." He takes a breath. "But I don't understand. This is perfect for you. I have other authors, if it's too much pressure. I know it's been a while since you've been under a deadline and this one is tighter than tight. But, after all that has happened to you, I wanted to offer it to you first." He holds up a finger. "Gage, I'll be but a moment." Then he says to me, "And it's perfect for you. You write the book. You get paid. Your name stays out of it. Isn't that what you wanted?"

"I have to think about it."

"Why?" he asks, appropriately confused while backing into an alleyway.

"I have a partner now."

"The sex guy? I assumed he was a professional."

"He is—"

"So pay him."

"I'll think about it."

Josh will never take straight money. We had a deal. A cut. A percentage. A byline.

"Don't think long. Email by noon tomorrow or I'll have to move on. This is one of my biggest names, and she's having a really tough time. It would help her to know it's all settled. Bridget, it's time to get professional."

"I know. Give me the day. I'll let you know tomorrow."

"You have until noon. But consider this decision carefully."

"I will. And Richard, thank you. You are like my"—I want to say fairy godmother but it seems potentially offensive, so I go with—"Glinda the good witch. You are giving me what I need when I don't deserve it. I hope you're not offended by the metaphor."

"Dorothy did deserve it. By the time she clicked her heels, she deserved it. And not offended if you'll follow the yellow—as in gold—brick road. Think of Toto!"

Bringing up Sally Girl is a low blow. But one that hits.

"Got to go," he says. "Think fast. And I need to midpoint!"

Then he's gone.

TWENTY-ONE

THE FIRST TENT POST

J osh texts to say he's about finished taking the ladies for lunch.

The fact that he goes to church every once in a while is irrelevant to me but the fact that he takes four octogenarians to their church of choice every other week is not.

The only way this man is not taken is because he doesn't want to be. As in *you cannot fall for him.* It's just the orgasms. And the writing. And the laughter. And now the lies because how am I going to tell him I've got to sell out.

Maybe you don't. Maybe you make the story so good you set the terms!

A new manifesto: When the story is good enough, great enough, can't be put-down enough, you make the rules.

This I can work with. And the strangest thing? It came from me.

It's been days since I had anyone else in my head.

I'm cured. Orgasms cured me from internalized debate. I can't give them up now. And one thing at a time. First, write through midpoint. Second, figure something out with Richard because I'm sure once we have time to talk we can figure out something.

Do the work. The rest will follow.

I text Josh.

> Me: I need you.
>
> Me: I talked to Richard. I need a midpoint! Can you help?
>
> Josh: Of course. Was heading that way regardless.
>
> Me: Really?
>
> Josh: I'm going to get supplies. We are not leaving till we have half a book.
>
> Me: Snacks! Yes please.
>
> Josh: Meet you at Bins and Barrels in twenty.
>
> Me: What's Bins and Barrels?

Turns out it's an independent health food store three blocks from my house, so I take Sally Girl for a walk and then to Bins and Barrels.

We're sitting at a bench out front when he arrives all dressed up in a white button-down and skinny vintage light blue paisley tie, gray flat-front pants and what look to be Cole Haan brogues. He's delectable.

"You look nice," I say.

"It's my chauffeur costume."

"Well, I like it. How is Nana?'

"Good."

"If you say good?"

"Right. Not good enough. Actually, I need to move her. The

place she's in is not okay. It was all I could afford when I was in college, but—"

"You've been taking care of your nana since college?"

"Uh-huh."

I stop tying up Sally Girl and look up.

"That must have been hard."

"What was hard was her getting hurt when I was gone."

I follow him in thinking I can't even take care of myself. Even now, my backup plan is Mom.

"You're a remarkable person."

He stops and turns to me, his self-deprecating smile making an appearance.

"No, really," I say.

"Stop."

He licks his lower lip, then bites it, and I heat. I bet that look has made it onto a cover.

"Come on. The sooner we shop, the sooner—"

"We eat?"

And the way he raises his eyes to mine, I know I'm on the menu.

"Don't scramble me in the store, or we'll never get out. And hey, where's the snack aisle?"

He points to a wall of bulk raw nuts.

"You are so weird."

"I like that. That you think I'm weird. That's different," he says, grabbing low-salt jerky. I throw in some kind of chickpea cheese curls.

"So why haven't you moved her? If you need to. Is the place not nice?"

"Like I said, it was what I could afford, but now she won't leave."

"Because of her friends?"

"Exactly. But I can't leave her there now. I'm supposed to go to L.A. in the new year. Sable has been begging me to give my career a go, and with the book deal—things look good for the book, I assume, if Richard is meeting on a Sunday—so who knows? If nothing else, if I go to L.A., I'll be able to interview without all the suns on set."

I laugh, remembering him dying on the cheery set of *Tampa Today*, trying to forget the choice Richard presented me only hours ago. I focus on his food choices, fascinated by them, to keep me from thinking about what's hanging in the air between us.

"Anyway, it's fine. I'll figure it out after the scar shoot. Which should pay enough to get her settled in The Oaks and take care of everything at least for a while."

"Wow."

He shrugs his shoulders.

I grab some sweets on the way to the checkout, not really happy with the haul. "So where's the wine? This sobriety thing is ..."

He pulls to a stop and looks down at me, and it's like I can see the last forty-eight hours reflected in his eyes.

"... the best fucking thing ever?"

He nods and moves on.

Josh's final haul is a dozen pasture-raised eggs, low-salt jerky, raw almonds, three kinds of homemade soup, and what he calls sandwich stuff. I have dark chocolate, fancy tea, three kinds of chickpea cheesish curl things, sour cream and chive dip, mango sorbet, and organic dog treats.

We pile into his truck, Sally Girl standing tall in the back, her hair blowing in the wind like this is the best thing ever for the three minutes it takes us to get home.

He parks on the street, and we walk past the offending yard.

I huff the way I always do when I see the mini golf course that's my front yard.

But he's heard enough about how I hate it. Every time we take Sally Girl for a walk, I curse it on my way out, so I keep my mouth shut for once. Instead, I ask something that's been niggling at me.

"It's not only the 'sensitivity' thing, is it?" We did get a nice bottle of Pellegrino. "And how do you know that women are more sensitive without alcohol?"

"I pay attention, of course. I watch. I listen. How else can I know if the pressure or speed is right, if she's a hard thruster or soft? If she wants an orgasm first or after? If she can get there without clitoral stimulation? If she likes to show me what turns her on? One of my favorite parts, I might add." Then he turns and winks.

Fucking winks.

And it makes me want to leave all the food on the astroturf to spoil and jump his Richard right here, right now, in full view of every neighbor.

What this man can do with one eyelid. I bet he is a great actor.

When he opens my door, Sally Girl rushes in knocks the bag in my hand with her nose and rushes inside.

TREATS!

I stand outside, not wanting to go in. Not wanting for this day to begin because then it has to end. He's still talking about the fact that he hasn't had sex with a woman who was intoxicated in years, oblivious to my missing him before he has even thought to leave.

"You coming in?" he asks.

I walk past him to take my bag to the counter.

"It's more than that," I say. "You're a great actor, but you have some issue with women who drink, don't you?"

"Okay. Okay. Once when I was in college," he says, putting my dip in the fridge, "I woke up, and the woman I was with the night before was gone. No note, no text, nothing. I don't want to sound ... well, that had never happened before."

"I bet not."

"Anyway, she was intoxicated—we both were; clubbing, you know—and I was afraid. I still don't know. Did I do something wrong? Take advantage?"

He pauses to put the tea in the cupboard, and I love that he knows where it goes. After a beat, he turns back with a face I've never seen on him. One that looks a lot like fear.

"I've resigned myself to never knowing, as I could never find her again, but I will never wake to that feeling. That I've possibly done something harmful to another person. There is no excuse for that and no possible apology."

How is he not taken?

"And then there is the vanity."

And friends, the cocky smile makes a reappearance. Yes, this is the same one I saw at the gym that first day when I basically called him a sex worker.

"Vanity?" I ask, feigning disinterest.

He puts six eggs on to boil.

"I fear that I put a good bit of my expansive ego on my ..." He shakes his head.

"Honesty, remember? And this is great for me, for the book, to get into a man's head this way."

"Fine. Prowess."

I swallow.

I don't know how he does it. Puts into a single word all the pleasure I'd never dreamed I needed.

Prowess.

What a word.

"Might be your best trait," I say. "But who knows? I don't know you that well."

His smile in reply is my favorite so far. The sly expression where he is trying not to smile. Like he's before the camera and the photographer tells him to keep a secret. It barely reaches his glacier-lake eyes—deep and elusive—but his mouth is quirked up, implying *I know something*. And yet those eyes let you know it is something you never will. This secret smile makes me want to dance and cry at the same time. If I could have Josh on the cover of my book, that's the smile I would want him to wear.

I pull out my phone and take a quick shot before it disappears.

"Can I do that too? Anytime *I* want?"

"Maybe," I say, somewhere between seductive and shy.

"Fuck," he replies. It's not even a word, more of an involuntary exhale. "Let's get to work."

We start by going back, reverse outlining the forty thousand words we have so far, tracing the plot points from one to another. He teaches me a trick. One he learned from the makers of *South Park* of all people. He attended their virtual teaching session for screenwriters, and their method is brilliant. Something I knew but could never put into so few words.

If the phrase that fits between your scenes is "and then," then it sucks, but if the word that fits between your scenes is "therefore," there is causation, or "but then this happens"—a reversal, Josh's specialty—then all is good in the land of pacing.

And it actually works. We move from scene to scene, checking.

Reviewing what we have written, it's clear his style is cinematic, as if he's creating visuals. It is sparse; every word, every movement has purpose. And I realize my writing is getting tighter. I'm learning from him. A way to condense emotion and heat. Sharpen it until the characters are practically bleeding. And his pacing is diabolical. I actually feel sorry for Jessica and Royce.

Now, the interiority he has issues with, which makes sense, as all of that comes from tone of voice and expression on the screen.

It takes hours, but by ten p.m. we know we have filled in the holes, cut what isn't necessary, removed the purple parts—mostly my overly poetic ramblings, but also some of his little over-the-top-sexy-to-something-almost-uncomfortable bits. At least some of them, but he argues hard to keep some. I almost leave those parts in. I mean, if that is how a man thinks? He reminds. I argue back, remember who my readers are.

My readers. It is a revelation.

The women who will read this romance are my readers. This genre's really growing on me. But he is quick to remind that men read romance too. Tells me to stop being sexist. I am appropriately chastised.

By eleven, we concede snacks will not cut it, and we still have not written midpoint. So we make sandwiches.

Josh can make a meal out of making a sandwich. Sliced, low salt, dill pickles, banana peppers, sprinkles of oregano, oil and vinegar, avocado, tomato, and turkey. I learned he once worked in a sandwich shop to make ends meet before he became the hottest cover model ever. Well, I'm assuming, as he has the scar shoot this week in Miami that Sable says is it was going to put him on the map.

He seems all over the map to me; scrolling through the romance section of Kindle Unlimited is like having a visit from him. But not everyone would know all those covers are of him.

They change him. Give him tats or dress him up in a suit—scorching! In one they gave him blond hair. I didn't like it. Not at all. Why would they make dark and dangerous look like Ken? But the abs are always on display, even in the one with the suit. And I know why, know those abs. Dear god, do I know them. But never the scar.

"No cheese?" I ask as he pushes the Swiss to me.

"Too much salt already, and the last thing I need is seven more grams of fat."

So matter of fact. So revealing. Just like that, he speaks to the struggle. I mean, it must be.

I look him up and down. His nimble fingers finish with a flourish of his knife—mustard, no mayo. Celery, no chips. And I see. Really see what it must take to keep him looking this good. The utter dedication. Does he *ever* treat himself?

I pull out a salt-and-vinegar chip, my favorite, and raise it to his lips, poke at them. He licks his upper lip and gives me the "I want" smile. I push it between his lips. They stay sealed.

"Come on, live a little."

He takes the chip, and when I go to pull my hand back, he grabs it—fast. Drops the chip to the counter. Brings my hand to his mouth and sucks the salt off first my pinkie, then works his way across them all. Slowly. Looking me in the eyes the whole time.

Fuck.

I let out a breath.

"Pointer-finger girl."

The sandwiches lay uneaten in front of us.

"Not hungry now," I say, meaning exactly the opposite.

"Trust me?"

"Yes." I don't even think, but it's what somehow is the absolute truth.

"I've been thinking, let's get out of here. Go somewhere."

"We still—"

"Trust me. You'll get your midpoint."

It's almost midnight, but I'm so worked up I have no room for sleep, and midpoint is still unwritten.

We agreed it needs to be brutal and tender, almost break them, as Jessica and Royce are about to be separated again by circumstances like when she left for college abroad. I suggested some options, but they all fell flat. I was getting worried we would not get it done by Richard's timeline, and this whole plan —a plan that's not really a plan—just a plan for the book to be so good that I demand our terms—a plan Josh is oblivious to of course—well, it hangs in the balance. But something in his eyes says he's got this.

"I trust you, but I only have until noon tomorrow to get it to Richard."

"We'll make it back by noon, with a scene, I promise."

Where does he think we're going this time of night? But I am all in. Aren't I?

He eats his sandwich while I get changed. Said he would make a mess if he tried to drive with it. Said he would pack mine for the ride. I hear him rummaging through my hall closet while stare into my bedroom one.

What does one wear to midpoint? Jeans? Too difficult. Then I picture him peeling them off me. No. Easier. Better access, but not too easy. Something …

I know.

It takes me a few minutes to find the denim dress with snaps all the way up from knee to neck and vintage cowboy boots, but when I walk out, I know I've chosen perfectly because his "want" smile is back in full force. I try to tamp down my own, but it's impossible, and a tingly feeling spreads across my face and down my body to my very country girl toes.

———

As we pass the sign that tells us we are leaving Pinellas County, I have no idea where he is taking me with my entire way of life on the line, but I sit back and listen to his country playlist. Said he was matching my outfit. And country is sexy, who knew?

And there's something brewing. We don't touch, but that doesn't diminish it. Like a storm building—that not-touching. Like once we do, we won't be able to stop. Because we are past editing; we are in the scene. I can tell. He's creating it. And he knows what he's doing. With his long looks and his not-touching. He is priming us for midpoint, for the scene that will carry the story to the second half.

The only problem.

It's not Jessica it's working on. It's me, and there be dragons.

It's what they used to put on maps to mark the edge of the world, before we knew what was out there, before it had been mapped, when everything past the horizon was a complete unknown.

And the thing about dragons, they're dangerous as hell, but who can resist the pull of them when they hide a trove of gold.

TWENTY-TWO

MIDPOINT

The next three hours are some of the longest and strangely best of my life. Longer than waiting to see if I passed my college finals, longer than waiting to hear if my debut sold, longer than the last day of school before summer. But so full of promise. Anticipation. Want.

The dark roads and rocking of the vehicle lull me to sleep. A door closing wakes me up. Josh has pulled into a gravel drive at a small ranch-style house. I look around me for some point of reference, but I can't see a thing. It's so dark only the red light on the porch breaks the blackness.

The car is still running, so I lower my window. Josh thanks someone, then heads back to me with something rolled up under one arm and what seems to be binoculars hanging from the other. Strange. The red light on the porch clicks off, and I'm suddenly sightless.

I hear him slide something into the back bed and then he rejoins me.

"We're here," he says when he sees I'm awake.

"Where's here?"

"You'll see."

The scene is so strange, so dark, I can barely make out his silhouette, but his eyes are bright with what looks like excitement. And then he backs out without turning on the car lights, and I wonder what is going on.

"Is this a dream?"

He reaches over and finds my hand. Lightly pinches the place between my thumb and forefinger, and suddenly I'm very awake and, suprisingly, very turned on.

"So, not a dream?"

His head moves back and forth.

"What's up with the lights?" They're red and line the road. We roll by them slowly, since he is driving with only the running lights. "Can you see?"

"I can see fine."

We pass a sign, lit with another red light, that reads, "Kissimmee Prairie Preserve, the only designated dark sky in Florida."

"Wait. Your going to show me the stars, aren't you?"

"Something like that."

And just like that, I'm in the scene.

"Kiss-a-me?" I ask when we pass the sign for the turnoff to the picnic area. I like the way the word sounds in my mouth.

"That's the idea," he says, with the just-can't-possibly-tamp-it-down smile I can barely see. He's so intoxicating. I want to bottle him up and drink him down.

"Kissimmee?" I say again. "Where is Kissimmee?" I shiver. I'm cold the way I always am when I wake from a nap. He folds up the divider separating us and stretches his arm along the bench seat of the truck. I unbuckle so I can tuck myself into him. He's so warm that I audibly sigh.

"East of us. And don't worry—I have a blanket."

"Wait I've been here before, years ago. Don't they have like alligators and things?"

"We'll be fine."

"That thing in the back? That's a big blanket?"

"That"—he gestures with his head to the back bed—"is a bed roll."

And I remember why we are here.

Midpoint.

A flash of heat washes over me.

"The scrub can be pretty prickly for only a blanket," he adds while playing with my hair, wrapping a length of it around his finger. Around and around, brushing my neck, sending chills that have nothing to do with cold down my spine as we drive slowly across what looks like flat scrubland to the day-use area. He says it will be more private than the astronomy pads or campground within the now-closed park fence.

"How did we get in if it's closed?"

"I have my ways."

I can't decide if I'm nervous, anxious, or plain impatient. I don't know what he has planned, and it makes me antsy. I make small talk on the short ride to our destination, which he says is less than three miles in.

Turns out the house with the red porch light belongs to a friend of his from graduate school who works as a researcher at the park.

"You went to graduate school?"

"That tone. I'm wounded."

"Where? What for?"

"USF. Kinesiology."

"What does that even mean?"

"The short answer is it's the study of human movement and

its effect on health. Niche, I know, but well-suited to me. Helped
me work through some personal health challenges."

"Makes complete sense to me. You might be the healthiest
person I've ever met and you clearly love to move your body."

"I do."

And again. What he can do with words. How he makes them
a promise. And how he moves his body. Like right now. Just one
finger, lazily moving up my neck to wrap a strand of hair around
it and gently pull.

It's something Royce does. When Josh first suggested it in the
book, I balked, but fuck it is hot. I lean into it. To the scene he's
creating.

We drive slowly, pushing wildlife—a hare, a heron—ahead of
us across the mix of small, still pools of black water, low palms,
and shrubby grassland.

He rolls down the window as we creep along the forest
service road, and I feel the air—not cold, not warm—on my skin.
Hear an owl hoot in the distance; it's almost drowned out by that
peculiar mix of swamp music. Frogs sing and crickets scratch to
make up the white noise of the prairie. I wonder if anyone has
ever recorded it. Made it an app. It is sleepy music, and as
languid as I feel, as late as it is, anticipation has made me not
even the slightest bit tired as he rubs that one finger along my
neck and every once in a while ... pulls and I know I, we, my
protagonist and me, are about to have the best sex of our lives.
Josh/Royce would give us nothing less at the all-important
midpoint.

When he pulls into what is marked as the picnic area, I can't
help but remember the last time I was here: years ago, a field trip
before budget cuts. Five buses, two hundred and fifty sack
lunches, and a miasma of talking, whining, singing, pushing,
bright-eyed children. Walks in the grasses and the swamps,

unending questions about tadpoles and alligators—how many teeth do they have? do people really make purses out of them? can you really eat them? what do they eat?—and on and on and on and on and on.

How different my life has become. Weeks ago, I would have been sound asleep at three a.m. with an alarm set, and when it went off I would be looking forward to the weekend already.

I don't really like kids. I don't. I'm a little ashamed of the thought, but there it is. And there are so many people who do. They don't need me.

I don't really like kids.

Quite the epiphany.

Then it hits me. I'm never going back to teaching.

He clears his throat.

"I'm about to stop this car, and when I do, I would like for all that chatter in your head to cease." He whispers to my ear, "Capiche?"

"Capiche."

When the car stops, all thoughts of my past, my job, those kids evaporate as commanded. They rise up and away like they never existed. Only one thing exists for me at this moment, and he is walking around the front of the truck to open my door.

When I exit the vehicle, I tilt my head back to take it all in. Stars—seemingly billions of them—dot the black sky, as if we can see the entire universe from here. I lean back so far I get dizzy. I step back, unstable. Josh catches me by my elbows, his body a wall of warmth behind me.

"It's better if you lie down," he says. He grabs the blanket and the bedroll.

I'm glad he brought the blanket. It isn't cold. The air feels almost skin temperature, yet I'm still glad for the blanket. I am feeling somewhat shy. Like my protagonist, as they haven't been together in a while. She might feel insecure. I go with it because Jessica is trying to get past her fear of intimacy, and she has finally confessed her brokenness to Royce. Why she left him all those years ago. How it is wrapped up in her lack of trust. Mostly due to her father abandoning her so young. And Royce is leaving her now, for opportunities, but also because of lack of trust. He does not trust her to stay, so he's leaving preemptively; she's like an impossible dream, and it is breaking his heart.

It's easy for me to move into Jessica's shoes, as they fit me so well. Easy to pretend Josh and I are two people who live only on the page. Almost too easy.

"Is this okay? You're very quiet."

"This is ... good?" I snort.

"I'll show you *good*," he says as picks his way through the low brush. Richard's joke has become ours. And this is real intimacy, isn't it? These little things that are only ours.

I am intimate with Josh.

The thought stops me, even as he moves away from me into the dark.

TWENTY-THREE

IMPOSSIBLE STAR

I follow him into the night. No path to guide us. His silhouette—that sharp hourglass that first drew me to him—a dark place surrounded by stars.

Extraordinary to think that not too long ago, this man was a stranger to me. Even odder that the person I *was* when I first saw him running that beach seems a stranger to me.

It's slow going. On the way I drop something off. My persona, the characters, everything. Like stepping out of a shadow, I choose to move even further away from all I have been. Step into a new point of view. Like I crossed a barrier in that scrub and stepped into a place where I could be myself with someone else. It's so freeing.

Oblivious to all that is rolling around in my head, he unfurls the pallet and drops the blanket. I see it in shadow play, in dark cutouts against the spangled sky—there is no other word for the stars covering the sky from horizon to horizon—not a sliver of moon in sight.

He steps up to me. So close we share heat.

"Ready?" he asks.

"For what?"

"Midpoint."

I feel it, the shift. This is for the book and not. Somehow, it is also ours. Our turning point.

"It's not supposed to be about us," I say, suddenly afraid.

"Too bad."

He runs a finger along my neck, wraps a thick strand of hair around it. Pulls. My head falls back to meet his eyes.

"Do you know who likes this?" He pulls again.

I take a shuddering breath.

"Jessica?"

"You." He breathes out the word, worshipful.

Then his take-no-prisoners smile locks me in place. A lick across my lips. Opening me up to him. A long, hard, deep kiss, all the while tightening my hair in his hand.

It tightens everything in me.

"Let."

A deep, devouring kiss.

"Go."

I relax so quickly he has to catch me to lower me to the ground, where he pulls apart the first snap with his teeth.

Josh has been passionate with me, but somehow always playful. But this is different. Intense. And all thoughts of playfulness disappears when he inserts his knee between my legs, pushing up against me, his hand wrapped in my hair.

Two more snaps fall open to his teeth, and he has yet to touch my skin. But when he discovers I have on nothing underneath he pulls hard. Baring my breasts. But not stopping there. Opening it all the way to where his knee is pushing against me. Then sits up, and in the low light, with billions of stars behind him, I see a brand-new smile. One that has an edge. One that lets me know I have never seen him unleashed. And I want to. Oh god, how I want to.

Then with one finger, he presses the cold metal of the still closed snap through my wet folds until he finds the point he is looking for. And presses, and presses, and presses.

"Fuck."

"In time."

Another press and his mouth is at the snap. My leg bends out involuntarily. Then behind my knee. A bite.

He pulls from the bottom. *Snap, snap, snap.* So that only that taut scrap of fabric, that one snap covers me, held by the most tenuous of connections. He leans in. Breathes me in. I flood onto his tongue.

A lick, a suck, a press of that metal against me, and I drench him again, the dress is ripped open and he is drinking me.

Fuck, fuck, fuck, fuck.

He pulls back. Then a warm breath across that point so sensitive it almost pushes me over the edge. Then a cold blow, then spreading me further. A warm exhale, a cold blow. An exhale, a blow.

With only air, he's balancing me on a precipice. When he inserts a finger, I lift off the ground, searching for his mouth to press into. Desperate. A cry, a pleading, and he takes my folds into his mouth and kisses my slit the way he kisses my lips, his finger moving. Biting, sucking.

Fuck.

I am a writhing ball of sensation about to explode. He stops. Everything. And taps—from inside—just taps—I pour onto his hand. He looks across my body to my eyes, his finger still buried inside me.

Fuck.

Like he can hear my mind screaming, he says, "No one to hear you. We're finally alone."

Tap. Tap. Pressing, rubbing, circling, flooding.

"Fuuuuck," I call out.

He adds another.

I scream.

"Is that all you've got?"

"Fucking faster," I say louder.

"That's right, let me hear you."

"More. Fuck. More. God, Josh, please."

"Your turn," he says and flips us. The loss of his fingers inside me fills me with anger. I want to hit him, beg him, fuck him senseless.

But he adjusts me to his will, till one of my knees is at his hip, the other between his legs. Until I'm straddling him diagonally. He lifts me by the waist high enough to find his tip and presses inside.

Our audible breath follows his progress, followed by a guttural sound when I am fully seated.

"Move," I beg.

"You move. Find it. Find it, and I will break you apart."

I know what he is asking. But I don't know how to do this. I start by moving up and down on him. Tilting forward using my hands on his knee to get traction, his hands at my hips taking my weight, helping me. Tilting, moving. Moving, tilting. Pressing, searching.

"Find it." A demand.

Dying of frustration, I press my mound against his leg, rubbing.

He pulls his leg back.

"Find it. Know yourself as I do."

I lean back against his other knee. And scream.

"Gotcha," he says smiling.

"Oh god."

"Move."

"Oh god."

"Move."

Small movements. I can't go far. More like pressing him against me and without thought I press my fingers to my front.

"Oh fuck, Bridge, yes. Move."

But he holds me still by the hips.

"Move." He forces the word out.

My fingers. They move in desperate circles, pressing my clit against his cock inside me. He lets go of my hips, and I move from the inside and the out.

Holy hell.

"Now open."

I spread my legs wider, frantic. To a moan from him as he presses up in small thrusts from beneath me. Hitting me right there. Right there. My hand frantic.

"Your eyes. Open them, Bridge. See."

He's barely hanging on. Circling faster and as the fiery ball inside me explodes with eyes wide open, I see the most impossible star. I blink, shuddering, crying out words that have no meaning as the star dives in slow motion across the sky, seemingly born of the scream that will not stop coming from me.

And for one moment, one space in time, I float in ecstasy.

Then Josh loses control. I'm a doll in his hands. He spins me to my back, holds me by the ass, thrusts with a punishing pace. Neverending. Holds me high off the ground, pulling me onto his cock as he thrusts inside me. Heartrending words spilling from him.

"Fuck. Fucking broken. Bridge. You fucking break me."

I look away from the star, to him, at the sound of my name.

He roars into the night. Birds scatter from trees, fleeing from the power of his release. Devoid of control, I'm lifted to only shoulders as he pumps into me as far and as fast as he can go— building again. It's transcendent to see him this way. Shedding control. Taking what he needs. Being for himself what he is for me. He roars again, and the sound has me following, begging, exploding again.

His head drops to his chest.

"Broken." Barely a whisper, and then he lowers me, curls in on me. His face buried between my breasts. I wrap myself around him, arms and legs holding. He keeps saying it—broken, broken me.

Funny that.

All I feel is whole, while watching the comet slowly disappear in morning's light.

TWENTY-FOUR

NONFICTION

W e walk quietly back to the car covered in dew. He looks at his watch. We both know I'll be lucky to get back by my deadline. He squeezes the hand he is holding and the wave of anxiety that threatens to wash over me recedes.

Once in the car, I stare at my open laptop, but nothing comes but the chattering fear of failure and the betrayal that will follow. And like he can hear those debilitating thoughts he touches my shoulder. His eyes forward on the road ahead."Do you get carsick?"

"No."

"At home, when you are alone, where do you like to write?"

"I generate on the couch or in bed, and I edit at the table."

"Then crawl into the back; stretch out like you're on the couch."

I look behind me, and sure enough, the extended cab is like a big couch, and the blanket could be a pillow. This might work. I scramble over the seat and reach back for my laptop.

"There is a plug back there."

"Helpful. Great truck, by the way."

"Romance readers bought me this truck. It was made to be a generative space."

I smile, amazed at not only his insight as to what I need as at his kindness.

Once situated, a seat belt across my lap required by the driver but legs still able to stretch out with the blanket that seems to hold all of last night in its soft weave behind me, I open my laptop to begin.

With the tinted windows, it's almost dark, which is perfect but too quiet. I can hear myself think.

Music helps me get out of my head to somewhere deeper where I can write and not care what anyone thinks. Where I can lose myself. Sometimes I play the same song for hours when writing, but I can't think of any song that could capture what happened in the field. It would almost need to be a symphony.

"Can you play something? It will help."

"What do you need? Acoustic, symphonic, relaxation? "

"Something soft. Words, but ... I don't know. Something about eyes." Because I can't stop seeing them in the dark, the cool, clear waters of them. Soft, hard, side-glancing, blown out —blown away—as I was. "But something I know well enough to not to need to listen to. Sorry, I know that's not very helpful."

"Spotify, play something soft about eyes from an '80s movie soundtrack."

He knows me.

Then a slow acoustic remake of that old Peter Gabriel song starts up. It's exactly what I need. I won't even hear the words, I know them so well.

And with the song cocooning me, I walk behind him through the dark field. The stars from horizon to horizon mixed in with the clouds of the universe. And like a switch, I switch off, no

longer seeing my fingers on the keyboard or even the landscape
fly by in the window.

---

*We lie side by side in the dark. An ocean of indecision and doubt
between us.*

*"Looks like we may have clouds," I say, and point to an almost
rainbow-shaped arch of them tinged with pink and aquamarine.*

*Royce takes the hand pointing at the clouds and brings it to
his mouth. Speaking quietly, his lips brushing the tips of my
fingers, stopping on the one he knows gives me chills.*

How can I let him leave?

Because he let you.

*And I remember our promise to each other, when we were too
young to make promises. When we were to young to know we
couldn't keep them.*

"Not clouds," he says. "Home."

*I turn to him in the dark; he tucks my hand into his arm like a
cocoon. I look into his eyes, confused.*

*"You know, home—as in our-place-in-the-universe. The Milky
Way."*

*"Oh," I say, and look back up at the sky. "Not sure I've ever
seen it. Not like this." He opens his arm wide so I can rest more
comfortably in the crook that I think of as my place—where we
joke about tattooing Jessica's Place but have never gone through
with it. Too close to his heart. Too permanent for two people who
can never seem to stay.*

*I wrap my leg around him—for warmth, I say. The Milky
Way arcs across the sky—towers of gas and light that as we watch
are birthing stars. And paradoxically, it grounds me, how small
we are, how large the moment feels.*

"Every moment an eternity," he says voicing that promise we

made when too young. And the hand holding mine brings our
hands together to a place over my heart. He lets go of my hand
and moves his to the vee at my neck.

"Is this what you want?"

I nod, afraid if I speak I will break. With a flick of his fingers,
the first snap releases and heat washes over me.

I snap out of the scene. The song has ended.

"Again," I say, desperate to be back.

Josh puts it on repeat, and I live it again. But this time with
the knowledge of what will happen, with the knowledge of the
comet rising in the sky to meet our ecstasy.

I build the scene slowly, moment by moment, like that comet
moving across the sky so many billions of miles away, but also
fast, so fast—feelings falling out of my mind so fast my fingers
can't keep up. I moan, beg, suffer, survive, all the while the
Milky Way watches to birth that impossible star.

It is only one night in the life of one small being, but as my home
spins across the sky making stars, I am changed. And regardless
of how far away we may soon be, what we created here will fly,
speed, burn ... forever.

I let out a deep exhale. Read back over the last sentence.
Almost purple, but I leave it.

"It's done?"

"It's done," I say with resignation.

"Should I change the song?"

He has been driving to *In Your Eyes* for hours.

"Sorry. You can turn it off."

"No, it's okay. I like it."

"Nobody likes the same song for hours."

"You do."

I stretch my neck, rotate my ankles, move to sit forward, having been locked in that position for so long.

"It worked perfectly. Thanks for putting up with it."

"It's from the Cusack movie. The one with the boom box," he says.

"Yeah, it is."

"The grandest of gestures. What everyone wants, right?"

In the rearview mirror, his eyes meet mine.

"You want the grand gesture?" I ask.

"Doesn't everyone? Don't you?"

I don't answer right away. He turns off the radio. We ride in silence.

What doesn't he understand? That *was* the grand gesture. What happened in that field.

But wait.

Oh. Oh.

And it all makes sense. The words he used. The brokenness. All of it. He was a character in a book in that field, and stupid me, I was me..

I was me.

Stupid, stupid me. I forgot why we were here. Thought that grand gesture was for me. But as grand as it was, it was for someone else. Someone who doesn't exist. A scene. Part of the story. *Their* story, not ours.

We don't have a story.

We have a job.

Tears threaten. I swallow them down. I sit up straight.

Why are you so upset? Isn't this what you wanted? What you asked for? What you needed?

And it is. The point of everything. And as promised, he gave me midpoint. Created, directed, acted a scene incredibly important to the story and my plan. And it was all I never knew I wanted. It was primal and powerful—even empowering.

But it was a scene. A wonderful scene, one Richard will gush over. But a scene still.

Once I'm ready, I crawl into the front. A little later, I say, "No. The grand gesture. I don't." Lying is becoming so easy for me.

And then I smile at him. Like nothing's wrong as we climb the bridge to St. Pete, the one that will take us back to reality. And it's okay. Because that moment, those moments we spent together. For me, even if they were fiction, they are eternal.

All the best fiction is.

He passes me his Topo Chico. I take a sip, knowing I will steal it. Pretend to take it into the house for recycling and instead put a tag on it.

11/17/25 — the field is eternal.

Then I will tuck it away. Hide it.

Or maybe I'll put it on the bookshelf, with the rest of the fiction.

TWENTY-FIVE

SPINNING

R ichard loved the new pages. How could he not. He raved. But when I texted that I wouldn't take the ghostwriting job his only response was you're making a career level mistake. Which pushed me into my bed too early on Tuesday. I didn't leave it all Wednesday except to walk Sally Girl who stayed snuggled up with me most of the time. I didn't even watch movies. I just slept and slept and slept. Missing Josh the whole time.

Ironically, I think at this point he was the only person that could understand what I was feeling. Mourning. But how could I possibly tell him that I was a complete and utter mess because for me midpoint was real. So real. Made me feel so many things that I was throwing away my security to keep. Because if I betrayed him midpoint would be forever marred by what came next.

Of course he texted. To see if how it went, how I was, if I needed anything. I lied. Said I was down with a cold. Since then, he has texted every day to ask after me. He keeps mentioning that he has to go to Miami on Friday for a shoot. And I can tell he wants to see me but I really don't think my battered heart can take even the smallest hit of him. Hopefully once he leaves he'll be too busy to bother with me. Because everytime I text better or getting rest he asks if I need anything. And I do. I need him. But I can't text that.

Now Thursday was better, thanks to "spin" class. I got into my body for a while and out of my head. It's nice being with people who don't really know me but like me just the same.

I wonder if they'd feel different if they knew just days ago I was a hairsbreadth away from betraying a truly beautiful man. Because even though my offer of royalties meant something to him it was nothing compared to our collaboration—to the offer of a byline. To co-authoring the book with me. That *really* meant something. That took his breath away.

And I know it's because of the boost to his credibility being published will give him, but it's more than that. It's almost as if no one has ever looked past the beauty of his body to see his drive as an artist and his talent as a storyteller. That was the gift I gave him, while he gave me—so much—passion I'd never once felt, pleasure beyond my imagining, in many ways the gift of my own body—to know it. So much. Too much.

And yet he was not giving it to me at all. But to the story. And for that I cannot blame him either. What did I expect from such a kind, reliable man but to get exactly what I asked him for?

No, I can't blame Josh that I got all turned around. Can't blame him for not keeping it business. He only ever did what I asked. All of this is on me.

It's not such a bad thing. I haven't let myself fall hard since Mateo, and I'm trying to convince myself the gains outweigh the losses.

For one, I can finally dance. Celeste said it was like dancing with a different person. I was so loose, so open. Sarah let me lead, and it felt effortless.

For two—my god, the fuss. So fucking much fuss. If I never have another moment of fuss again I will have had more than most. That he gave to me. And even more.

Something in me has changed. And even though there is only a small possibility that Richard can sell the book on spec before I'm three mortgage payments behind, I can't count on that. Can't count on anyone but myself. Somehow this experience gave that to me. Time to find a day job. Because after all Josh gave me, I knew the moment I sent Midpoint to Richard I would not betray him.

Now fail. Fail I can do, but not betray, use, lie—for that is what he will think—what I would think if the roles were reversed. No, it's time to grow up and be the person I want to be, not damn the consequences, but in the cold hard light of them.

And the cold hard light of my refrigerator this morning showed me I had no cream, or eggs, or butter. No food. So after a trip to Barrell and Bins this spectacular Florida winter Friday morning, I pull into my driveway and do a double take.

Get out of my car, not trusting my eyes.

"Richard?"

He is sitting in the old paint flecked rocking chair on the porch, I'd like to call it distressed but it's actually dreadful, looking out at the ocean.

"I see the charm. The yellow is a bit happy, but the view is serene if one can ignore *that*."

Of course my front yard mars his aesthetic. It mars mine. And yet I never considered he would see my front yard.

"What are you doing here? Please tell me it's good news."

"Of course it is. I'm your George. I'm here to help—to talk

some sense into you. Help me help you—in the grand tradition of perfect sidekicks."

I sigh. So not good news.

If you say good, it's not, I hear in Richard's voice.

Exactly, I think.

When did I start having imaginary conversations with people that are right in front of me?

"Richard, no means no."

"Can we go inside? I'm melting."

He moves toward the door but I hold up my hand.

"Give me a minute to put Sally Girl up or you'll be covered in fur. Why are you in a suit? And why are you in wool in Florida?"

"It's wool because it's winter, not that you would know that in this season-forsaken place."

"This from a man who wears linen after Labor Day," I say under my breath.

"Air-conditioning? Please."

I slip in and put Sally Girl in the laundry room with a treat and open the door for him. He stalks past me to find there is really no room to stalk. So he turns on me.

"I can respect no. But I wouldn't be a very good agent if I didn't make you think twice about a cottage-saving opportunity."

"Fine, say your peace. It won't change a thing. There are some lines I can't cross. But I'll get you some iced tea."

"Beware drawing lines. Life is a moving target." He sits at the kitchen counter. "I'd love some tea."

"It's sweet."

"I've been to the southland before. No need for cultural education."

I grab two glasses and fill them at the fridge's ice dispenser.

"I've reached back out to my principal. You know, to see if

anything can be done about the suspension. Maybe I will negotiate to quit. And if they wipe my record, I can get another job teaching somewhere. Even keep my retirement."

I pour each glass full and add a squeeze of lemon.

"Bridget, why would they do that?"

"Because I've given them ten good years."

"And they're good people, loyal people over there at SCAB. That's been your experience, right?"

I picture beady eyes. Then remember I told a subcommittee of the State Board of Education to suck cock.

"I'll find something else."

"But you want to write."

"What difference does it make if it's not mine?"

"I'm so confused by you. Do you know what you want?"

"Obviously not!" Sally Girl must sense my unease as she turns the knob with her teeth.

"Oh, shit." She bursts into the room, and I have just enough time to put my body between her and Richard.

"That is quite the pet. And as intrigued as I am to put my hand within inches of that line of sharp teeth, but the suit. Where's your en suite?"

I point to the bedroom and crouch down. "He's a friend. It's okay." I grab a raw bone out of the freezer, knowing the treat will keep her occupied for at least ten minutes.

When he comes back out, his hair is slick and he looks cooler. "The mirror against the wall is an interesting touch. So are the roots."

I touch my hair.

"But I don't have time to *Queer Eye* you. Sit down." He points to my couch. "I'll be late now, regardless."

"Late to what?" I sink into my couch and pull the crochet blanket over a section for him.

He looks down at Sweetie's multicolor acrylic thread throw and grimaces, "Don't think I'll risk it since I'm marrying the richest man in Hollywood this weekend."

"You're what? Congratulations! Wait, I'm not invited?"

He rubs his face. "Not making myself very clear. I blame coach. You see, to come see you, I had to forgo a private plane to Ft. Myers and fly into Tampa instead and *drive*." He says the word like it means *clean up shit*. "And I'm not *getting* married, but marrying a lovely couple, my boss and the aforementioned Mr. Big. So this is a grand gesture, which I need to continue with but *the hair*. I'm sorry, it's hard to think looking at you. Who knew you were a ginger?"

"I know I look like a pink skunk. I can't afford the salon, and I'm afraid to do it myself—so many colors, who knows what to choose—and the temporary wash my hairdresser recommended to cover the roots irritates my scalp so I stopped using it. And no one to see it. I don't really care what I look like right now."

He shakes his head. "This is not the problem I came here to fix."

"Why *are* you here?"

He's here to talk some sense into you, Bridget. You really must learn to take care of yourself first.

And the second-worst part about avoiding Josh because I don't think my heart can take another "scene" right now, is Mother is back. No, that's the third worst. The second worst is I *really* like him. And orgasms. I really like them too.

She's right, you know, Richard's voice adds.

"You're in my actual house!"

"Astute. And by the by, once we have you some money, I think domestic assistance is in order. That bathroom."

I take a deep breath and let it out. "Richard, drop me if you need to. But I just can't."

"You can and you will. That"—he points to my bedroom—
"experiment went south, I infer from your pages. Fine. You got
caught up. But it's not too late, because after reading the first half
of the book the publisher is offering more, more than they were
giving *her*. We're talking six figures for *ghostwriting*. Bridget, this
is not something an unemployed broke school teacher walks
away from."

"Wait, you're a priest?"

"Stay with me, and of course not. I'm a Unitarian
Universalist—for a weekend. And charismatic, and great in
pictures."

"In St. Pete?"

"We really are off track here. Captiva Island. I will be captive
in Captiva for an interminable weekend. Sign the papers." He
pulls them out of his jacket pocket and passes them to me.

I shake my head.

"It's not only about you, Bridget. Think of the author. She's
having a really hard time. And if you don't care about her, what
about me? Or of the money the publisher will make that funds
debuts? You know that, right? They have to sell the big names to
give people like you ten years ago a chance."

"I know that."

"What about the cover designer who will get stiffed? Not to
mention the model; holy hell, he has been on the hook for weeks,
and his agent Sable is breathing down my—"

"Did you say Sable?"

"Yes. Sable Smith. Talented agent. We use her for movie
pitches sometimes."

"You know Sable?" I ask.

He looks at the sky and takes a cleansing breath, holds, and
lets it out over four beats.

"Better?"

"Remarkably, yes. Bridget"—he takes my hand—"Your book, *Scarred*, is in the middle of a publishing machine and many, many cogs in the wheel are counting on it. Including me."

"What did you call it?"

"*Scarred*. Bizarrely, the publisher let the art decide the name. Usually the other way around, of course. But we need the second half yesterday. So get your boy toy and give me some heartbreak to HEA."

And then it hits me. I can't believe it took me so long.

It's Josh.

The Miami shoot. The one he is headed to right now.

He needs this cover. This cover will get him what he needs for Nana, what he deserves for himself, money for L.A., a shot. I have no choice, and yet I'm between a rock and an impossible place.

You can do this. You can even continue to work with him if that's what it takes. You'll tell him. He is a good man, a great man. You'll offer him money. You can worry about the pieces of your shattered heart later. It's time to go to work.

"Okay."

"Okay?"

"I'll get a pen." I click all the way back to the table where the paperwork lies.

Richard stands to leave right after I sign, looking confounded. "I didn't think it would be that easy." I walk him to the door, still clicking.

"Best wishes to the happy couple," I say like it's a funeral.

"They're likely to be happy for the life of a fruit fly, but kind of you."

"I thought you were a romantic?"

"Oh dear, I am. That's why I'll never marry. Speaking of

romance, where's your Richard? I would love to see him in the flesh."

"He's out of town. Miami."

"Perfect." He reaches into his back pocket to pass over a black AmEx with STONE STREET LITERARY written in font you can barely see.

"Join him. My treat. Part two could use some sex in a city before you make them cry."

Before I can blink, he's at his car. How do men move so fast?

"Richard," I call out. "The shoot, the cover—it will happen, right?"

"Getting the contract signed tonight. And the model is Sable's plus-one so I get to meet the meat."

"That's pretty offensive, you know."

"Sorry, weddings make me pissy. But look at you,. When did you start getting all defensive for the professional Richards of the world? Speaking of, might want to wait until after you're finished with him to break the news about the royalties. Silly girl. But all will be well; you'll have plenty of cash to put in his hand."

Oh god, what have I done?

"But my part in this. No one will know, right."

"You just signed a contract that says if we tell a soul, we forfeit the funds and more. We'll be sued to within an inch of our lives. I'll be ruined. So, no one can know. I thought I made that clear in my earlier conversation."

He's walking back to me. I stop him with my hand.

"You'll be late. I understand. I know what I have to do."

PART 2

JOSH

TWENTY-SIX

NOT FINE

I sit in the parking lot, pulling myself together before entering my former home, South Lakes Juvenile Residential Treatment Facility. From the outside, it looks like a hospital with a high school attached. There's even a football field with stands now. But on the inside are locked doors and angry faces. At least, that was my face for the first twelve months I lived here.

They buzz me in through the main door, and no matter how many times I've been here, the background checks, the fingerprints, I have to wait for Gretchen to escort me. And today she doesn't even know I'm coming. I actually passed the exit, driving to meet Sable to talk business and hopefully transact some, but I did a U-turn at the next exit. I figure I have an hour to not be late for Sable and our pregame meeting before the fancy wedding where I am her date having been talked into coming as my scar contract is coming too exactly twenty-four hours before the shoot. Such a rollercoaster this one has been. I'll be glad to get it over with.

It takes longer than normal for Grechen to come get me. To walk through the door of the treatment wing and into reception, and when she does, I can't help but notice how gray her hair has grown. I shouldn't be surprised. How many kids like me has she counseled in this huge facility? How many classes of boys has she worked with? How many stories—horrible stories—ones to make my orphanhood seem small? Too many, and yet here she is, still tough as nails while being kind in the way we can take it. We boys. And for the not first, fifth, or even fiftieth time, I wonder what in the hell mess I would be in without her.

She holds the door open for me, and as I pass, she asks, "And to what do I owe this unexpected visit?"

"I'm not doing so well," I confide. "I had an incident."

"Come on."

On the way to her office, she pops into the director's, and when she comes out I say, "I'm sorry. You don't have time for this."

She looks at me with her dark, almost black eyes and says, "I have time for you."

———

She has a desk in her office but never uses it. It's pushed up against the wall and covered with books and papers, coffee cups and chip bags. I see my old chair, the one with it's back to the corner but I'm too anxious to sit. She leans on her stool. I asked her once why she never sits. She said sometimes she has to move fast. Smiled and showed me her gold tooth. Told me how it happened. I broke many things in this office, but thank god it was never her.

"Hey, Gretch, it's been too long. How are the boys?"

"Not as much trouble as you."

"I was your worst."

"You *are* my favorite. Why do you think I keep talking to you ten years later? So what's up? It's been like six months."

My initials are still scratched into the armrest of the chair.

"We talking?"

Same thing she asked me every day for nine months. I didn't even answer no for the first six weeks. Just scratched my initials into her chair with a pen. But once I did, well, this woman saved my life.

"I'm struggling."

"Okay. Tell me."

"Do you remember when I left the detention center to go to Brazil for that week, when I came back, how I was?"

"Of course."

"It happened again."

"How long?"

"Only a minute. And it wasn't 'I'm fine,' it was darker."

"Whatever it was, you needed to hear it."

"I know that. Logically I do. But I was afraid it wouldn't stop."

She passes me the ubiquitous Skittles bowl. I shake my head.

"It always stops. But what stopped it this time?"

"She held me. We slept."

"She?"

Gretchen waits to see what I might be willing to share, knowing I always share eventually. Her patience knows no bounds. She slurps on the bright blue slushy she gets in the cafeteria. I swear she likes them better than the kids.

"Are we talking?" she asks.

I walk the length of the room and back. "I'm broken. That's what I couldn't stop saying, that I was broken."

"Tell me what happened."

"We were together. Gretchen, there are no words for how I feel when I am with her like that, and it was ... Until it wasn't."

"Tell me about her?"

"She's brave. Has these piercing gray eyes that don't take shit from me. It wasn't like that at first. She was—"

"Dazzled?"

"She's polite and a badass. Sexy as fucking hell. The chemistry is off the charts."

"Good. Chemistry is good. Bodies speak truth."

I take a deep breath and walk to the window. "So we had this night like no other. I won't get into the details, not that you can't handle it—certainly heard it from me before."

"No shame. Look at me."

I turn.

"For you, sex is medicine."

"Yeah, that. I haven't gotten a test since the day I met her. Usually I test the first Monday of the month, or every other Monday if I am feeling off. So I should have tested the day this all this went down but I was so gutted I went to the gym. Twice. So, yeah, now that I think of it it's been almost three weeks since I tested. That means it's been three weeks since we met. How is that even possible?"

"How do you feel?"

"Physically? Even. I'd say I'm at like 950. Emotionally? Broken."

"Let's start with the first. That seems high. Is a testosterone level of 950 really okay for you?"

"Anything below 1000."

"So, you don't think it has to do with your hormonal issues, this feeling of brokenness?"

I draw lines on the white board, in red pen, then blue.

"We done?"

I turn back to her less than patient face. And I know exactly how long she can hold the I'm waiting face—forever—so I continue.

"After we were together, that night, I broke down. I felt broken. I said I was broken, over and over. It was too much. Does that make sense?"

She gestures to my chair and I sit. I can't believe it is still in this corner. I trace my name with my finger while she asks a couple of pointed questions noticing someone added below "is a dick."

"So what you're telling me, is after a varied and active sexual life, you have found someone whose sexual pleasure takes you to a place of emotional transcendence."

"Didn't feel transcendent. I mean, it did. But it also made me want to curl in on myself." I look up at her. "Made me feel fear."

"And you think this 'broke' you, but that's not what you were telling yourself."

"Isn't it?"

"Let me ask you this." She rolls her shoulders. Cracks her neck. "Back then, when you found yourself repeating 'I'm fine,' were you?"

"Hell, no. The opposite."

"Exactly."

"Oh."

"What if this woman didn't break you but instead broke you open?"

"Isn't that the same thing?"

She smiles wide. "Not at all. One is heartbreak. The other, well, you'll just have to see, won't you?"

"What if it happens again?"

"You'll tell her, when you're ready, about this very rarely

occurring behavior, and if she is worthy of your heart, it will all be well."

"But Gretchen, she knows nothing about me."

"Whose fault is that? Until you let someone know you, you will never know why they stay. We've talked about this before—your belief that people want you only for what's on the outside."

I look down to trace "dick" with my fingers.

"I've been content with my life. Enjoyed women as they've enjoyed me. It's worked. Kept me balanced. Why does it have to be more? I don't need them to stay. I'm stable. I'm fine—"

"And there's that word again. I think it terrifies you how much you want more. And you know why. Own the scars."

I take a deep breath and brace myself for what I am going to admit.

"Oh god, Gretchen. With Bridge I don't just want more. I want everything—every smile, every breath, every look, every touch, every minute of her day. Do you have any idea how hard it was to leave after we got back? But she wanted me gone. Gretchen, she wanted me gone. And since she has avoided me, pretending she is sick. I am so confused. Maybe she's sick of me."

"Hey, you don't know her wounds. You have no idea why she's acting the way she is. Did you ask?"

"No. I was afraid of the answer."

"You got to use your words. But since you didn't, what do you say you give her the benefit of the doubt?"

I nod.

"I love you, Josh."

At that, tears prick my eyes. She ends every session that way. Never lets one of us messed-up boys leave her without knowing we are loved.

"What do I owe you?" I say to keep it light.

It's our joke, because her continued therapy is always free. I know I should get another therapist. I can't keep leaning on a woman who has not been paid to treat me in ten years, but I've never been able to talk to anyone else like her.

"A visit. That's my price," she says.

"Next week?"

"Perfect. I need you to talk to these boys. This bunch needs inspiration and you are a shining example of what we hope for you boys when you leave these walls."

"So they're troublemakers?"

"Troubled."

"Like me."

"For good reasons, just like you. But this class can break a heart."

"Speaking of. I think I hate being broken open if that's what this is."

She reaches up to ruffle my hair as we walk to the door. "It's not an easy place to be, openhearted, and of course it can lead to brokenhearted, but if you imagine what else could be on the other side, you may feel it's worth the risk, worth the possibilities. And remember benefit of the doubt. Least you can give someone who gave you such a gift."

"If this is a gift, why wouldn't I wish it on my worst enemy?"

"Because you like to be safe, and this is not safe—not by a long shot. It might even be a long shot."

She walks past me out the door. I follow.

"Great. Sounds wonderful—feeling all messed up and regressing to mental health places I thought were in my past and staring out into the complete unknown."

She pats my back on the way out the door.

"Welcome to life, Josh."

TWENTY-SEVEN

GAME FACE

I meet Sable at her hotel on Captiva, and it's like there's a shoot. The room is full of wardrobe and makeup and hair.

"It's just a contract signing," I say as she slips yet another jacket off my shoulders.

"No. It's your best shot at being seen since you won't take my advice and move to L.A. I wish it was a pool party. Someone bring me safety pins, please."

I know where she's going. "Don't you think it's tight enough and without the undershirt almost pornographic? I can see the outline of my nipples in the mirror."

"On a body like yours, it can never be tight enough." She pins the back of the shirt, pulling it tight across my front.

"I like it, but no jacket," she adds.

"Isn't this a formal occasion?"

"You'll stand out."

She goes back to the rack, flipping through shirts till she finds one that will be so tight I'll have to keep an eye on the seams. She tears it off the hanger.

"And cufflinks," she says, almost to herself.

As I try to get it over my biceps, I say, "You know I would expect a bit more professionalism from one of the big five. How is it that I am just now signing a contract for a shoot that is happening tomorrow?"

"Who knows? But as long as it gets signed, that's all that matters. The exposure, given the publicity plan for this book, combined with this co-authoring situation, which I need to know a whole lot more about—" She turns to me with an accusatory look.

"Let's get through tonight. We'll talk Monday." Since Bridget doesn't seem to be talking to me. Hopefully that will change soon. I've sent three slight touch texts this morning but still no response. "You're still staying a few days after this shindig, right?"

"Yes. There is much for us to discuss." She tugs on my collar. "And just so you know, last minute change to the contract. We have editorial approval on the photo. I wanted to make sure that for the scar, you get to decide how you are seen. Do not underestimate the power of being seen. Particularly tonight."

"I am nothing, if not viewed."

She turns to me and tilts my chin up to meet her eyes.

"I see you. I see your talent, your beauty. Josh, I've seen you since you were sixteen. I will protect you. But this"—she releases my collar and gestures at my outfit—"is a necessary evil."

It will button, barely. But I push off the checkerboard cufflinks she tries to hand me and roll up the French cuffs messily.

"Oh, yes," she says. "And two buttons."

"I know what you're looking for, the afterparty look."

"Exactly."

"But no makeup. This is not a shoot."

She looks at me, taken aback. "Makeup's for me."

I wave bye to the hair tech, who is done with both of us, and sit on the settee in Sable's suite. From her chair at the portable vanity the makeup artist brought in, she says, "The director of that Scottish epic will be here."

"They're already filming. That one is lost."

"Never say never; it is a big cast—one more won't hurt. When I found out he was coming, I called the casting director to let him know you would be here. I think you were his choice for the role, but, well, maybe the star didn't want the competition. That's the hardest part about repping you for film. No one wants to compete with you. But the star of this one is a real professional and big enough that if his ego is in order, you can't compete. Maybe we can turn no into a yes tonight."

Walking across the wide lawn to the huge tent set up on the beach, Sable turns to me. "Show me your game face."

"What are you looking for?"

"I'm looking for the face of a man who is already the star."

I unbutton one more button, muss my hair, and put on the one I like to call Mr. Discerning. The way he looks at the world, it's as if everything and everyone is there for his perusal and pleasure. I pull him out for billionaire romances. If Bridge were here, she would say something like *A bit on the nose, don't you think?*

"Perfect."

I still don't know how I left her Sunday. Not after she let me read our scene. I don't know how she let me leave. But she did without a glance—seemed to want me to leave. And since then, one word texts meant to put me off. Now I'm thinking I made a mistake by leaving.

I should have just given her some space. Crashed on the couch. But she was like a zombie, turned off, unfeeling—cold, even. It was such the antithesis of what I was feeling it was hard to take. But I could have, would have, if she'd wanted me to stay. But she didn't. Everything she didn't say told me to leave. So I wrapped my arms around her as she stood there like a statue. But I held her just the same because *I* needed it. And she needed me to leave.

I'm not sure of much else two days later, but of that I am positive.

Benefit of the doubt, I remind myself. We each have our own way of dealing. She was exhausted, so much on her plate. She needed time to process.

Sable is giving our names to a petite man at the door of the tent.

Before we enter, she looks at me and mouths, *Game time.*

So I stuff myself in the corner and become him.

TWENTY-EIGHT

MEETING THE MEAT

Dinner is over. Most guests are drunk. Sable is angry because we still haven't seen hide or hair of Richard.

"Finally," she says, as a tall, attractive man in a well-cut suit walks into the tent like he's not two hours late.

"So this is Richard Piner?" I say reading between the lines.

He finds us in the crowd and smiles, nods, and then veers toward the head table to make his excuses or apologies. The couple, two men in their seventies, are laughing before I can push away the dessert that lands in front of me.

Sable gets up to join a table closer to the front—you are seated by importance at these things—and she engages in conversation with a director I would give my eyeteeth to work with. Knowing my role, I pull out bored and smoldering.

Richard comes over and takes Sable's seat.

"Joshua Anjo Silva, as I live and breathe. What's Anjo mean?"

"Angel."

"More like devil. Too bad you don't play for my team."

"Don't hit on my client, Richard," Sable says from over his shoulder.

"I would never."

"You just were. Now, where are we on *Scarred*?"

"There's a little library just inside the resort. Let's adjourn."

————

Once we are sitting in the well-appointed library, it takes less than three minutes for me to become sixty thousand dollars richer. But I had to agree to keep the scar off other book covers for ten years and do publicity with the author, for which I will be further compensated at an hourly rate.

Once we're done, Sable says, "Richard, don't you rep Bridget Stanton? My client is working with her on a romance of all things, and she promised him a byline. I need a contract for that, obviously."

Richard's eyes lock with mine. He takes in my features. With a sigh he says, "I do. Will get back to you ASAP on that."

"Like this kind of ASAP." She holds up the contract. "I expect better given my longstanding relationship with Stone Street Literary."

"Of course. *Scarred* has taken up too much of my time as of late. I must attend to … other matters." He sounds upset. He doesn't like the idea of the art getting a byline. Too bad. But I know better than to cut Sable off at the knees, so I just add, "It has been an honor to work with her."

"I'm sure," he says, but it feels like a slight.

"Josh minored in screenwriting—is quite the talent himself. Quite good at it."

"Good, such a weak word. I'm sure he is great at what he does."

Again, I don't understand the context unless … fuck.

He knows.

I stand.

"I've got to go," I say.

"Have fun in Miami," Richard adds with a smile that doesn't reach his eyes that are boring a hole through me.

"It's work, Richard. I'll do my job."

Then he stands. "Sable, a pleasure. Sorry for the delays. Now I must call an author; they can be so much trouble." But he's still looking at me.

My pocket buzzes. I lean in to give Sable a peck and Richard also stands to leave.

"Nice to meet you," Richard says to me. "Sable, talk next week."

We walk side by side until the door. Then we each gesture to the other to go ahead.

My pocket buzzes again so I take the offer.

I'm pulling out my phone before I even break the doorway. It's her. She wants to meet me in Miami. I'm so relieved, tears prick my eyes. I rush to the truck, wanting to get the hell out of here and to her—and my hometown. I can't wait to show Bridget my favorite place in the world.

———

The drive is long and dark, taking me through the Everglades. There are few exits on the section of I-75 called Alligator Alley, but I take one of them. Turn off the truck. The lights. And just listen to the sounds of the swamp. The moon is almost full, so the stars are not as spectacular as at Kissimmee. But if I close my eyes, I can be back there with her.

One more day.

One more day, and this time I don't care what happens—I'm not leaving her again. Not like that. I am going to use my words. There is so much to say.

TWENTY-NINE

WHAT HAPPENS IN MIAMI

I lean back so far I can see the shore, sigh, and pick up the twenty-pound weight to start on my abs, which can take my mind off anything, as tight focus is necessary to do right by them. The trick is to get them all—every dip and bump, which is not as easy as it might seem. Takes seven different moves on the bench, plus the hanging leg lifts I did earlier, to touch it all up. I watch them flex and release, check them off, make sure I get them all. But I'm careful. This is an area where I need HD-level definition but no bulk. My look is slim. Angsty—at least, that's what Liane, the photographer, called me before she sent me to the gym to get ready.

I could have used the one at the hotel, but I love working out outside. Liane said I had forty minutes to sunset and "to make 'em count."

I like her. She likes women but knows her way around a male torso. According to her, we might go three hours to get the "money shot," which is longer than I remember anyone shooting me, ever. Usually, it's like twenty minutes and "we're good," but not for this shoot. Because finally, after more than a decade of modeling, I'm letting someone show the scar. And they are paying for it. Wow, are they paying for it.

We're doing it at The Aura, at my suggestion, and it is quite the production. I got us the penthouse suite for the night, and after oiling me down, they have me take a shower and then without even drying, walk onto the penthouse deck that overlooks the city. She looks at my tight, wet, pornographic Skims.

"Fold them down."

I do.

"Once more."

You can see my hairline. The woman setting up the reflectors clears her throat.

Liane looks at my dick, then my face. "If that grows, it will ruin the shot."

"Don't worry about the Richard; we've done this a few times."

"Named him, have you?" she says.

"Shakespeare did it for me."

But really Bridget did it for me.

"An intellectual—my favorite kind of sex on a stick."

"So you like the Smart One?" I ask.

"If that's like the Chosen One but Smart, yes, that's my kink."

She is the perfect photographer for this shoot—super talented and no interest in the goods to muck it up. I've had photographers spend more time hitting on me than shooting me. No, Liane is a professional.

"Let's get the wet one done before he dries."

The makeup tech rushes in with a brush to highlight my abs.

I let them do makeup. Helps with shine and lighting. But my contracts specify no CGI, not even a touchup. No one is going to take what I work so hard to maintain and give me an arm in the wrong place or a strange optical illusion leg thing. Nope, it's *au naturel* with me.

Better not to follow that line of thought. Don't want to ruin the shoot.

The tech is touching up again. This can be an issue for some —the touching, the brushing, the applying of oil all while being objectified. Nothing new for me. Been objectified since I was about thirteen.

"So how'd you get it?" the tech asks. She means the scar, of course.

"Shark bite," I answer, as that one usually makes them laugh and we can move on.

But she looks at me side-eyed and says, "If so, it needs braces?"

I laugh. She power shoots, so she must have gotten a hundred frames. But that's as original a response to a pat line I've ever heard. Clearly I need to find a new one. But I can see from her eyes her interest is not going to wane.

I hate it when people ask about the scar, and after this shoot there will be a lot more of it. A publicity tour for a book called *Scarred*.

Only three people on the planet know how it came to be: Gretchen, Nana, and the doctor who stitched me up, and I am very happy to keep it that way. Some things don't need to be known. Some things change the way people look at you. And my income depends on people wanting to look at me.

"No, really?" she asks.

"It's personal," I say.

I can be truthful since she has no intention of asking for my number or my social accounts. I overheard her hitting on the hotel concierge when I arrived. But I could see why. The concierge is tiny-curvy, a combination that's usually my MO, but

I can't stop thinking about a woman so complicated she colors stunningly sunset-kissed hair brown.

I cannot even imagine why someone would cover such a remarkable and rare gift. My Richard follows my train of thought, and I swallow, shake my hands, think of the nursing home, then refocus.

Liane has turned off the flash and angled me toward the multicolored lights of the Carrier building, and I can see where she is going with this. The building has a kaleidoscope of lights that after dark it shuffles through, like a rainbow. I wonder how I will look with a pink glow, a green glow, a blue glow. Will it highlight the scar? That's why we're here after all.

"Josh, I need those sultry, half-mast eyes and a soft mouth."

Tilting my head to the left, I look at the photographer like I want her.

"Whatever you are thinking, stop," she says, horrified. "Look at *the camera* like it holds a video of the best sex you've ever had. Watch it play."

Easy.

Stars fly above my head, her body beneath me, my cock still hard inside her. At that place between—the place in the middle where we were perfect and I tried to fight my need to move inside her just to never leave that place.

"Perfect."

I blink. Coming back from the waking dream.

"And just in time," she chuckles.

I look down to see the promised land has grown considerably. Unashamed, I shrug my shoulders, "Danger of the profession."

"I'm almost not gay right now."

I laugh as she throws me a robe. But as I walk back into the penthouse suite in one of the most decadent resort hotels in Miami, I realize I don't want to be here. Not alone.

All night I can't help looking at my watch.

The next morning, I buy a ticket to Orlando for forty-nine dollars on Spirit Airlines just so I can get past security. I leave at noon and valet park but the line is long and I don't have precheck, so I arrive at the gate at 1:15 P.M. just in time to see her plane taxi to a stop. It's one of those end gates for the puddle jumpers. Doesn't even have jetways, so I get to stand at the second-floor window and watch her walk down the gangplank. She's wearing a bright yellow pinup-girl polka-dotted sundress, a big hat, and shades like she's a star. And in my world she is. She takes my breath away. I plan to take hers too.

She walks into the terminal, pulling a red-tagged roller bag. I wait impatiently in her direct line of sight. When she sees me, it's like Christmas morning. She drops her bag and runs to me, her hat flying off on the way. I catch her. I'll always catch this woman and kiss the ever-loving hell out of her.

There are whistles and catcalls, and she pulls back with a breathtaking smile. "I've missed you."

"I've been going out of my mind."

We realize her dress is bunched up under my hands on her ass. Someone clears their throat, and I let her slide down.

"Let's get out of here."

"Let's do. Jessica has been looking forward to this."

I take a moment. Because what I plan for her on our balcony —what happens in Miami—I want it to be about us.

"Let's be us while we're here," I say.

"Richard says I need sex in a city."

Pulling her along with one hand, her roller bag with the other, I say, "You'll get what you need."

THIRTY

WHAT IS IT ABOUT ELEVATORS?

"I flew first class. They give you champagne," she says as we walk out the sliding glass doors.

"Even on the baby planes? Wish I'd been there."

I hand my tag to the guy at the valet stand.

"I toasted us." She holds up her hand like she still has it, and I realize she's a little bubbly herself. "To great sex," she says.

"To great sex."

The valet attendant's eyes go wide, and of course they do. In that dress Bridget is a shock to the system.

I'm in black jeans and a black V-neck that I had housekeeping dry on high. Reminiscent of that first night. The night of the mirror.

On the way to the hotel, she's stares out the window on my sexy city. Some think Vegas is sexy, but Miami's one better—sultry. Sultriest city in the world, if you ask me. Her hand is in mine, resting on my thigh, I trace my finger along the pulse at her wrist to feel it speed up as the city shines in the bright winter sun.

Yesterday I was feeling whiplashed by the hot-or-not nature

of our relationship, but today she is downright giddy, and for at least the next twenty-four hours she's mine. And if this is only a job, and I have to consider that it might be, I will make sure this is one trip she will never forget.

She opens her clutch and removes a lip cover—pale and glossy, thank god, as covering her lips is a crime. I might just reapply it later, slowly, holding her chin as she kneels on the bed, right before she takes my cock between those shining lips. Because if there is one thing that is not in doubt, Bridge loves my cock. And he and I are going to do everything we can to make sure she can think of nothing else. And I'm not even getting ahead of myself. We discussed the scenes she wanted on the phone last night right before I violently jerked off—twice.

But I have an ace or two up my sleeve.

"What do you think about using Jess and Royce for this trip?"

I look at her, surprised. "For real?"

"Will make things easier. Less confusion."

Or more. So much more.

"I've a better idea. What about just Bridge and Josh for a change?"

She's silent, so I risk a glance, in Miami traffic.

"You okay?" I ask.

"The names aren't important. We know this is make-believe."

No, I don't, and not quite anger rises. More like a challenge—like I'll *make* you believe. I crack my knuckles, steering with my knee, and wonder what my number is right now. I need to blow off some steam.

I pull into The Aura, my black truck almost an eyesore next to the Maserati's and Lamborghinis.

"Fancy," she says as I open the door. Her dress rides up her thighs as she gets out. I give her a hand and pull the dress down, letting my fingers slide against her skin.

"I'd worry about someone seeing my panties, if I were wearing any."

"Fuck."

I grab her hand, practically dragging her down the short walk to the door.

"My things," she says, turning back.

"They'll bring them." I march her past the guest elevators to the concierge desk.

"I did something different down there for you," she whispers.

Now *my* eyes are wide.

She mouths, *Brazilian.*

"What?"

She barely lifts a shoulder.

We aren't going to make it to the elevator.

I call out, "Ernesto," and he comes from around the corner. I hand him a bill and say, "Bags in the truck, need a card for—" I cut my eyes to the staff elevator. "Give us thirty."

She looks at me askance when the elevator door opens to padded blue walls, but I hold her back and let the hospitality staff coming from the basement take this one.

We wait in silence, holding hands that can't stop moving, caressing, while we watch the lights go all the way to the top and back down again.

When the doors open, I say, "Your turn."

And before the doors can even close, she's glad for the padding, as I've thrown her up against the wall.

"I see," she says when I drop to my knees. Throw her leg over my shoulder and before she can even get a sweet little "Oh" out, her skirt is up and my mouth is on her velvet skin.

"Hold it," I say into her pussy needing my hand.

She moans. Takes the hem and bunches it at her chest. She loves it when I talk to her pussy so I do. Tell it all I'm going to do to it between sucks and licks and thrusts.

We have thirty floors, so I try to take my time. But her lips are smooth as silk. Her clit between my tongue and teeth. I squeeze. One, two, three. Then press. Hard.

Two fingers inside, and her head hits the wall.

Her hands join her head, pushing her pussy onto my mouth. And that's when she starts with the filth. What she's going to do with *my* cock. What she wants me to do with it. And I almost press the fire button and fuck the consequences. It's Miami— money can take care of a lot. But I need time. So much time for what she's begging for. I stop playing around. Throw her other leg over my shoulder and stand in one movement.

And up against those padded walls, I eat her the fuck out. She writhes against my face, but when I slip my pinky in her backside, she comes in a gush all over me. And it's so hot. So fucking hot.

Panting, she looks down at me like a deer in the headlights.

"Game on," I say. And lift her at the waist to bring her to her feet as the bell rings.

She straightens her dress, and I use my shirt to wipe my face, all the while looking into those dark gray eyes, making sure she understands this is just the beginning.

The door opens, staff waiting. But I lean in, pressing the zipper of my jeans between her legs to let her feel what she does to me. Kiss her on the neck, feel her pulse racing.

"Game on," she challenges. "Our room better be close."

"Just here," I say, as I pass those waiting. There are only four rooms on this entire floor.

"I need a pen and paper," she says.

"You can write tomorrow." I pull her into the room behind me.

"But—"

"If you forget, I'm happy to remind you. Actually …" I push her up against the door because after five days apart and a taste, I am fucking insatiable.

Three hours later, the room is a disaster. The couch is slanted across the penthouse living room, every pillow on the ground. The bed cover is halfway out the bedroom door, and I'm pretty sure one of the sheets is torn, but I don't know if it was her or me.

And I feel *a lot* fucking better.

She is devouring a burger, and juice is running down her naked chest. I inhaled two, minus the buns, which she made fun of while sipping from a comp bottle of Piper.

I will need to get the house staff in at some point just so we can sleep. But I can't help the urge—grab my phone and snap a shot of her wrapped in a white sheet, the sun shining against the mirrored buildings in the background.

"Fair enough," she says with her mouth full. "I certainly have taken a few of you. But what's it for?"

What's it for? For me to stare at hour after hour so I can relive everything over and over.

But I say, "You. This. It's beautiful. The sun and the city behind you. You'll want to write it. I want you to write it."

She looks behind her and says, "Wow."

But she is by far the wowest thing in the frame.

And don't get me wrong, I love sex and have had a lot of it, but this, what we have, is unprecedented. She makes me unhinged. There is no norm, no moral line, I wouldn't cross to have her under me, above me, rubbing that fucking soft-as-satin pussy up and down my abs. I mean, that was ... I have no words, because she seemed unhinged too.

I know beyond a shadow of a doubt that not only has she broken my heart wide open, she's taken up residence. Which is terrifying.

Talk to her, I hear Gretchen counsel while I watch her tip the bottle back and let bubbly run down between her breasts.

I reach for the bottle to take some liquid courage, and while I'm trying to find a way to break the ice, she lies back against pillows at the foot of the bed.

"So how did you get so good at sex? I mean, I don't need the details, the body count, as I'm sure it's in the hundreds."

"Not hundreds." I try to emphasize the S.

"What you do, it's more than just practice."

"Okay." I turn on my side and put my head on my hand. "Here's the story. I started early and had an experienced teacher."

"How early?"

"Early."

"How experienced?"

"I don't know her age, but likely as old as you."

"Were you— Was it—"

"Kind of, but not really. I was taken to a whorehouse in Rio. My father left me there for the night and told me not to let him down."

"Shit."

"It was the way things were done. Strangely, he saw it as moral. Didn't want me to spoil any young Catholic girl. And maybe it was for the best because my libido was ... overactive."

"Still is."

I give her a pointed look.

"Not complaining."

"I learned fast that night. One never wanted to embarrass my father."

And I see the interest, the curiosity in her gray eyes, like she is turning me into a story. That's what she does. For her, everything is a story.

"Do you remember her name?"

"Allesandra. She had hair the color of obsidian. And her teeth were clean and straight, which I was grateful for, as all I knew how to do when I got there was kiss. She taught me much that night."

"How old?"

"Thirteen."

"Thirteen's like ninth grade."

"Eighth for me. It was spring break. But I was sexually mature, even then."

"I barely had mosquito bites in eighth grade."

"I looked pretty much like an adult."

This is it. You can do this. Tell her your secrets in this bed you rumpled with her. This is where intimacy happens.

I lick my lips, shake my head, and she saves me.

"So what did she teach you?" she says, poking me in the pec.

"To listen, to notice. She kept saying *ouvir, observe—listen.* Over and over, in Portuguese."

"That's hot. You speaking Portuguese."

"O que está quente é um pequeno mamilo rosa aparecendo por baixo das cobertas."

I reach out, circle her nipple. I'm unsurprised by her little intake of breath.

"What else did she teach you?"

"She told me to cover up. That if I didn't, my dick would fall off."

"She didn't!"

"She did. And since my dick was my new favorite thing, I followed instructions. Until you. If you make my dick fall off— Well, it will be for very different reasons." I'm still circling her nipple. "I'm glad to have had Allesandra. It could have been horrible. And she taught me that every woman is different. Needs different things, different places touched, different pressure."

I squeeze her erect nipple between thumb and forefinger, and she arches toward me.

"You like this." I squeeze again.

"But *this* even better." I lean in to press that nipple between my teeth and lip and receive a full-on moan for my canny observance.

She doesn't ask many more questions of me after that, except how to say *harder* in Portuguese.

THIRTY-ONE

THE PRETTY WOMAN

"I f we don't leave this bed, we will never leave this bed."

"That makes no sense," I say, staring at the ceiling, trying to catch my breath.

"It's your fault." She rolls over, flinging her arm out but still not reaching the edge of the California king. "Josh Silva, you have fucked me senseless."

I chuckle, but she's right—we are sated to the point of insensibility.

"I'll start the shower," I say.

I get out of a bed that is not just rumpled but ravaged. You should have seen Ernesto's face when he brought in the bags.

"You'll shower alone," she calls out after me. "Can't get pulled into your nakedness again. It's like gravity. On Mars!"

I step under the rain shower.

"What do you want to do now?" she asks, turned away from me like she doesn't know every inch. She's wrapped in a robe, sitting on the vanity bench.

I sniff the hotel products. Nope.

"Hey, pass me that black zipper bag on the counter. Please."

She rustles around.

"If it's not on the counter, look in the top drawer. It has products."

"Products? As in multiple. You crack me up." But she passes it through the mist.

"So what's on tap, Mr. Miami? Want to club it?"

"Sure. As long as I pick the club."

"X?"

"No. Just no."

"Why not? It is the hottest club—"

"It's not. Trust me, it's not your scene. If I read you the rules, you would picket the place."

"But it would make a good scene," she whines.

I peek around the glass. "I think you have enough material to hold you for a while."

She's trying not to smile, but it sneaks in, and it is bashful and makes me feel like the creator of the universe.

I pass back my black bag, and she fiddles with it while I wash off.

"Your turn," I call as I wrap a towel around my waist.

"You carry your shampoo *and* bodywash. Even I'm not that fussy."

"I'm sensitive to smell," I say, noticing I need to shave. I bet she has a rash on her thighs.

"I see." She drops her robe and steps into the fog. "So what do I smell like?"

"If you want to go out, it would be best if I did not think too hard in that direction."

"You say the sweetest things."

"Let's do something authentic, like as in our authentic selves. Take a night off from role play. What do you say?" She can't see me, so maybe she can't see what the question cost me.

"I like role play," she calls out from under the spray.

"As do I. Obviously. But I want to take you somewhere special. And I would like to take Bridge, if that's okay."

"Bridge will go anywhere with you."

"Now who's in the third person."

"But I don't know if I have something to wear. Clubbing is not normal for me, Mr. Miami."

It's not true. I've seen what she brought, and it would be fine for where we are headed, but I can't resist. Not knowing how much she loves old movies.

"Okay, then one more scene," I say. "Let's do the *Pretty Woman*."

She squeals.

Once we are dressed in jeans and T-shirts and headed down in the actual guest elevator, I explain how we're going to do the *Pretty Woman* with Richard's card, since I covered the room.

"I figure we have at least a thousand to spend. We can even do it in character—too good not to use—Jessica?"

"Fine, Royce."

I laugh. "That name was supposed to be a joke. I don't know if we should keep it."

She stills.

"You okay?" I ask.

"I'm good."

But we both know what good means. What did I say?

I take her hand, and we walk around the back of the hotel to the causeway bridge that will take us into Brickell proper.

"How do you know so many old movie references anyway?" I ask as we cross the canal.

"Me? What about you? But Sweetie loved old movies—well, old to me—and she couldn't afford the quote, unquote, good channels. She was a real romantic. Liked to say there was never enough time to love all the men she wanted to. Didn't even care when they didn't love her back. A tragic romantic. What about you?"

"Maybe. With the right person."

It just hangs there between us, for so long. I have to move on.

"And same as to the money," I say. "But Nana used to put movies on at night to help me sleep and to help her learn English. When she moved here, she didn't speak any. She would say, 'If I learn English like on TNT and USA, I will be very American.' Sometimes she would fall asleep in the chair next to my bed, watching some old thing. She loved anything black and white all the way to the early nineties. After that, she said they got too violent, and honestly, I have to agree."

"Me too. Old movies are simple and a whole lot less bloody."

We're still walking hand-in-hand down Brickell's wide palm-lined sidewalks.

"You know you look perfect," she says. "You don't need the *Pretty Woman*. But let's do it for you too. A twist on the trope."

"One to talk," I reply.

She's wearing a wide-brimmed hat to keep the sun off her face, held with a red silk sash wrapped around her neck. She looks right out of Turner Classics in skinny white capris and a pale pink boat neck that highlights her delicate clavicles.

I'm loving the look. I can't help but picture what she would look like in this outfit with her ripe strawberry-blond hair.

She nods toward a couple coming toward us.

"He looks like an Italian prince," she says in a whisper.

I whisper back, "Quite possible in this neighborhood. J Lo lives here."

Really? she mouths.

I nod.

The couple passes us on the sidewalk. His companion is in a

lovely shirtdress with strappy sandals that crisscross her calves, oversized sunglasses, and what looks to be an Hermès scarf tied in her dark hair.

"That's a good look," she says once they're out of earshot.

"That scarf would look great on you."

"What about here?" It's a men's store.

"A little too buttoned-up, don't you think?" But the couple has given me an idea. If there is any place besides Hermès where you can find a selection of their scarves, it's Fifi's on Fifth. "I have a better idea."

I take her down a few side streets farther off the waterside. Looks like Richard's card is going to get a break today.

"Where are we going?" she asks as we wind through an almost industrial area.

"Fifi's on Fifth," I tell her and pull her to a stop before she crosses against the light.

"There's a Fifth in Miami?"

"No. It's not on Fifth, as there is no Fifth Street in Miami proper, but the one in New York is where this establishment began.

"Duh. My mother takes a load every season."

Interesting.

"Hopefully my cousin is working today."

"Kissing cousins?" she asks.

"We only kissed once; I was, like, eight."

"You actually kissed your first cousin?" She sounds horrified.

"Not cousin in the genealogy chart sense. More like neighborhood cousins, like the way everyone on your street is your cousin, you know?"

"I don't. If I did, my cousins would be mostly lecherous white men." She pulls me to a stop. "Just the once?"

"Just the once. Over here." I pull her toward an unadorned awning.

"It's like a speakeasy."

"If you know, you know," I say, opening the door for her.

Ana's at the counter. She runs at me like I'm a long-lost brother, hugs my neck and pulls back to take a look.

"¿Qué bola, primo?"

"Falta el 305."

"¿Cuánto tiempo? Te ves lo más sexy como para comer. ¿Quién es la chica?"

"¿Un amiga?"

"¿Buena amiga?"

"Sí."

"Hagámoslo chévere."

"Si."

"Hagamoslo divertido."

"¿Champán?"

"Perfecto."

I lead Bridget to a plush gold-accented lounger, and she seats herself with an inquisitive look on her face. Removing her hat, she says, "Spanish too? I didn't know that."

"There isn't much you *do* know about me."

"Ouch."

"It's true. Other than knowing I'm great in bed, was deflowered by a sex worker, have sixteen layers of abs, and a scar like a lightning bolt pointing to 'the promised land,' as you're beginning to sound like Sable, you know nothing about me."

"Hmm. How does one learn the secrets of Josh?"

"Stick around."

And I mean it. It seems like just when things are getting

good, she runs. It's upsetting, and annoying, and confusing as fuck. But what is *not* confusing about all this?

When are we in a scene? When are we not? When am I me? When am I Royce or whatever the fuck we decide to call him?

That's why tonight is important. Tonight, I want Bridge. And tonight she gets *me*.

But oblivious to my need for honesty, she is pouring champagne. She stands with her glass and moves toward a rack, but I shake my head.

"I've got this."

"*You've* got this? I am great at this. I'm a thrifter extraordinaire. Teacher's salary."

"I have been modeling since I was fifteen. I could be a stylist at this point. Watch and learn."

With Ana's help, I fill a rolling rack with so many looks for her, it can barely move. My selections for her are modern and sleek. For myself, I'm thinking old Hollywood—the movie Bridge was somewhat watching while we dressed. *Roman Holiday.* Must have rubbed off on me.

It takes me five minutes to choose a pair of Tom Ford slacks and a thin cream vintage sweater that accentuates my attributes —didn't say I fought fair.

Takes Bridget fifteen to pick a dress, but she chose my favorite: a chartreuse designer shirtdress, Celene, I think, with gold strappy sandals almost the twins of the woman with Italian royalty, and the sweetest yellow-and-green Hermès scarf I've ever seen tied at her hairline with a square knot at her nape. I want to eat her for lunch. I don't even let her put her clothes back on thankful that Fifi's only accepts the newly drycleaned. She demands the same.

I top my ensemble with a vintage Cuban canotier with the tip of a peacock feather in the band. The boater cost more than everything else combined, but not many men can pull it off and I happen to be one of them.

And given the little whoosh of air that escapes her as I come toward her, there is no need to look in a mirror. I smile, the kind for the camera, and she says, "I think my panties fell off."

I hold her eyes. "I hoped you weren't wearing any."

She winks.

"In that short thing? Are you kidding?" I ask, but she just sashays out the door. I follow. Jesus, we better not go back to the room. And absolutely positively no elevators or we will never make it out tonight.

We return to Aura to drop off a bag of clothes at the desk. I'll have Ernesto take them up as I was serious. If I lift the hem on her dress and there is nothing underneath, our night out is shot.

We talk about getting a drink, then head back toward the city. We have to stop at the base of the causeway bridge because it's up. Looking out onto the city's skyline, she says, "It really is an exceptionally nice place. So clean."

"Miamians are proud of their city, and Cuban Americans, well, I cannot wait to take you to Little Havana tonight."

She looks up, holding her hat to her head. She took off the red sash, as it clashed with the Hermès. She's staring up at the glass deck jutting out from our suite, hanging in midair. And I know exactly where I want tonight to end.

Then she turns to me, serious, just as the bridge horn announces to a waiting yacht it can pass under.

"How can you afford this?"

When I'm about to tell her not to worry about it, the reason I can stay in the penthouse of The Aura passes below on a hundred-foot yacht, screaming at me.

"Josh, baby!" Kayla is sunning on the deck.

"No way," Bridget says.

They pull into the berth right next to the hotel—a parking space for yachts—as The Aura is that kind of hotel. And the owner of that yacht owns The Aura.

"Her godparents own it," I say, waiting for some kind of reaction, explosion, something. It wouldn't be the first time my friendship with Kayla rocked boats.

"So Kayla is how we're in the penthouse suite?"

"Yes."

I wait for what comes next, but Bridget just waves at Kayla, who's in a bright but barely there Brazilian bikini. "She looks nice in yellow"—she tilts her head to me—"don't you think?" Bitchy as hell. Bitchy I can handle. Bitchy actually suits her.

"She's like a sister to me."

"Not the same as *being* a sister."

"Obviously, and yet it is in this case."

"Come on!" Kayla yells from her spot splayed out on the deck.

I glance at Bridget, who looks like a billion dollars, and raise an eyebrow.

"It would be impolite to refuse," she says.

"All right," I say in a normal voice to Kayla. No need to scream when she is right below us.

We walk the short distance past the hotel and the cars parked out front just for show. The boat is rocking so I hold Bridget's hip as we walk up the gangplank. She doesn't even blink, and I realize she must come from *real* money and wonder if so, why the issue with her house? Which reminds me I still don't know what's up with Richard and the book. Shouldn't I know that by now? Sable sure thinks so. But there is no way I'm asking tonight. Tonight is for us.

As I muse, she introduces herself to Mr. and Ms. Paloma,

who graciously agree to show her around the yacht. I stay on the foredeck with Kayla.

"Still playing the prostitute? Oh, wait, are you even getting paid?"

"Hello, Kayla, how are you?"

"Not as hot as you right now, which is pissing me off. Cream is a good look on your skin, and the butter-yellow loafers are a nice touch."

"Bridge and I did some shopping, and no, I'm not being paid. I'm the talent on this one, co-author. And well, our process is unique."

"I'd say. Did *she* dress you like this?"

"I can dress myself."

"So I'll assume you picked out that sleek light-green shirtdress and strappy golden flats she's wearing."

"Indeed I did."

"The scarf adds something special. She looks like money."

"I think she might have come from it."

"Good, because you should be expensive."

"It was a misunderstanding."

"She called you a whore."

I sigh, as nothing is going to convince Kayla this arrangement is a good idea. And I get it. We get treated like that sometimes, models, like there is nothing we will not do for money. But there is, for both of us. A line neither of us has willingly crossed.

"Kay, she really is quite amazing." I'm looking up to the second deck, where she is being led with her hat and glasses in one hand, a flute in the other.

"She's pretty, I'll give you that."

"She's exceptional."

Bridget looks down at us, and I lean away from Kayla, pretending to take in the view.

"This will end badly."

"You don't know that."

"I do. Because it began badly, and all things that begin bad end that way at some point."

"It was a misunderstanding."

"Well, she seems lovely if you like entitled, self-centered, emotionally stunted bitches."

"I'm changing the subject now. I got the proofs back on the shoot. Thanks for the penthouse."

"And?"

"Sable says it's going to launch my career. She's been showing the proofs around. Just showing; no one gets to keep them."

"Then you should be concentrating on this"—she touches my stomach—"and this"—and shakes my chin—"not that." The person she so sweetly refers to as "that" is walking toward us.

"I want more." I whisper.

"Josh, my love, you have the audacity to want everything."

"Nothing wrong with that. Kayla," Bridget says as she stretches out her elegant hand, "so good to finally meet you. Your godparents are lovely."

"Where are you off to?" Kayla asks.

"Think we will go dancing; you know the place," I say.

"Bold choice," Kayla says.

"Shall we?" I offer my arm to Bridget.

"Indeed," she replies, suddenly a cold sophisticate. Either she's a better actor than me, or maybe I'm only now seeing the real deal. The thought unnerves me.

How well do I know this woman?

Maybe only as well as she knows me.

THIRTY-TWO

CUBANO

"The secret to a great café is not the coffee. Just about everyone in Miami uses one of two brands." I take her hand and lead her down Calle Ocho after exiting the Uber. "It's the sugar, and the literal hole-in-a-wall here uses a proprietary blend of white and dark akin to a state secret—trust me, I have tried to fuck my way into that recipe—but it is the best Cuban coffee in Miami. And that's saying something."

"Color me intrigued."

"I'd like to uncolor you."

She stops.

Shit.

"What do you mean by that?"

I want to back out carefully, but it was her idea, on almost day one, the honesty.

"Okay, I am sure I'm going to regret this, but, Bridget, I do believe that you might be the most natural beauty I have ever seen, and given my line of work, that is saying something—"

"But?"

I step back against the brick wall behind us to let some kids pass. She's facing me.

"But. You are a natural strawberry-blond. And I cannot imagine with your skin tone and eye color a more perfect shade for you. And yet you color it."

She takes a deep breath, and I'm sure I have overstepped now. I try to fix it somehow.

"I don't mean to say I don't love you as a brunette. I think I might love the look of you if your hair were blue." She is not happy.

"Sorry, it's none of my business. I'm a fool. But you were the one who started the honesty thing."

She tilts her head. Thinking.

"Fine. My mother told me young my fiery hair would get me in trouble. The kind of trouble her mother got into and she followed. You see, we don't know my grandfather, and I haven't seen my father in two decades."

Wow. That is some big truth for a sidewalk.

"Sorry about your dad. I have father issues too, as you know, but I'm more sad your mother said those things to you."

"*Says* those things to me. And look at me, all Kate Middleton brown." She twirls a lock of hair around her finger. "And here you are, more trouble than even she could see coming."

"I'm trouble?"

I let her make light of the situation because this kind of truth hurts.

"*Please.* Now, come on, if you are not letting me go back for a nap after all the 'trouble' earlier, I need this best-in-Miami Cubano."

She pulls me by the hand off the wall. I take the opportunity to wrap an arm around her back, gripping her hip, wanting her to feel I'm here. She knocks my hand away, seeming to think I'm feeling for a panty line.

"No cheating."

Side by side we walk, crossing at the light.

Then out of the blue she turns to me.

"How did you get so comfortable with sex? I mean, I realize I'm not a great comparison as I've had less than a handful of partners since college, none of which even got me there, but you are actually comfortable with it. All of it."

"As are you, as far as I can tell."

"I am?"

"Extremely. And even though I hate that you did not have satisfactory experiences in the past—makes me want to find that not-handful of partners and shame them into getting their heads out of their asses—but I would be lying if I didn't admit I like that your first orgasm was with me."

"It's kinda like *the* first, isn't it?"

"Wow. That makes me feel …" I put my hands in my pockets to keep from touching her. "It's hard to describe how that makes me feel and too embarrassing by half to try. But you have one of my firsts too so we're even."

I stop.

"We're here."

She looks around the string of maybe fifteen people we stand behind.

"There is always a line. But it goes fast. No need to order; just say how many you want. No half-caf mocha lattes with whipped cream here."

"I can do that."

We shuffle up a few feet.

"Where do people sit?"

"They don't. They just sip as they walk or even take it to share."

"It's like four ounces?"

"If you went in there"—I nod toward a local nail place—"with one of these to share, well, that would be very Miamian."

"Hmm. I do need a pedicure."

"You do not."

"There's no color on my toes."

"I like your toes the way they are. Nail polish tastes funny."

"Then no polish."

And just like that, we are next in line.

"Dos, por favor," she says with a horrible gringo accent, and I smile down at her misplaced smugness.

We end up on a sidewalk bench not twenty feet from the shop. We stay long enough to watch the sunset turn from pink to purple and plot almost to the end of the book, her making notes on her phone. I throw in a few reversals she loves, and we talk about screenwriting and growing up in Miami and Rio in the summer and modeling, and by her third Cubano, she's wired as hell and I don't know any more about her than when we sat down two hours ago. But regardless, I know her better. Like the facts of her life are unimportant when compared to what makes her laugh, what makes her furious, what makes her blush.

"I feel like I'm high on cocaine," she says as she stands. She is moving side to side.

"Lightweight. Have you ever been high on cocaine?"

"No."

"Well, trust me, that is not what you feel like, and thank god."

A raised eyebrow.

"Trouble, remember. And look at you, so jacked you can't even stand still."

"If caffeine-overdosed Bridget doesn't dance soon, she might explode."

"Salsa?"

"Really? Please."

"Dirty?"

She stills. Smiles the wickedest smile I have ever seen and says, "As long as you promise not to cheat."

THIRTY-THREE

LA CANDELA

We Uber back through the streets of Little Havana with
the windows down, so different from Miami proper
with its high-rises and glass. Little Havana is all squat buildings
crowded against each other, lights pouring out onto the
sidewalks as every door and window is open, music pouring out
of every establishment. Even Spanish talk radio, as couples
stroll, kids eat alfresco at food carts and run the streets. It's a
cacophony unique to this corner of the world. And La Candela,
is the center of it all. An institution continually operating since
Batista was run out of Cuba. I've always thought it seemed to
hold the hope of a newly freed people and their celebration—
frozen in time.

Tonight the place is lit, so many people they are spilling out
onto the sidewalk. Some gather under the brightly striped
awning to smoke, even though the building is open to the air.
You can see the red hot pepper logo spotlighted on the brick
behind the band, its members moving as one as they play the
horns, silver and gold, shining in the light.

Bridge is nothing less than giddy when she sees the place, so

I'm surprised when she waits for me to walk around and open her door. The SUV is high and she is short, and the pleasure of seeing her legs wrapped in gold straps almost to her knee—the bright yellow-green of her very short shirtdress highlighting skin so natural to a redhead—I want to tell her to stop, as one foot extends to the pavement, her hand reaching out for me. Like a director, I want to control the scene, but she keeps coming with bright eyes that are stealing my breath and the eyes of every man within sight.

Bridget with a messy head in bed is beautiful, but dressed to kill she's lethal. And what's more, she seems to know it tonight, taunts me with it. And I still don't know if she has anything on under that shirt we're calling a dress.

Once she stands on my other side, I close the door and knock the roof to let the driver know he can go.

"Why did you do that?" she asks.

"It's helpful to know when passengers are clear," I say.

"Do you drive?"

I want to say I've done almost everything to keep my tuition paid and my grandmother safe, but I just smile and nod.

"Jack of all trades?"

She has no idea. I even danced in a club in downtown Tampa for a while.

"So this is the place," she says.

"Might be my favorite place in the city. Definitely my favorite place in the city to dance, which is ironic since there is no dance floor, per se."

As we shuffle through the crowd, her hips move to the samba beat played by the house band, one I know well. Not a man in it under sixty, but a sound so tight you can't help but move. I lift the hand that holds hers, and she spins away from me, I tug a bit and she rolls into my chest. Smirking up at me—like a ringer.

Then she goes limp in my arms, and I lead her across the room one spin at a time until we are in front of the band with room enough to move. And can she ever, facing away from me, my hand across her hips, hers keeping time with mine.

"Girl knows how to dance," I yell over the music. She gives me a mischievous smile, and I spin her out. Tug her back against my chest. Pull, and she's turned to me, and when I step between her legs, she drops her hips to circle against my thigh.

"Girl knows how to dance *dirty.*"

She circles again. Fuck, this is going to be fun. But we need room, so I spin her all the way out, and the crowd moves to contain us. Candela loves a show. So song after song, we move together like fucking Katey and Xavier from *Havana Nights*—the better of the dirty dancing movies in my estimation and where I learned some of my signature moves.

Before long, my sweater is on a speaker and my hat is on the lead drummer's head, and we still don't stop. My hand runs over every part of her as I pull and push her to the beat. All except her panty line, which she notices with a wink. I am no cheater.

With absolute abandon, we move in a seduction that has us both dripping wet—the crowd now visibly parted, giving a lead couple room. We own the floor.

I call out when she is again against my back and she grinds against me. "Why did you keep this a secret?"

"Keep you on your toes."

And I drop her so low her hair almost skims the floor, her pelvis against mine as I pull her back up to press against me. A moment to catch our breath. Mine in her hair, hers on my neck. A touch of her tongue that sends a jolt down to the place I press against her as I drop to circle my hips, cupping her ass, and I'm rewarded with an almost mewing sound I feel more than hear. Then the tempo picks up, and she is spinning away again.

We can barely catch our breath and still can't stop, intoxicated with each other's skin. It's better than sex—it is the place right before sex, the anticipation of it, the certainty, the moment before the climax. Pure wanting and completely reckless in that dress. I only pray she's wearing something beneath, but my hands have felt no hint of it. And yet the way she flies back to me lifts her knee against me so I can drop her low, holding her back, and leaning in to take a kiss like I just got home from the war that morphs into something so real and raw —catcalls egg us on as she holds the dip, wraps her hands in my hair, and gives it back to me as good as she gets.

Until the lead singer calls out, "¡Un descanso! ¡Demasiado caliente!" to laughter.

We wake out of the frenzy to a lot of watching faces. She curtsies, so I bow, and then we laugh our way to the bar, me shrugging on my sweater, her calling out, "Mojitos!"

"Where did you learn to dance like that?" I ask from behind her, still amazed, holding on to her hip. Not wanting to let go.

She stands in the crush around the bar, which is opening up to let her through. She turns her face back to me and says, "Sweetie had these Saturday night dance parties in her living room with martinis and cigars and, more often than not, Latin men and women and children. It was a free-for-all. That's where I learned to love to dance."

She takes the tall glass full of minty sweetness ready for her when she arrives and pulls long on the straw. I call out to the bartender for water as I sip mine, and holy fuck, the sugar. I can't help the moan that escapes me. She trades the straw for the bottle of water, and we empty it in two passes.

I clear a stool of some coats at the end, parting the crowd to hang them by the door, and she sits primly, legs crossed, her secret still a secret, at least to me.

Like she can read my mind this woman, she says, "And do you want to know a secret?"

I nod.

"It was a girl, Juliet, who taught me. We were seventeen. She was the second person I ever kissed."

"Just stop. I can't think about you dirty dancing with another woman. Not at seventeen. No. That is off-limits to this brain."

"Want to know another one?"

"Desperately."

"Now I partner three afternoons a week with two women, trading off between them."

My mouth will not close. "But wait. We are, just us, during this time. Supposed—"

"Sucker. It's a dance class at the Treasure Island Community Center and almost always completely queer. And the women in question are partnered—together—but they love me."

"I'm sure they do."

I hold up my hand for another drink for her, as she sucks on ice. She swivels her stool so her knees are on either side of my legs. It's a bold move given the other secret I still don't know.

"What about you? Where did you learn?"

"This place. Right here, this band. From about the age of fifteen."

I look around, remembering.

"Want me to tell you a secret."

"Please do."

"It's where I came to pick up women. Back then, I was ... Well, I couldn't date girls. But here, older women, I didn't need to worry about them."

She turns her head, and her eyes go soft.

"It wasn't easy, was it, being you. Growing up so fast." Then she stops for a moment and really looks at me. Like me now and me then, and says, "I'm sorry."

This is something no one else has ever even acknowledged outside of Gretchen. To everyone else, it looked like I was living the dream. Modeling in high school, sex with women twice my age, never carded, allowed anything and anyone.

"It was and it wasn't. It was both," I admit.

"Is it hard being back here?"

"With you ..." I take her hand turn it over trace a line across her palm. She shivers. "I do believe this night will change my memory of this place. Want some fresh air?"

She nods, so I walk her back through the throng as the next act starts up. Past the kitchens and the bathrooms to the hidden back door and the walled patio the band members and employees use for breaks and to hang with the owner.

The house band that just played is out back, smoking cigarillos. They look at each other when they see me. Then in unison stand up to leave.

"No, no tranquilos," I say, but they just smile at me and file back into the club, each giving Bridget a nod on the way. The last player still has my hat.

"Looks better on him anyway," I say once the door closes behind them.

We sit on an old metal rocker under the pergola with hibiscus flowers dripping down. Over the tall concrete wall of the patio, a large yellow moon hangs in the sky.

"That moon looks as languid as I now feel," she says.

"That's Miami, at turns sultry and languid—at others frenetic and sexy. I had forgotten how much I missed it."

"Why did you move?"

"I had to live in a dorm my first year, and it was too

expensive for Nana to be in a home in Miami. So, soon after I went to school, she came with me. Tampa is where I live, but Miami will always be home."

Now that we are alone, it feels like a first date. And I realize it is our first date.

"Tell me something," I say.

"What kind of something?"

"Something small."

"I wondered after Juliet if I might be bisexual but never followed up on it."

"That's small?"

I use my feet to rock us as fragrant pink petals fall into her hair.

"Okay, now you tell me something, something big, like the scar?"

"Try again."

"Kayla?"

I turn to her. "A sister, I swear."

"Now or always."

"Always."

But she looks at me like she doesn't believe me.

"But you've seen each other naked."

"Not completely. But we've been modeling together since forever."

"And you are perfect together," she says under her breath. And I can't disagree.

"Sure, the camera loves us as a couple, and we look like we love one another because we do." I make sure she is looking at me before I add, "We just don't *make* love to one another."

"Her tastes point in a different direction?"

"No." Now we are getting very close to the truth.

"Then why? You can't tell me you're not attracted to her

physically. That would be like not being attracted to you, and that is literally impossible. You both are the ideal personified."

"Is that all we are?" I say under my breath.

"Of course not. But it makes no sense, seeing the way you look at each other—"

"I can't give her what she wants."

"And that's?"

"Not for me to tell."

"Okay, fine. Then the scar."

I stop the rocker. She looks at me. Then her face drops. And I see where her mind is going.

"It happened a long time ago. It is not something I talk about, and if I'm honest I don't really even like looking at it, so I never let anyone photograph it."

"I don't even know how that is possible the number of covers you've been on."

"Well, now that you know where it is, look again. A hand, a shirt, a turn. I manage."

"All because you don't want to see it?"

"All because I don't want my scars out there in the world for anyone to see."

I stand up. Angry. Unaccountably angry. "Let's go."

She faces the moon. "If you say so, but this would make a pretty nice scene."

Adrenaline floods my system. My hands fist. Tighten. There is a planter in front of me. I see it being lifted, hear it crash against the wall, feel the cuts on my hand.

I blink. Release the air I'm holding. The planter is still there. Intact.

"I've got to—"

I don't remember how I get to the men's room. Don't know I'm there until I feel the pain and look down to see splits in the

skin over my knuckles and blood running down the wall.
Terrifying. I haven't blacked out in a decade.

I enter the stall. Wrap tissue around my fist. Call an Uber.
Text her to meet me out front. See a flash of my face in the
mirror; turn away. I look just like him. Just like my father.

Leaden, I join her, but when the car arrives I sit in the front to
hide the evidence of my illness. It came on so fast, I don't even
know what set it off.

But I am lying to myself. I know exactly what did it. A word.
Just one word, and I could have hurt her. I *did* hurt myself.

Scene.

Tonight was not supposed to be a scene.

Tonight was supposed to be us.

"Josh," she quietly says behind me, but I can't. Not right now.
I'm not right.

I think of how I had planned to finish this night—on the glass
balcony, with her bathed in the kaleidoscopic lights of the city—
what I had planned for us there that she would take and put in
the fucking book because it wouldn't even be us to her.

Kayla is right. This isn't going to end well.

The city slips by, and I drown in our silence.

When we arrive at The Aura, she slips out. Taps on my
window. I shake my head, staring straight ahead. To the driver I
say, "South Beach," and he pulls around the circle. I hear my
name but I wonder if she even knows who she is speaking to.
The tint on the windows protects me from her view.

I'm afraid. Afraid if I go with her, up there, and it's not me
she sees ... afraid of what I might do.

And I know I'm being an asshole, that I can't be upset at her
when she doesn't even know the way I feel. But how can she not
know the way I feel? After midpoint, how can she not know?

No, this is all on you. You had plenty of time to tell her

anything you wanted to. This is all on you. And you have completely blown your regimen since you met her, have no idea your number.

Tomorrow. I'll get a blood test. Figure out what's going on. Apologize. Talk to her. Tonight I could use a few milliliters of my emergency cocktail, but my case is in my suitcase and I am not going back to get it.

"¿Adonde?" the driver asks.

"Noveno y Océano," I say, staring at the window, ready to break glass. Because I know I've broken something tonight. Even if I didn't break anything, I did.

———

I stay at the South Beach gym and work out in the sand, stripped to my boxers, until almost dawn. I'm not alone; I have a spotter in a cool dude who works third shift at MIA. He looks up her flight for me. It doesn't leave until ten, so I sleep in the roots of a rubber tree until I'm woken up by a guy named Joe, one of the many unhoused people who stay on this stretch of South Beach. He brings me sweet black coffee from the Hotel Florida, which hands it out in the mornings when the workers scrub its pink patio clean for the next wave of tourists.

I take a few sips, the sugar spiking me and making me uneasy, so I chunk it and buy some cold water at an open stall selling breakfast empanadas. I drink some and then hold it against the swelling in my hand. Nothing is broken—wouldn't have been able to work out if it was. I'm lucky. They bleed on the bottle, and I wonder how much testosterone is leaking out of me. Not enough.

I walk through the inner neighborhoods where locals live in low concrete apartments, past parks and people walking dogs, across the bridge to the city and the few blocks back to the hotel. I look up and see our balcony, Bridget staring out over the city with what looks like a cup of coffee in hand. I can't go back up. Can't join her.

I text her *with family, back later* and walk onto the yacht's gangplank to crash for an hour in one of the myriad guest rooms.

———

Two hours later, I'm arguing with Kayla, who is stretched out on the bow, working on recovering from a better night than mine. Actually, it was the best night of my life until it wasn't.

"There is something not right about all this."

"I'm fine. It's work, that's all."

"Sex is not your work. And she doesn't see you. Has no idea what you want."

I sit down and pull her feet onto my lap. Her toes are the color of Bridget's *Pretty Woman* dress. I hate that I notice.

"Hard to know, when I don't let on."

"She could ask."

She could. Or I could tell her. I think all this while struggling to keep down black acidic coffee.

"It would help if I knew what I wanted," I admit.

"You want respect. You want a career, something that uses your extraordinary talents. You want a family and house and a fucking picket fence. You want it all."

I rub my face, my tired eyes.

"On the patio, I felt like we were getting somewhere, to someplace real, until I realized it's all a scene to her, regardless. I'm not real to her. I'm some—what did she say?— ideal."

I pour the rest of the coffee over the side into the blue waters.
"She's very interested in you though," I say.

"She's jealous of me, and who could blame her? You are the fucking catch of a lifetime."

She moves around so her head is on my lap, pulls down her oversized sunglasses.

"But she is using you. Using you up, I'm afraid."

The bridge horn blows behind us.

"What if I'm not, you know, a catch, and *this*." I don't have to explain *this* to Kayla; I don't have to explain much to her.

"If she can't, or won't, look past your particularly stunning package—"

"You said package."

"Package, package, package," she yells out to the cars backed up, waiting for a multimillion-dollar sailboat to pass through the causeway opening.

"What if that's all I will ever be, to anyone?"

"It's a great package. In and out. Someone will realize what I have always known. Josh, you are real, not some fucking ideal."

Fuck. Tears prick my eyes.

"Why aren't we together?" I croak.

She sits up and takes off her glasses. "*Josh.*"

"You want it too—all of it—and you know me and you know the worst parts. I almost … I could have hurt her. By accident, but it … And I know you want kids as much as I do, but if I don't work, there … there are so many who need someone, or a donor. I don't care, if you don't care."

She leans over and pulls me into her arms. "I care that you're in love, but not with me." Then she kisses my cheek, my nose, my forehead. "But you'll always have me, and hey, if we have not made it happen by the time we're forty, sure. I'll marry your ass and make you miserable."

"You could never make me miserable."

"I'll make you miserable because I'm not her. God almighty," she yells at the sky. "You've been with more women than most men in ten lifetimes, and you have to fall for some ... writer!"

"That the worst you've got?"

"Closed-minded—"

"Creative genius. Really, her way with words is unparalleled."

"Stuck up."

"Stood up for me, I think, with Richard. I'm sure of it. He's the dick. He's the problem. I mean, I know I'm the problem, too."

She gives me a side-eyed glance.

"It's not that. Not the curse." That's what we call it—the shell. What it makes people do and say. And the curse has never hurt me half as bad as it has hurt her.

"Is it too much to want to be seen?" I ask.

"I see you, baby."

I shake my head, swallow salt.

"I've got to go. Don't want to make her late for her flight."

"Can't believe you care."

She walks me to the gangplank.

"I'm always here."

And as I hug her bye, I realize Kayla is really all I have. There's Nana, but she will leave me, and Kayla may leave me too one day. No signifigant other of hers will put up with me. I wouldn't.

Walking past the show cars, I decide if this doesn't work, I might as well go to L.A. It seems like the kind of place to be alone. Because I have a slowly melting heart held in a body that wants nothing more than to salsa a feisty redhead in and out of bed for the rest of my time on this planet.

What the fuck, Josh?

Work and love.

Rookie mistake.

When I get back to the room, I call out for her.

"Bridge. Bridge, I'm sorry. I'm here. We should go in the next hour. Bridget?"

Walk into the bedroom, and it's trashed. Everything I own on the floor. My suitcase across the room. My other black case open on the bedside table. Laid open. Waiting for me. A syringe sitting open in the crease.

Cold dread fills me.

I round up my things. Stuff them in the bag. Zip up the case with my meds and put it away. Not thinking. Not thinking of the invasion of my privacy. Not thinking about what she must be thinking.

I have four hours to beat her home. Longer if there is traffic on the bay bridge from Tampa. I pray there is traffic on the bridge so I can be there when she gets home. So I can explain everything.

But I can't risk it. So I take time I don't have to stop at a Rapid Screen in North Miami. Pay out of pocket; don't even wait for a script. Then drive like my life depends on it.

THIRTY-FOUR

WHAT DO YOU WANT FIRST?

My testosterone isn't high. I mean, it's always high, but not high for me. The results came into the portal, and I can't believe. I have nothing to blame for my behavior last night. Which means that was all me. I picture my face in the mirror last night while blood dripped from my hand. What it means.

Could that only have been last night? It feels like a year since we were dancing.

When I'm almost to the bridge, Sable calls. I answer, and her voice fills the cab. I turn it down.

"I have news."

"Good news, I hope."

"I'm on speaker."

"Yes. I'm in my car."

"So first, I heard the shoot went great."

"That the news?"

"No. I have, well, great news and disturbing news. What do you want first?"

"Not sure."

"Okay, great news first. You got a part in the Scottish epic. They need you there next week."

"Lines?"

"Fourteen."

"Sable. You're amazing."

"You're amazing. This is your shot. I feel it, and I'm going with you. I'm going to make sure everything goes to plan."

"I don't know what to say."

She clears her throat.

"Maybe pull over for the next part."

"That's not ominous. But I can't. I'm in a hurry."

I look at the phone on the mount. Her flight is running late. Now my ETA is a little over forty minutes after she arrives. But she has to navigate TPA, and on that small plane, she will be at the end of the gate. If she takes a taxi, she might beat me. If she waits for an Uber—

"Josh. Are you okay to talk? This can wait. It's about Bridget."

"Tell me."

"She's been stringing you along. There is no byline. No royalties."

"What do you mean?"

"Listen, there are things I can't tell you. Had to sign an NDA to hear them myself, but there's no byline for you, never was. Richard didn't even know she offered it. Do you hear me? She didn't even tell her agent."

"Fuck Richard."

"It's not Richard. He's playing by the rules. She's not. She's a wild card. One it's best for you to cut ties with."

"Sable, it's more than that now. More than professional." I stare straight ahead. Try to process what this means. All the while remembering her in this truck days ago.

"All the more reason to cut ties. Josh she's been using you. She's known for a while there's no hope for a byline for you, no royalties either."

"So? I always knew she might not be able to sell the book."

"She sold the book."

I listen to the road. To the sound of the truck on the road to not hear what she just said.

"She's no good for you."

I won't break down with Sable on the line. But I'm breaking. "Got to go."

"I'll call later with travel details for Scotland."

All I can manage is "Kay."

Once she's off, I walk back over it all, her asking for help, offering the cut, the weekend, and the writing—together. How good we are together. The offer of the byline, and how much it meant to me for such a talented writer to share that with me. Then her not going to church, her call with Richard, how she was afterward, and all the chaos that has happened since—both good and bad. It all leads me to one conclusion: something happened on that call with Richard, something big enough to keep her from her promises. If I'm giving her the benefit of the doubt, it has to be that.

And yet, she should have told me. Whatever it was, in Miami she had ample openings. She should have told me. Unless she needed me. Needed to finish the story first. Unless, like everyone thinks, she was using me.

If she thought I would stop helping her for any reason, she doesn't know me at all.

It's too much. Too much information. Too fast. Too much to process. I feel like I'm going to self-destruct. So I reach out for my lifeline.

"Call Gretchen—cell."

She picks up on the first ring and I realize I'm going ninety. I set the cruise.

"I'm sorry for calling like this."

"What's wrong? You never call my cell."

"Because I respect your boundaries, of which I suddenly have none."

"Are you driving? You sound like you're driving." Then the notification that she wants to move to video call comes over the screen.

"Answer," she says. "I want to see you. That's better. Tilt it to the left. You sound like you've had a difficult day."

"That's an understatement," I say while adjusting the phone.

"There. That's good. You don't look good. Have you slept? What are your numbers?"

"My testosterone is normal for me. Which means when I punched a wall last night"—I hold up my fist—"to avoid I don't even know what, I had no excuse. Other than I am my father's son."

"We need to meet. Come here."

"I've never been to your house."

"Well, then, it's about time."

"I can't right now." The sound beneath me changes as I hit the bridge. "I have to see her. I'm trying to beat her home. I lost it. Blacked out. She saw the syringes."

"Did you hurt anyone but the wall?"

"No."

She lets out a breath.

"I don't think we should do this now—like this. We should break this down, what triggered it."

"I know what triggered it. I'm nothing but a job to her. A scene she needs to write. A means to an end. And she doesn't even respect me enough to tell me the truth. I knew something

260

was wrong. That Richard, her agent, was up to something. But whatever it was, I wouldn't have cared. I would have helped her anyway. Shit, Gretch, I love her."

"Of course you do. Bodies have wisdom; bodies know. And the way you are together, well, I bet it's like your souls are talking. Probably doing more than that."

I laugh around tears.

"But I can't trust my body. My body can hurt." I shake my head. What am I going to do? "I have to go. Almost there."

"I want you in my office tomorrow at ten. I love you, Josh."

"Fuck. Don't do that. I'm right around the corner."

"I love you, Josh." And with that, she clicks off.

I park across the street from the house. What now?

THIRTY-FIVE

NOBODY KNOWS ANYONE

I decide to text. I don't want to scare her, not after how I behaved last night

> Me: Can we talk? I was an asshole. I have issues.

> > Bridget: I'm headed to my mom's for Thanksgiving.

So she really doesn't want to see me if she is using Thanksgiving which is not for three days as an excuse. But I can't force it, can I? No. I'll give her some space. As much as I hate the idea I don't really have a choice, do I?

> Me: Okay. What about this weekend

> > Bridget: Leaving for the mountains right after, with mom. She does December in Highlands. Maybe we can talk when I get back.

> Me: In a month

Bridget: Might be for the best. Give us both time

Me: Time for what?

Bridget: Just time

Then a car pulls up. The driver helps her with her bags.

I get out and walk across the street. My feet moving before I can even think.

"Can I be here?" I call out. "Can we talk, Bridget, please?"

She looks at me, then turns back to the house, walks in like a zombie but leaves the door open. I don't cross the threshold, and fuck.

"What happened?" I ask.

"I'm taking her out back," she says.

I think that's as close as an invite that I'll get, so I follow her. It looks like someone broke in. Like someone was looking for something very small. Pillows torn apart. A couch cover, feathers all over the laundry room, floating in the air as I walk through to the open back door.

Sally Girl runs in circles in the back yard, if you can call the empty lot of sand and weeds a yard. Bridget is sitting on the steps.

"What happened?"

She turns to me, eyes dead.

"What happened here?"

"She does this, sometimes. When I leave her with someone else. We are all each other has."

That hits me like a fist to the chest.

"Like you, she just needs to work it out sometimes," Bridget says. Then pats the stair next to her and wraps her arms around her knees, pressing them into her chest, like she's holding something in.

I go to sit beside her, and brush her arm. She leans away. I'm careful not to touch her again.

"I saw your issues, Josh." She swallows. Nods her head. Tears dripping on her knees. "The syringes. It shocked me. Scared me."

I will not cry.

"That's private. That's why it was in a closed case in a zippered pocket, Bridge."

"Don't call me that," she says. Eyes downcast. "Not right now. Please."

"Okay." I nod. "Okay."

Sally Girl comes up and bumps her hand. "I'm okay, go run."

She takes a deep breath and lets it out. "Did you get the money yet, for the cover?"

The question surprises me, and then I realize, that's it. It's about money.

"If this is about money—"

"Just answer the question," she says harshly. "Please," she adds softer. She's trying to keep it together but I can tell she is coming out of her skin. I answer thinking it doesn't matter what we talk about as long as we are talking.

"The first half will hit sometime this week. Then the book comes out in May. I get the second half then. And then more for publicity. So if you need it, I have it. I have whatever you need."

She looks at me, confused. "Publicity?"

"You know. Appearances with the author. Romance bookstore signings. Whatever the PR department comes up with. Just being the body. But I get paid, handsomely, so there's that."

"I'm glad for you." But her voice is so flat. Like she's in shock. I know what that feels like.

"Can I get you something, some water or something?" She shakes her head. "Bridget, if it's about the money, you can have it. I know I was an ass. I have ... issues ... sometimes, with control but—"

"I know about your issues." She is looking right at me but through me at the same time. "I can't believe you shoot steroids. I can't believe it, but I know it. I saw it. But it's just not you."

"Not me. And yet you believe it?"

"I know what I saw. What you brought to Miami."

"Again. What was in a closed case in a zippered pocket of my suitcase."

"It wasn't intentional. Thought it was products. You see I got angry after you left. Trashed the room. Just like her." She nods toward Sally Girl, who is tearing up a toy. I was actually going to throw your stuff off the balcony." She laughs, but the sound makes me want to cry. "Can you believe that? Me?"

I rub my face. "This isn't how I want to do this. You don't understand what you saw. I should have told you. Should have explained. I know—"

She holds up her hand to stop me.

"I'll tell you what I know." She looks me directly in the eye. "I don't know you at all."

I close mine. Nod. "On that we can agree."

Give her a chance. The benefit of the doubt. One chance. I stand and walk down the stairs. Turn to face her.

"So, now that you think you know all my secrets, have you got any of your own?"

She wraps her arms around her head. Rocking, shaking. "I hate this," she says. "I don't cry. I never fucking cry. Until I blew up my life and yours."

"Bridget, what's going on?"

"I don't know what to say to you. There is nothing I can say to make this better."

"You could give me the benefit of the doubt," I say.

"That's what I did, and you deserted me. Did you think I wouldn't notice you bleeding? I see every single thing about you. Always have."

She stops rocking. Stands. "You were happy before you met me. Be happy again." She opens the back door. "Come on, girl." Sally Girl rushes past me.

"Bridget, don't do this. We can talk. We can work this out. I'm ready to hear anything you have to tell me. I'm ready." But that's not true. I'm terrified to hear her say it. Say she was only using me. But I wait. Hoping it is anything but that.

"There's nothing to tell," she says with finality.

I want to grab her, shake her, use my fucking words, but my chest is hot with pain that I don't want to feel anymore.

She turns back to the door. "Go to L.A." She steps through, feathers floating around her. She doesn't look at me when she says, "Take care of yourself. Figure it out. Stop hurting yourself. And maybe when you get settled, I know I have no right to ask, but maybe let me know you're okay."

"No. You *don't* have the right to ask," I say to her back.

A gasping sob comes from her. I force myself to go. Walk around the house. Across the street. I tell myself to get in the truck. To leave.

But I can't.

I strip off my shirt and run.

THIRTY-SIX

TWO MOTHERFUCKER DAYS IN
A ROW

B ridget told me her grandmother loved to love men who weren't good for her and who didn't love her back. So I guess Sweetie and I have something in common.

I'm at the gym, doing back-to-back motherfucker days because—yesterday. Jesus, yesterday. I ran until I couldn't and then pulled a motherfucker day. And here I am again. The sun is high. Dehydration a real potential. But it seems I have only two iron-clad coping mechanisms: sex and the gym.

My way of coping might need to catch up to my age, intelligence, and experience. But not today, as there is an undercurrent of rage in me I recognize as a warning sign. It's still low, controlled, but present. And it might just be me. I probably should test again but I'm afraid to learn I have no excuse for the violence of my feelings.

I drop down before my arms give out. I shake them out. Know I pushed too hard. But bourbon doesn't help—tried that. Even talking with Gretchen didn't help.

I told her I understood why Bridget did it. How she didn't want to disappoint me with her failure to champion me.

And I know that's what happened. Richard shot her down. Not about the book. He loves the book. About me. I was the issue, I know I was. But that's not the problem. I'd write books with her for nothing. I'd write any book she ever wanted to write. It's not about the book.

It's certainly not that she promised me things she couldn't deliver. I always knew that was a possibility; she did too. No, it's that she went to Miami and she made me fall in love with her—I was halfway gone, but she pushed me over the edge, all the while lying to me because she still needed something from me. A scene. All the while, while she was making me love her, it was just a scene.

Gretchen called me on that.

"She can't make you do anything. Least of all fall in love with her. Take responsibility for your own emotions. She's not perfect. And neither are you."

She ended with *I love you, Josh* like always. But for once it didn't make me feel better. Feel loved. Because I don't need Gretchen to love me. I need Bridget to. To realize everything else is nothing. That it can be her and me against Richard, publishing, acting, the world.

And even more fucked up, after the test in Miami, I might have to face the fact that I'm more like my father than I want to admit. We talked for a long time about that fear, Gretchen and I. And I don't know when I'll test again. When I won't be afraid to.

Seems I'm afraid of everything all of the sudden. I was certainly afraid to use my fucking words yesterday. But that's okay too. Gretchen supported me on that. To not tell Bridge while she was angry, to be able to decide when and how and under what circumstances I will be vulnerable. Because it's hard for me to talk about it. It seems like a little thing—hey, I make too much testosterone—but it's not. It affects every aspect of my life, my future.

So I work my lats, telling myself this is the best thing for me right now. That I have empirical evidence to prove it.

"Hey, T, give me a spot?"

"A minute," I grunt at Mink. I have at least seventy-five crunches in me. But I don't count. I never count on MF days. Makes it hurt worse. But when you train as much as I do, you have to mix it up, trick your body into feeling pressured to act, to tear, then build.

"Hey, T. That spot?"

I realize I've been lying here, staring at the sky. I roll off the bench and head for the press. Mink is in position with three-sixty on the bar. More than I would attempt, as Mink's look—Chippendale meets Harley boss—is bulkier than I need. But I can spot him.

"Twelve," he calls out to let me know his plan.

"Ready."

He is straining by seven. I keep my hands on the bar in case he needs an assist, but he pushes through and puts the bar back on the rest with a resounding *clang* at twelve.

"Impressive."

"You motherfuckering it today?"

"In more ways than one," I say, replacing his fifties for twenties for a much lighter two-eighty. Lying down myself, once he wipes the bench.

"Didn't you take it to muscle fatigue yesterday?"

I ignore his rational thinking. "I'll let you know when I need you."

He grunts and I began. Breathe in on the down, exhale on the lift. In on the down, out on the lift, in on the down out on the lift, over and over until there is nothing in the world but the bar, the threat of muscle failure, the danger, the zone.

It comes on fast. I grunt, "Hold."

Too fast.

I'm too tired to be fucking around with an MF day. But Mink is good, didn't go far, and has the bar easily in the cradle while I catch my breath.

"That was a little too close for comfort, my man, not like you. What's up?"

"Distracted," I say as I rise.

"Well, don't try that shit alone. And speaking of, my schedule's about to change. Will be here earlier. Left my shit-ass job and started a biz."

I smile. It feels funny on my face. "That's great," I say. "What kind?"

"Fencing, and with the help of my baby cousin, landscaping. He is like a botanist or something—knows all the plants, talks about xeriscaping and shit, but he's good people. Going to be great."

"Funny that. I have a friend who needs a fence. Sod and landscaping too. The whole yard. Front and back."

"Well, what do you say you let them know I'm in business."

"I'll try."

"Don't do me any favors."

"She's not really talking to me right now."

I set up for weighted squats. He is swinging big alternate singles. The bar feels heavy on my neck. I should probably call it a day before I get hurt. When I know if I go down I won't be coming back up, I stop.

"So it's like that."

"Like that."

"Okay, just let me know. Pretty open right now."

I don't know why I even ask. "If I get you some pictures, can you get me a quote?"

I walk over to the table to get my water, ignoring the curious look on Mink's face as he follows. Cheryl passes us on the way to the weights and nods.

"T. Mink. How's it hanging?"

Mink says something graphic, and I keep my peace. I like Cheryl. She's a regular. A firefighter who was once competitive in bodybuilding. Could kick my ass. Definitely has pounds on me. I've known her for years, as she also studied kinesiology at USF. We even shared some classes. Her thesis was on muscle failure. How the body can push through it in certain circumstances. Like when a father can lift a tractor off a child, and such things. Her dissertation was fascinating. Normally, I would take some time to talk shop, but I'm not very good company today.

Mink sits at the table while I pull on sweats.

"Sure. If I have measurements, but why? Shouldn't I meet your friend and talk to them directly about their yard?"

When he puts it that way, it does seem a strange request.

"Maybe get me a quote, and I'll see what she thinks?"

He squints at me, like I'm pulling something on him.

"Is this some reality TV shit? *Supermodel Sod*? Oh, or does little T have it baaaad."

At six foot three, only Mink calls me little.

"Some shit like that."

"This I've got to see. The little fish that hooked the shark."

I smile and show all my teeth, walking backward to my car.

Mink has four kids, and they all need braces. He thinks it is the universe punishing him for past misdeeds, and he can't believe mine are unaltered. But I've never let them mess with my teeth. Some models' teeth are so white they actually seem to glow in the dark. Against my skin tone, mine are plenty white, just like my father's.

Although he didn't smile much—not that I can remember. Nana says he smiled all the time when my mother was alive. Couldn't stop. But since we lost her when I was three, I didn't see very many of his smiles. And he became angry with the entire world the day she left us. Then he left me. Left for *his* home, not mine, not hers, and buried her there. And never came back. Once a year he would send Nana a ticket for me to visit him.

Once a year I would see her grave.

Once a year he would size me up but never look me straight in my mother-gifted eyes.

Once a year I could see all the ways I was becoming him, until at fifteen he didn't send a ticket. By the time I was sixteen, he was buried next to my mother, thousands of miles away. Then bad things started to happen.

It's hard to accept you're an orphan when you never saw either of your parents buried. That's why Nana took me to Brazil, which led to my eventual breakdown and breakthrough.

I went to see my mom. I never really wanted to see him. Nana said he wasn't always the man I knew, but I could not remember anyone else. And my eyes might have been my mom's, but I got plenty from him. My dangerously high testosterone was inherited from him—well, we believe that based on his symptoms and early death from prostate cancer.

So I think of him every time I get a blood draw to see how my T is doing. Because the last thing I wanted to inherit from him is his temperament—erratic, mercurial, violent. Which makes me thankful for Nana every day. Without her, I would have lived in Brazil full-time with him from the age of three. Would have grown up in the shadow of his loss, which he seemed to think was greater than mine. I would likely have never known I had a congenital adrenal disorder because that's just "what Silva men are like." And damn proud of it, for no good reason at all, I might add.

I wonder what my mother saw in him, beyond his face I wear every day, reminding me not to be him. But Nana said when they were together he was better, happy, even-keeled even, which is hard to imagine. But maybe not. Maybe intimacy was medicine for him too. I'd like to think that a mother of mine wouldn't be with someone like he was in those last years.

When I look up, I'm in my parking space at my condo. For how long, I don't know. I'm staring at the glass on my building reflecting Tampa Bay's waters when my phone notifies me of an incoming text. I check as it might be Nana, or maybe even Bridge.

Sable: How are you

Me: Hanging in there

Sable: Sorry. Richard and I are both sorry.

Me: Don't say that man's name to me.

Sable: It's not his fault.

Me: Don't care.

Then a picture of my itinerary arrives.

Sable: Find some warm clothes. It's winter somewhere.

Shit.

THIRTY-SEVEN

GHOSTS

"It's Josh," I say into the antiquated speaker box. The door buzzes my request to be let in. It bothers me every time. The fact that they lock Nana in here. But not for long, if I can convince her to leave. Of course I haven't told her yet, as she will pitch a fit, say she's fine—but she's not. Her suitemate, the one she shares a bathroom with, has issues, and I will not have my Nana cleaning other people's messes just to use her own toilet so I've had the move in the works for months. And now I should have enough to get her settled, even if I decide to give L.A. a chance.

But I don't even know if I want to make it there, whatever that means. I guess I'll do the Scottish film for Sable, but at this point I don't even know if I want to act, and I certainly don't want to be the body on a publicity tour with an author I've never met, but I do want the money. The Oaks is not cheap.

Of course, I wish she'd live with me. But she won't, refuses to "ruin" my life. So I tell myself, for the hundredth time, that the only other option is assisted living and that she is safe, if not happy. And even though Nana does her best to keep her spirits up, she hates not having her own home, misses her car and cats —her life. And I question for the millionth time if I should have just relented. Not fought her when I went to school when she wanted to keep her place.

But she would have hurt herself or someone else by now. Too many car accidents, too many stove fires, too many close calls.

But there are better places than this Medicare facility. I hit the buzzer again. I mean, the staff is okay—some are even wonderful—but the place is drab and the people less active than Nana, who still has such a zest for life. And the smell. That one is hard to get used to.

At The Oaks, she could safely live much more independently until she can't and then move gradually through the layers of care as needed. Where there is a pub and a movie theater and outings to more than Walmart.

The door relents with a click. A med tech I don't know lets me in without even asking my business. I sigh. Wondering why the locked doors if they don't care who comes in.

As soon as I enter, I see one of my "friends," a euphemism I use for clients because I don't charge the residents I work with here and the home can't have me giving free physical therapy. How would they make any money off me? And honestly, some have become friends.

"Hello, handsome."

Ms. Olive is at the door as usual.

"Good Morning, Ms. Olive. How are you today?"

"'Bout as well as one can expect."

Ms. Olive is futzing about in her wheelchair today when we both know she needs to walk. But I never berate a client in the halls for not following my advice. That can wait until we meet in her room next Wednesday. I wish I could manage to see her more than every other week, but I do what I can.

"My son is coming to see me today."

"That's nice," I say because I always do. Just like she is always waiting for a son who hasn't visited in a year.

"Have you seen Nana?" I ask.

"In the courtyard with Gammy most likely."

"Of course. Have a nice day."

"Sweet talker." And she swats my ass with a newspaper.

I shake my head, unable to banter with Olive today. I don't even want to be here today sure Nana will again see I am out of sorts. Thanksgiving was brutal. But November 30th is the one day I will always visit.

I find Gammy and Nana in their rockers. Their special seats under the magnolia where they can watch the birds. All of Nana's bird feeders from home are hanging from the tree. There are over a dozen, but two of them are empty. I'll need to get that squared before I leave.

"Nana," I say softly. "Sorry I'm so late."

"The church is always open," she reminds.

"Are you ready? Hi, Gammy. How are you?" I kneel down to check her legs for edema.

"I'm fine. Don't need you fussing." And she bats me away.

My grandmother looks anything but fine. She is all in black, her head covered. I wonder how long she has been waiting for me.

"Ready?" I ask.

She stands and takes my arm. "See you after," I say to Gammy. "I'll stop by and see about that knee."

She waves me off, but she fell last month and has been favoring it.

———

The ride to the cathedral is quiet. And I never know what to say. I don't miss my father—how could I? I see him in the mirror every day, and that's been particularly brutal as of late.

We bless at the entrance, the water warm but the church cool and dark. There is a small chapel at the east with the Virgin Mary where Nana likes to go to pray. But on this one day a year she goes west, to St. Joseph, the patron saint of men, fathers, and families.

I pass her a bill, which she stuffs in the box. I light the match, and she takes it and lights a tall pillar. Then kneels.

I light my own and kneel next to her. Her head is down, her thoughts her own. My normally garrulous grandmother is always quiet on this day. Almost like a penance, like she is punishing herself for something. I can't imagine what. She is the most thoughtful and giving person I will ever know. Of that one fact I am very sure.

Her mumbling prayer has me looking up, away from her grief, to St. Joseph himself, holding a young boy. Did my father ever hold me that way? Before Mama died? If so, I can't remember it.

There is a prayer one says here, for fathers, but since I don't remember ever having one—not a real one, not one who stuck around—and since I doubt I'll ever be one, no need to pray it, I just wait, listening to the wax crackle, until Nana has said her peace.

When she moves to stand, I get up to help her. Lift her from under her arms as she struggles, cursing myself that I let her stay on her knees too long. When she is up and steady, she looks up to me. Touches my face with her small hand.

"I know it's hard," I say. "That when you look at me you see him."

"I see *you*, Joshua Anjo Silva. When I look at you, I only see you. But it hurts that he never saw the man you became. He loved you. He told you that; you know he did."

And because it is the anniversary of his death, and because I'm in the chapel of St. Joseph, and because I would never willingly hurt my Nana, I don't tell her what I'm thinking.

It doesn't matter what people say. The only thing that matters is what they do.

It takes less than a moment to decide. If I can't see Bridge—if I can't be with her—I can still do something for her. Something worthwhile. Something that will help her. Something that will make her happy. With the money I set aside for L.A. Mink could make it amazing.

So I'll settle. So what. Give up the dream of writing movies and finally really use the degree it took me six years to get. I could be happy working in homes, doing physical therapy, being useful. It would be refreshing to work in a profession where I'm unlikely to get hit on. Where I would know where I stand. Where I wouldn't be so fucking confused. I don't have to leave. And if I stay, I might see her now and again on the beach. And with time, who knows?

You do. There was no crack left in that door. No room for any hope. But it doesn't matter. I want to do it anyway. I want her to open her door every single day and smell jasmine, the scent of her favorite tea. I want her to be able to leave the beast, get out, do things, whatever and not have to worry about the menace or her furniture.

I'll text Mink as soon as I get Nana settled. I feel better already.

PART 3

JOSH AND BRIDGE

THIRTY-EIGHT

BAGGAGE

Mom's huge attic is as empty as I feel. It echoes every movement to remind me there's nothing here but a small pile of my stuff in a corner. I don't dwell on the fact that she has storage space out the wazoo below and only my things are up here. I focus on the gabled windows that look out on the golf course. I envy the sod.

You'll have plenty for sod, I tell myself. Plenty for everything you want. Plenty to write another book—anything you want this time. A sequel to *Red Bridge*. A memoir on how to ruin a life in a weekend. Bet I could pull that one off. Or maybe a duology: *How to Start a Life in a Weekend,* followed by *How to Ruin One in the Same Amount of Time.* Shoot, I could move on to *How to End a Career in a Week.* Or *How to Ruin Your Love for Your House in a Day,* because I will never walk down my back steps again without remembering all I didn't say and all he did.

But I already have a book to write—for someone else. A book I loved and, more than that, was proud of until a couple of days ago. Now I don't feel like doing anything but falling into bed and not getting out. And yet all this falls apart if I don't write the second half. I have to find a way to care. And the only thing I can grasp onto is Josh getting his money. All of it. For him, for Nana, also for me and Sally Girl, because if that one day away from each other taught us anything, she needs me as much as I need her.

But Josh was right. In the end, it's all about the money. For everyone.

I still can't believe Richard's author is going to do publicity on a book she didn't write. Such a strange world, publishing. Makes me want to move in with Mom. Write for myself and no one else. Hide from the world. But that's a cop-out. And I'm going to try very hard to never cop out again.

Speaking of, Kimberly has called five times and texted ten since I got back from Miami, and I can't find a way to respond other than to say I'm headed to the mountains with Mom. I'm a shitty person and a shitty friend. And clearly a glutton for punishment for choosing to go to the mountains with my mother for Christmas.

But I can't write in my house. Not yet. Hopefully, in the pristine, cavernous, nondescript mountain house I can get the book finished even with their deadline pushing down on me. It will be easy to break them apart, the bitter taste of our break being still so fresh, but how the hell am I going to find enough hope to put them back together again.

Out the window, Sally Girl is running on her lead. The only place she is allowed at mom's after "the incident" in the guest house. But I'll sneak her in tonight—no one will know—and have her back on the lead before we leave at five because John husband-number-four Stanton is an early riser. Said we will be in Highlands by tea time. He doesn't drink tea.

Back to the task at hand I search each carefully stacked plastic bin and finally find the one with winter clothes. I pull out some fleece-lined leggings and a few sweaters. Snow boots, just in case, even though it rarely snows in North Carolina in December. But I remember one year we had a white Christmas. I've never been more thankful that Christmas at my house is only about decorations. But mom knows this is a work trip for me. She's so happy I'm writing again. Can't wait to read it. And once again I keep up appearance for her because she will never read this book. She'll never even know I wrote it, that we wrote it, as it's still as much his as mine. The outline we set out in Miami, I have to follow. I have no inspiration at all. But the thought of writing the final reconciliation, well it feels insurmountable.

"Are you all right up there?" my mother's voice calls up from the attic stairs.

"I'm good," I call back to her.

The irony of the word choice is not lost on me.

———

I leave my phone on the table and move into my bedroom to pack. I don't know why I would expect her to reach out when I told her she didn't have the right. I was so sure on those steps that there was no way back from what she said and thought about me. But in hindsight, and with some therapy, I realize they were not without merit.

No, I left because it hurt. And I didn't want to hurt anymore. I left because I was a coward. But even with Gretchen helping me to understand that I get to choose when I'm vulnerable, and I was not ready to get into all of my issues with her while she was so I closed off. So judgmental. But now it feels like that might have been my only chance.

She's clearly gone—her house is closed up tight, and even her rocking chair is inside. But I have no idea for how long. And no matter what I do, how I beg, Sable will not tell me one more thing about it. I know she knows more. Knows what Richard did. But I guess her loyalty to Richard's agency is more important than her loyalty to me.

No, that's not fair. She said it was confidential business. That she couldn't discuss it. And I have racked my brain for what could possibly be so cloak-and-dagger in publishing. But clearly I don't know anything about how it really works or I wouldn't be in this situation. I blame myself. I should have talked to Sable sooner, asked for clarification from Bridget—should have taken care of business. Now not taking care of business is ruining my life, because since the first moment that feisty blushing redhead said she'd never pay for sex, I have wanted her in my bed and now in my life.

But she's seemingly moved on, and maybe I need to as well. At the very least, get my head in the game. I would be lying if I said I wasn't nervous, and reading the script, it is clear that my abs have more lines than I do in this Scottish period piece, but I do have lines. Fourteen of them. Careers have been made from less—Brad Pitt had ten lines in *Thelma and Louise*. At least, that's what Sable tells me. And yet I don't even know if I want this career. I don't feel like I know anything.

I pull out the air-removal packing bag that has been under my bed since a ski trip two years ago. I crack the seal, and it expands. Makes me think how nice a deep breath would be, but I'm holding on tight and if I let go, I will lose it.

I still can't believe we're done. I guess I served my purpose. I'm not so desperate as to beg.

I pull out hats and gloves, sweaters and thermals, trying to understand. When it's all laid out on the bed, I'm hot just looking at it. I sit in the mess and decide to plot it like a screenplay.

Opening Image: Bridget turning beet red while asking if I will fuck her for research. Priceless.

Set-up: Me not able to stop thinking about her freckles. Her eyes. Her ass.

Theme Stated: I try to get laid and can't get into it, must break off. All I can think about is a short powerhouse who said no.

Catalyst: Her kitchen island. Fuck. Moving on.

Debate: Her kitchen table. What is it about kitchens? But that is where we became partners. Or I thought we did.

Break Into Two: That's me all right, breaking. I can't even finish the thought, it's that insipid. Work, sex, love—I know the deal—it's like water, gasoline and a spark. Everything burns. But the ever-hopeful side of me is wondering if this is just both of us heading out for a B story and we will come back to the promise of the premise later. Except it feels more like midpoint is behind me and I'm sitting squarely in the dark night of the soul.

Well, if this is the dark night, then I wonder if this acting gig is my B story. The part starts out, as most things do, with me as a body, but maybe it ends with someone saying, "Hey, I think he can act." We shall see. And more importantly, I may like it at this level. Maybe things will be different working on a film. Maybe I will be able to see the process from the inside rather than just in my dreams and decide if it is even for me.

And who knows, maybe this melancholy will be just the thing. And since it seems there is nothing I can do to make us real that I didn't already try in Miami, I might as well use it as this film is one giant dark night of the soul for my character, who shows up in one scene and is killed in the next.

I look down at the mess around me and realize the bag

doesn't even have what I'm looking for. I search the top of my closet for the one wool sweater I own. Cream, cable-knit, iconic, given where I'm going. I sniff it experimentally. It smells like the back of a closet in Florida. I'll let it air out tonight and, I guess, wrap it around my waist tomorrow, as there is no way the thing is fitting in my roller bag.

Speaking of screenplays, I'm taking my most recent, an actual paper copy that I plan to "work on" on set just in case someone asks, like the co-star of this film who is perfect for the female lead. It was Sable's idea.

So, it's time to retreat, for both of us, me metaphorically and Bridge actually. Well, me actually as well since most of the movie is tracking the retreat of a Scottish force that is decimated in the end. Clearly an art pic or we would need a happy ending, but the production is top notch and well funded and could turn out to be an Oscar darling—at least that's what Sable thinks. Which is hard to believe given the script. I would make more than a few changes in my character—and in the story in general—if anyone asks, but they won't. I'm just above an extra with no shirt in a kilt. But I get to die sacrificing for the clan, so there is that.

It's funny—at the audition I thought of her as my good luck charm. If I'm honest, when I dared think I could get the part, I hoped she might come with me. Which is ridiculous.

But the beast. Always the beast. Likely would eat the entire house if she left for that long. Maybe we could get her signed up as a comfort animal, but can you imagine the beast on a plane? You'd have to buy her a row.

No, the beast is not the problem. And even if she is, maybe I can at least solve that problem. Yet if this is the end of Bridge and me, if this retreat leads to more and more distance until we are nothing more to each other than body and beauty, I'll miss the scratchy, curious-eyed monster.

I look at my watch. Shit, I'm late.

I drive to the beach and meet Minx and his cousin at Bridget's house.

They firm up the quote and walk me through the plans. It's a bigger job that I originally envisioned. But I can see her face in the doorway looking out on it all and it's worth whatever money it takes. I can't think of one thing better to do with the L.A. money. And as for the potential of a career in film it will either happen in Scotland or not at all. And maybe it's best if not at all. I could be happy helping people like Gammy and Olive stay mobile and active. It's not grand but it could be a life. And as for my prior method of keeping my T in check, at least as to sex, I think I'll take a break. Take meds if necessary. Not feeling like I care about the consequences at this point.

"Hey, how long do we have?" Minx asks, breaking me out of my thoughts.

"I don't even know. At least two weeks, maybe four. She didn't say exactly how long she would be gone."

"Then we'll get to work today."

"Thanks, and hey it needs to be pretty, but cool, you know, different. Like a redhead," I say.

"I gotcha T. Sublime."

"Exactly."

"And you're sure the owner won't mind? Not normal to work this way, man. Not going to get me in trouble, are you?"

"I promise, she is going to love it. And before I leave, I will put in the doggie door. I know where the key is hidden but don't feel comfortable, you know."

"Seems like a lot of money for some broad's dog."

"She's not some broad. She's ..." But I can't go on.

"Shit, man. Sorry. It's like a curse, the love."

"No. Not like that," I say, but the reality is I'm spending a huge chunk of what I made on the money shot to landscape a yard for a woman who is ghosting me and lying to me and to fence in a yard for a dog I'm still a little scared of. So maybe it *is* like that. And if this is all I'm ever able to give her, I want her to have it. I want her to have it all. The home she wants. The life she wants. Even if I will not be in it.

THIRTY-NINE

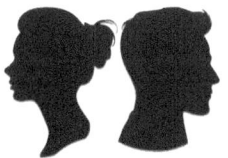

HIGHLANDS

Mother knocks on my bedroom door, "Dinner's ready." I stand, crack my back, and open it.

"Can I have it in my room?"

"But you haven't been out all day."

"Under deadline."

"Then of course. I'll have Carol bring it up."

It's been bothering me, so I say, "Mom, doesn't Carol have family, someone to be with over the holidays?"

"She's headed home on Christmas Eve. We're going out. Won't that be nice?"

"Not sure I am staying to Christmas," I say. Not sure I am staying one moment past finishing the manuscript but the setting has allowed me to get words on the page. Not sure how good they are but I will finish.

"We have weeks to worry about Christmas. But maybe …"

She touches my hairline. My roots are at least an inch long, maybe longer. I've stopped even trying to hide them from myself. When with her I've been wearing the thick band I use to wash my face but I ripped it off in frustration sometime earlier today and forgot to put it back on.

"A woman needs to be careful about letting herself go."

"It hasn't been important."

"Well, I have a scarf. One you can wear to dinner Christmas Eve or maybe we could find a little place to do a touch up."

I nod. I can make excuses for that later.

Hours later, when I walk into the well-appointed kitchen to wash my dishes, Sally Girl follows. She's barely left my side, as we are in an unfamiliar place and she seems to know that if she is not with me she has to be crated. It was a requirement of her coming. I didn't even know they made crates that big. But there was one in the huge SUV we drove here waiting for my girl. So hard to have her in it for hours so I gave her a little something to help her sleep.

After working for a few more hours I realize the house is quiet. John goes to bed early, so Mother does as well. Amazing how she is able to change her circadian rhythm for whatever husband she's on. But then again, she changed my name for every husband, and that seems more extreme. And it goes to show how I have always acquiesced to her that I haven't changed it back. I was born Bridget Rose—Sweetie's name, my mother's maiden name. I never had my biological father's name, and so be it. But I would like to find a way to be more of a Rose than a Stanton.

Speaking of Sweetie, she is so quiet, I'm afraid I let her slip away. I mean, she still talks to me, but it's in my voice I hear her, not hers. Like an echo of her in me. It's not the same. But given I'm living much more like a Stanton than a Rose, should I be surprised? I wonder if she is as disappointed in me as my mother is proud.

I had to lie. Told Mom I was under contract and the money

issues are all in the past. I'll figure out the rest later. It's done—I'm contractually bound, and I can't blame Richard. He did exactly what I asked, looked out for me as an agent should, got me what I needed. He did his part, and I did mine. I looked after myself as I always have.

I am safe. Sally Girl, who is eating crumbs under the table, is safe. And safety makes us happy, right? It has been my guiding star. So why do I feel so blah? Like all the colors have mixed together to make that icky brownish-gray. That's what my life feels like—drab. And I wonder if I will ever see color again.

———

I'm incredibly happy to be outside, regardless of the biting wind. It's already getting dark too early in whatever the hell time zone I'm in, which would explain the atrocious set times. And I'm still not done with my travel for fourteen measly lines.

At least I'm breathing outside air and feeling slightly better than before after talking to Gretchen during my layover in Atlanta. But she is encouraging me to get a therapist, not that she won't talk to me anytime I ask, but because her specialty is kids and I am not one anymore.

"These are adult problems, Josh. Ones you need to address or else."

"Or else what?" I ask.

"Or else you may never know what an amazing human being you are and what a glorious life this can be." This is coming from a person who has worked with seriously troubled kids her whole career. And all I have to do is look pretty.

I thought about that a lot on the plane. There are some parts of me, the physical parts, that I know are extraordinary, but she is right. How can I expect anyone to respect me when I don't even fully respect myself?

I'm waiting for the bus to the Isle of Sky that the production company arranged. I can't help but think, looking around, that unlike me, Bridget would fit right in here. With her precious upturned nose, and every third person has grayish eyes, but not like hers exactly. Actually, I just can't help thinking about Bridget. How things went from wonderful to wrecked in a heartbeat, leaving me with no idea where we go from here, if anywhere.

Another actor sits down next to me. You can tell. There is something about actors, like they are always in a scene.

She is pretty in that English way. That no-nonsense, got-good-cheekbones, serious kind of way.

"You too?" she asks.

And since we're acting. "Aye."

"You're not local."

"So obvious?"

"No one in this country is as tan as you. It's a goddamned crime."

"Josh Silva." I extend my hand.

"If that's a stage name, then well done. Sarah Callahan," she says, and shakes with a firm grip.

"It's the real thing: Joshua Anjo Silva."

"That explains your lovely color, but how'd you get cast in a Scottish period piece?"

"Bite your tongue. I'm half Scottish on my mother's side, but I live in Tampa." Then I add, "Florida."

I let go of her hand after possibly holding it too long. Testing, but as striking as she is, I feel not a shred of attraction. Not like when Bridge propositioned me, all feet squirming in the sand and pink cheeks and scattering of freckles. I shake the vision off.

"What's your part?"

"The Mourning Whore. No need for euphemisms, it's in the script."

I laugh.

"And what a script it is," I deadpan.

"Indeed." It is clear she feels the same.

"Well, then, I'll see you on the field," I say. "Alas, I will be dead."

"And I will mourn you. Have some experience there, coming off a long run as Ophelia in Inverness."

"So a *real* actor." That gets me a laugh.

This is what it can be like. You can meet someone and talk and not have a contractual relationship and, well, not be so fucking confused all the time.

"Ever worked on the stage?" she asks.

"Not worked. I minored in theater, but we had a fairly small stage. Once I played Fortinbras, though."

"Nice role. Tight, as they say. Our Fortinbras is an asshat, so if you want another gig before you return to *Tampa*"—she says it like it's a foreign food she's not sure she would like—"let me know. I'll have Laertes knock him off. My understudy would thank me for bringing you into the mix."

We're flirting. Easily. And I feel like a traitor.

"There she blows," she says, and sure enough a little white squat bus is pulling up with SPOTLIGHT PRODUCTIONS taped on the front. "Went all-out for the whore and the dead man," she quips.

"Aye."

She laughs. "Something not right about an actor from Tampa having that good of an 'Aye.' I hope it's not your only line."

The bus pulls up, smelling of diesel, and we gather our roller bags.

"Fourteen, if, and only if, aye is itself considered a line."

"Quite the star."

"Aye."

She is laughing and shaking her head as she steps up the short stairs in front of me. It could be this easy, talking for real, learning about each other. I bet after another fifteen minutes on that bench, she would know more about me than Bridge ever cared to ask.

Maybe it should be that easy. And there is nothing easy about being ghosted by someone you can't stop wanting to touch. I took it for granted that I could reach out at any time and feel that strange but right feeling whenever we even casually touched.

The bus jerks to a start, and I take out my phone for the too-many-times and go back over the last things we said to each other. When in a weak moment I texted her in the middle of the night.

Me: I owe you an apology

Bridget: You owe me nothing

Nothing since. My fault as much as hers as I didn't respond, because what do you say to that? And I feel every one of the thousands of miles away from her. And decide it's the worst feeling in the world—love. Wouldn't wish it on an enemy.

I look at Sarah; she smiles, and it is clear there is interest there, but I feel nothing.

FORTY

FLIRTING WITH DISASTER

I t's four a.m., and I have a call at six. But maybe it will work
for me. The exhaustion, since I've been on the battlefield for
days. Another kind of battlefield—one where I fight the urge to
call her, hear her voice, see how it's going.

But she's not asking me for help, and she's not wondering
about me.

Three hours later, after my last lines, I lie in a truly stunning
scene, if I ignore the guts pouring out of my body. Really
disgusting. But since I've already died, the acting is over. Now I
have to lie still while the star laments my loss. And even though
my eyes are closed, I can tell he is killing it—well, as much as he
can without a decent script, but no one asked me.

Yesterday I lay on set with my guts hanging out, waiting to
moan, for like forty minutes while the star argued with the
director about his lines, and it was all I could do not to revive
myself to agree.

"Cut."

Thank god. I take a deep breath and swallow. Blink my eyes.

"That's a wrap."

———

Over drinks that night with Sarah, we talk about careers and trajectories and inherent bias against abs and women, and got very drunk, which I rarely do. It has been a long time indeed since I've drunk this much. On the way to the elevator, I know I will be a perfect corpse in four hours, which is tomorrow's call.

We had such camaraderie that when she leans in just after the doors close, I am sluggishly surprised to find her lips touching mine.

"We're drunk," I say.

"I'm a Brit and can hold my pint."

Another kiss.

I try. I hold her head and lean into it. I let her press me up against the doors. Her hand slips beneath my shirt. I move mine to do the same. But like a robot. You do this, I'll do that. And I know if we continue, it would be robotic. She's a smart, alluring woman who clearly wants me, and I feel absolutely nothing.

Worse than nothing, I'm acting just to see if I *can* feel something for someone else ever again.

Suddenly sober, I step back. "You're partnered." She told me about her girlfriend over drinks. "And I am as well."

"I thought you said—"

"In here." I place my hand on my chest.

"Poor boy." Then she leans in and kisses my cheek.

The elevator opens to her floor. She holds the door, an invitation.

"See you on the set. I'll be the dead one," I say.

"I'll be the whore."

The door closes before I can correct her.

I slog back to my room and realize this situation is much worse than I originally thought. I thought I had fallen in love with a woman who was going to ghost me, disappoint me, and I would be hurt, but I would move on.

Now I wonder how long it will take until I can. And more terrifying still, if I will.

As I enter my room, my suitcase by the closet catches my eye, and I think, *Pack, go. You can win her back,* and the urge is so strong I sit on the floor with my head in my hands for a long time, trying to talk myself out of it. In the end, it is her silence that decides it.

I had left my phone in the room to keep from compulsively looking at it all night long. But all that waited for me was a picture from Nana and her crew with margaritas, of all things, toasting my "stardom," a few urgent texts from Sable about some opportunities and confirmation that payment had been received for the cover, and even one from Mink, saying the fence and landscaping would be done in the morning. But not one word from Bridget.

I take a shower and go to bed. The next day on set it feels like it is my heart that is outside my body, beaten and bloody, as I hold my guts.

FORTY-ONE

WITH MY GUTS HANGING OUT

"What are you about? Looking at a girl, are you? That face. So pleased with yourself," Sarah says when she joins me on the hill with two cups of coffee during a break in the filming. Things were back to normal with us after she apologized at breakfast. I said no need, that I was flattered. She said I was one of the good ones. But that word.

"No, really. What has you so downright pleased?"

"This." I show her the picture Mink sent me of Bridget's backyard.

"A fence? It is a very nice fence—good touch that extra bit on top. Very cottageporn."

"You think that is yardporn, what about this?" I show her one of the front yard with lime-green grass, the walk lined in jasmine, and a red rocking chair by the door where she can see the sea.

"So Josh lives in a perfectly cottageporn house?"

"Josh's …" Josh's what? "Someone I know does, and she has this beast of a dog that I kinda hate, so I built them a fence."

"You built a fence for a person you *know* who has a dog you hate?"

"Yes."

"That looks like a pricey fence."

"But now that person can leave that beast of a dog and know they are okay. And that beast of a dog can go outside and run and rip the heads off things and do what beasts do. Even, say, if she doesn't come home one night. And there is this feeding and watering system here." I show her another picture.

"Brilliant. But again, why?"

"Because I wanted to. Because it makes me happy."

"Josh Silva, I do believe this *person* makes you happy. I will go out on a limb and say this is not just any person. This might be *your* person."

I shake my head, and she pats me on the leg and asks, "Got anything on under that?"

She means the kilt, and I bark out a laugh.

"Skims. Want to see them? Everyone else has."

"Oh my sweet, so have I. Looked you up. Saw your covers. I'm reading one of them right now. *Spicy.*" Her eyebrows move up and down.

"I need the Dying Highlander and the Mourning Whore on set, pronto," comes from a bullhorn.

"Time to die," I say.

"Time to whore," she responds. "Let's both do our best work today. Won't it be fun to take our persons to this movie one day?"

"That would be fun." But I know it's not going to happen. It doesn't seem fair that I found my person just to lose her.

You could chase her? You know how to get her back.

And yes, certainly as a bedmate, because what we have in that department is incendiary, but I want more. Like Kayla implied, I'm ready to anchor someone and have a bond that can't be broken. Bridget clearly is not. She is avoidant and detached, almost heartless. How in the world did my heart fall for a person without one?

But no, that's not it; she has a heart. I just don't fit there. I'm not the one who keeps it beating, not after we get out of bed. I have to face the fact that I am not her person. Oldest story in the world. Wouldn't have movies without it. No grand gesture for me. No happy ending.

In the movies they never move on, not well. And if they do, it's never the same. And in this moment I agree with her, wish I'd never met her on that beach. That she had walked on by. Because those who say to love and lose is better than not loving at all are sadists.

The director sees me and says, "Perfect. Keep that face. Brilliant. Desolation."

So I use it. I writhe on the ground, holding in fake guts, but it is us that's dying.

I nail it. Best scene I ever shot. Because it is not an act. I'm actually dying inside.

When it's over, the costume artist comes over to take my picture so we make sure my guts look the same tomorrow. As she does, she whispers, "You're better than him." I know the him she means, the him that is the reason this movie is being made.

"Thanks," I say, spitting out the bag of blood that I burst at the end. "I'm good at dying."

"I've seen a lot of actors over the years, and dying is the hardest thing anyone will ever act. To get there, you have to let yourself feel it, and an ego like his will never let that happen. Think they are immortal, the stars, but you? You died on this set today—let yourself feel it—own it. You're good. What's your name?"

"Josh Silva."

"Josh Silva, I will say I knew you when."

"Thank you. Really. I needed that today," I say as I hand her my guts.

She goes to help me up, but I shake her off. She has her hands full.

"I'll give these back in the morning."

FORTY-TWO

WELL HELLO RED

As had become my habit, I head downstairs after Mom and John have gone to bed. I find an open bottle of red and pour myself a glass. Open the large glass doors to the deck and step outside, closing them behind me to keep the heat in.

It is cool, but not too cold, and the dark forest chirps and scratches and calls. I look out on the Blue Ridge Mountains, pressing into the distance. The moon's full, and under it, they look like waves, making me think of home.

A stick breaking below me has my heart racing. A huff and another stick breaks. I follow the sounds with my eyes, reminding myself that I'm fifty feet off the forest floor. Eyes flash yellow in the dark, reflecting the motion sensor lights below the deck that have just come on to reveal what I think is a fox.

It's not like any fox I've seen on TV. It's tall, and its tail is long and majestic and the color so bright. It stares at me. I don't move. The fox doesn't move. It looks up at me with reflective eyes and, I swear, judges me. That's what it feels like. Like that red fox is judging me. Then it flicks its tail dismissively and slips into the night.

I dream of the fox that night. It has a little vest and stands on two legs. And a pocket watch like the The Rabbit in Alice in Wonderland. I follow it into the forest but it drops to four legs and moves too fast for me. I try and keep up. Ignoring the briers that scratch at my face and limbs. But it's no use. The fox is gone and I am lost. I sit down to catch my breath and find I am before a still pool. Round in shape, the surface like glass. It seems to call to me. To look in, to see myself in it's reflection but I back away.

Sally Girl wakes me with howling. Even with the blanket I draped over the window she knows. I clip on her leash and walk her out onto the streets of this sleepy mountain neighborhood past monstrous houses thinking why didn't you look. What were you afraid to see?

———

That afternoon, I fine a *Steel Magnolia* kind of place with a hairdresser named Dot who has an opening. Her hands are gnarled, but she holds her scissors like she knows what she's doing.

"So what are we doing today?"

"I don't know."

"You really need to touch up the roots, but I don't have time for a dye job. Could you come back Thursday?"

"No dye. I want my hair."

"I see. Well, you have about an inch and a half of it."

"I know. If you cut it shorter, I could go get some dye at the drugstore until it grows out I guess."

"Hmph."

The noise lets me know she does not approve of this plan.

"Do you trust me?" she asks.

I have no idea what to say to that. I've known her four minutes. But I nod bravely.

"I'm going to give you a Mia Farrow. Your hair is a bit darker, more fiery than ginger, but I think it will be the cat's meow. Hold on, this might be distressing."

And it is. I gasp as huge clumps of hair fall around me. She works quickly, like a dentist. Like I might bolt from the chair. She talks nonstop to distract me.

"You see Mia Farrow, a very young Mia Farrow, had married Frank Sinatra, a bit of a pecker, but quite the looker. Anyway, as the story goes, he would not take Mia to see his children, the ones he had with Ava—Ava Gardner—you know of her, right?"

"Sure."

Oh my god, it's raining hair.

"They resented how young she was."

I'm trying to follow when a huge chunk of hair falls in my lap. I close my eyes.

"So Ava treated Mia abominably, and one day Mia was fed up with being treated like a child. She was about to do that scary movie, somebody's baby—too scary for me—but as the story goes, she got fed up and took scissors to her almost waist-length hair. The hair Frank loved. She did it herself—a wonder it came out so well. Although, I bet the studio had someone rush over to clean it up after Frank got a look. Bet he choked on his martini that night. Good for her, I say. Good for her."

She stops.

"Go ahead," Dot says, gesturing at the hand mirror in my lap.

An older woman under the dryer looks at me, smiling, nodding, encouraging, so I pick up the mirror. But like looking down when crossing a height, seeing all my dark brown hair all around me makes me dizzy. Like ripping off a Band-Aid, I pick up the mirror, do it quick.

Well hello, Red.

My eyes are brighter. No longer competing with my hair, which is barely more than an inch of fiery pixie. My freckles stand out across my cheeks. And it's like looking into the pool. It's what I think I would have seen if I had the courage to look last night in my dream. It's me.

"The bangs are a little pointy in the front." She touches them and says, "We'll get some Dippity-do and fix that right up. You look just like her, if I do say so myself."

Tears prick my eyes.

"Dot, I love it. You're a genius."

"You're a lovely girl. Now, you go tell your Frank to go to hell in a handbasket."

"How did you know?"

"Just a guess."

I stare into the mirror. "Dot, this cut is not to give me courage to tell off my Frank but to tell him the truth. About something hurtful. This cut is to give me the courage to try to get him back. And if not him, then me. Does that make sense?"

"Doesn't have to."

And as if the universe decides that moment to accept the loss of my hair which no longer seems to be a sacrifice to me, my phone rings. It's Kayla.

FORTY-THREE

FIGHT WITH A BOMB

"Well, hello, John. That's what they call them, right, the ones who pay for it?"

This is not going to be easy. I walk away from Dot, holding up a finger.

"Thank you for returning my call."

"Would you have stopped sometime today harassing my godparents' hotel staff if I hadn't?"

"Probably not."

"So what can I do for you?"

The question comes with so much sarcasm I almost hang up but instead I say, "I know what you think of me—"

"You don't. If you did, you wouldn't have called me. Bridget, what do you want?"

"I want to speak to Josh."

"So call him."

"It needs to be in person. Can you tell me where he is? There was this picture on Sable's IG of him somewhere green with rolling mountains—not Tampa. Do you know where he is?"

"Far, far away. And if his pictures to me are correct, hanging out with another whore."

"You're lying."

"*I* don't lie."

I fall into the chair at the hair-drying station because she has me there.

"Listen, I don't believe Josh to be what you think I do. I was confused the day you first saw me, confused and upset. I understand why you hate me. I have friends I would protect exactly the same way as you protect him."

"We are more than friends."

That takes me aback.

"So what? You're a thing? Going to get married one day?" My voice drips with sarcasm.

"Funny you'd say that; he asked me in Miami."

I stand. Start to pace.

"I don't believe you."

"I don't care."

"So then why don't you?"

"A hundred reasons."

"Like …"

"Like he is a brother to me, like he knows how much I want kids. Like—"

"He doesn't want kids?"

I don't know why I said it like that. *I* don't want kids.

"You stupid cow. I've never met anyone who wants them more. You know nothing about him, do you?"

"I know he shoots up anabolic steroids," I bark back.

At that she laughs, but an angry laugh, a very angry laugh. It makes me nervous. I pace back to the hair wash station and bite back.

"And *cow* is a bit below the belt don't you think?"

"Cow is perfect for a bovine that will stand in a field to drown while the water rises because she can't see what is *right before her fucking face*."

"And what, per chance, is that?"

Dot passes me with raised eyebrows. I hurry into the little pink bathroom.

"The stupidest reason in the world for why I can't marry Josh. The fucking stupidest reason there ever was."

"Which is?"

"Inexplicably, he loves you."

I'm speechless.

"You might try to get to know him or leave him the fuck alone because you have him in knots. Can barely concentrate on the set. And this is his biggest shot ever."

"Set?"

"Where have you been? He's on the Isle of Skye, shooting his first real part in a real movie. The biggest thing to happen to him in well—ever. After all the time you've spent together, how is it you do not know this?"

"He didn't tell me."

"Did you ask? Have you ever left your own little world long enough to give a shit about his?"

I stare at the toilet and know beyond a shadow of a doubt what I am.

"No."

"Wow. Didn't expect truth."

And the truth hurts.

I close the lid and sit down.

"You're right about me. I did think he … gave women sex for money, to help with their books. And I do think he has a problem with something or why the needles. And I know he likes me, but it's all mixed up, because I didn't know if it was me

313

or just acting—if he was only playing a part. I could have asked, and also, he could have shared. But I really do want to know him, and it seems you know him better than anyone. So please. Enlighten me."

"Not one fucking chance in hell. I'm wishing you screw up so bad he can get over you and find someone who deserves him. And have you ever screwed up? I spoke to him last night, and he knows. Knows you lied. Knows everything. How you used him to get what you needed. Promised all kinds of things—a byline, royalties—and then screwed him left, right, and center, as if that's all he was good for."

Oh, no.

"How?"

"He spoke to Sable."

I put my head in my hand. I feel like I'm going to be sick.

"I'm going to make this right."

"I assume that means you are going to leave him the fuck alone. Now lose my number."

"Wait!" I know she is going to hang up on me. "Wait, please. I'm so confused."

"You're a smart girl. If you need answers, start at the library."

Then she hangs up on me.

The *library?*

Dot knocks lightly on the door. "You okay, honey?"

"Yeah."

When I come out, she's cleaning up the mess, and I'm unmoored as she sweeps all that hair into a pan.

"Want to save a lock?"

"Nope. I'm done with her. Hey, Dot, where's the closest airport?"

When I walk in the door to pack, Mom looks aghast. Her countenance mars the put-togetherness of her perfect gray slacks and pale cashmere sweater, a holiday motif silk scarf around her neck. Even the heavy gold chain on her wrist sparkling with diamonds that match the carat and a half in each ear cannot compete with her look of utter—surprisingly, not disgust—but astonishment.

"What have you done?"

"What I should have done a long time ago."

She shakes her head, and I see it for what it is. That's fear in her eyes—not judgment. She's scared for me. And she has every right to be.

I step up to her. Take one French-polished nail in hand.

"You're right to look at me that way. Things are about to get messy. But Mom, safe—" I shake my head. "It might work for you—and I'll try to stop judging you for that—but not me. I need more. More everything. I can't do safe. It's keeping me barely alive."

She nods. Her nude pink lips pursed, *causing wrinkles* I hear in her voice. For she is even critical of *herself* in my mind. Then she takes both of my hands in hers.

"What do you need from me?"

"Your support. Your faith. But not your money. Not his money. What I need is your belief … in me."

Another nod. Takes me to the couch. We sit side by side by a roaring fire, and I tell her everything. Well, almost everything. Leave out that I watched us in the mirror and became the me I see. But I give her the broad strokes. Enough for her to understand what *we* meant to me.

And surprisingly, she does, and I wonder if she had this with the one who gave her me.

While I pack, she transfers enough miles to get Sally Girl and me home, and I take them, because how else am I going to do it? and technically it's not money.

She doesn't take me to the airport. They have dinner reservations. But she kisses my cheek and squeezes my hand so hard it brings tears to my eyes—not from pain—but how hard it is for her to let me go to likely be torn apart by the world.

But she does. She lets me go.

Sally Girl's already drowsy when I put her in the back of the Uber XL that is large enough for her crate.

I wonder how long Mom stood at the door after I left.

FORTY-FOUR

CUNNING LIKE A FOX

"Foxes are omnivores. They can live anywhere," I tell Kimberly on FaceTime, walking to my gate. "They're cunning. The females are known as vixens. Once they get something in their mouth, they don't let go. They have red hair and in folklore act as a disguise for female spirits."

"And why are we having a documentary on foxes?"

"Because I saw one. And I think Sweetie sent it. And it taught me something. Reminded me of something."

"And you think it was Sweetie because ...?

"The *hair*."

"So then you did your own hair—and again spectacular."

"Thank you." I find a seat by the gate and put in my earbuds. Kimberly is at home on her couch. *Home* is something I will not have very soon.

"And, Kimberly, they can live anywhere, on any continent but Antarctica."

"Is someone moving?"

"Probably me. But first, I need to figure out how to get out of my deal with Richard."

"Your publishing contract?"

"Not exactly."

"I'm so confused."

"I'm not." I'm in a crowded regional airport. Strangers everywhere. About to sell a house I love. "Everything is crystal clear."

"You're off your rocker."

"No. I'm cunning like a fox."

"Doesn't seem cunning to me. Flying home just to turn right around. Why didn't you leave Sally Girl with your mother. And what, pray tell, do you hope to accomplish with another trip to New York?"

"She'll be better at home. And if you can stay for just a few days then I can get myself back—or the version of me I was becoming when I got scared. Get the brave me back. The red-haired me. The fiery me. Somewhere along the twisty path of the last month, I managed to wake up to me. A me who can't believe she ever considered groveling to SCAB to get her job back, a me who can't believe I let strangers whose only concern is their bottom line talk me into sinking to rock bottom. I want the me who is brave enough to behave like a fool. That's what I get in New York. Hopefully. Me. Maybe for the first time."

"Well, if that's it, then you go. I'll be here to pick up the pieces when you come home ... or celebrate your triumph."

"We'll be home by six p.m., but I'll be headed to New York tomorrow."

"Quite the jet-setter."

"Mom gave me miles. I really had no choice but to accept them. She is probably already thinking up an important reason for me to rush off that she can tell her friends. But it was nice of her to transfer the miles."

Then they call my flight over the loudspeakers.

"About to board. See you soon."

And in the few minutes before we take off I text a former teacher turned real estate agent. She is thrilled to get the listing.

FORTY-FIVE

GRAND GESTURE PART 1

Every exterior light I own is on now, thanks to Kimberly.
And as soon as the Uber pulls into the driveway, tears
drop because there is only one person who would do this, only
one person who knows how much it means.

She finds me on the front walk, breathing in jasmine, finding
the lilac bushes sprouting bloom after bloom, a red rocking chair
I fall into to see the moon over the ocean across grass as delicate
as a golf green.

How?

When?

But I guess I've been gone long enough, because it's here.
Sally Girl is still a bit groggy from the sedative for the plane but
sniffing everything. Kimberly comes to stand behind me.

"Girl."

"I know. It's the grandest of gestures. It's"—I look up at her
—"I haven't even texted in more than a week. I left him in
Miami. I am—"

"Speechless."

I nod.

"And honey, you haven't seen the back."

I look up, wide-eyed.

By the time I have walked the Frank Lloyd Wright-inspired fence, the food and watering station, the letter from Mink's Fence and Yard explaining every plant species and their water and nutrient needs—and that each was chosen for color, scent, and specifically because none are toxic to canines.

There is even a special plot of grass that they "seeded" with her feces that will encourage Sally Girl to use that area to relieve herself, with a sprinkler self-cleaning system.

They even put in a doggie door—or horse door, as they call it —off the laundry room. Sally Girl is in heaven.

MINE. MINE. MINE.

Marking everywhere. Already leaving a prize for the cleaning system.

This must have cost a fortune. And since I'm giving back the money, I can't possibly pay him back. At least not until after the closing. The agent I agreed to list with will be thrilled. Josh really upped the curb appeal.

I pull out my phone. Kimberly puts her hand on my arm and, with her other hand, holds out a credit card.

"In person."

I book a next-day flight, promising to repay her somehow. She just kisses me on the cheek and heads home.

In the middle of the night, I wake up. Sit up in bed. Mind churning.

Instead of dialogue running through my head, as so often happens when I'm writing, what comes to me, what I know beyond a shadow of a doubt, is *I have to go to the library.*

I never get back to sleep. I listen to the crickets outside and Sally Girl snoring, and with the window open, the Jasmine scent subtly swirls in the air with the peonies blooming under my bedroom window. They are a deep shade of pink, which along with lilac has quickly become one of my favorite colors. And in these quiet moments, my house has never felt more like a home. Even if only for a day. The realtor hasn't even seen it but says in this neighborhood it will go quick.

I look over at the untouched half of my bed. I don't even need to pull out my phone to see him in the half-moon light, head on his hand, his eyes shining, a crooked smile turning up rose-colored lips. Dark brows, deep shadow that will be soft no matter how sharp it looks, high cheekbones, strong jaw, single dimple, perfect fucking ears. My god, he has the most perfect ears. I whisper, "I'm coming."

You will be.

I swear it is his voice.

I pack while it's still dark, make sure Sally Girl has everything she needs until Kimberly comes by in the afternoon, check to see when the University of South Florida library opens, and I am waiting at the door when it is unlocked.

Joshua A. Silva has a master's thesis, *The Effect of Routine Sustained Sexual and Physical Activity on Abnormal Male Testosterone Levels*. I copy every page.

On the flight to New York, I learn Josh's master thesis is about himself. I learn more in the introduction than I have in all the weeks we have known each other.

He put it all out into the world—all his struggles, all his fears—in the name of science. He made himself into a lab rat and experimented on his body to help others with diseases that raise testosterone rates to unhealthy levels. He was looking for a way to manage the condition, particularly to help preteens to avoid the experiences he had. Which he lists dispassionately with bullet points:

- explosive anger
- violent behavior
- self-harming behavior (e.g., cutting, punching walls, headbutting)
- sexual exploitation
- sexual cravings at a very young age (eleven)
- high pain threshold
- excessive masturbation (can also be treatment if shame cycle is addressed)
- self-hate

I find out his father died in his forties of a cancer associated with high testosterone. His mentally and physically abusive father who exhibited "symptoms of an illness he was never diagnosed with." He dedicated his thesis to his grandmother, who never gave up when it came to finding him help.

His type of excessive testosterone disorder is so rare and fluctuating that it took years for him to be diagnosed. He produced so much so young, he looked like a full adult at thirteen.

That I knew.

He's been taking intravenous medications to reduce his testosterone since he was sixteen.

When I read that, I want to slap myself in the face. In Miami never even looked at the medicine in the black zippered case; I just jumped to conclusions. I am more like Kayla's view of me than I'm comfortable with.

And the gut punch—his words, not mine—the medicine is making him sterile. He wants kids. A lot of them. I pack that up and put it away for another day.

To avoid the drugs, he tried diet, different physical activities, different duration and frequency of sexual encounters—so many things—but eventually he found the "prescription." Proved his premise, if only on himself, that "sustained physical activity combined with regular sexual acts—regular being frequent, almost daily—assist in regulating excessive testosterone production." And taking sugar out of his diet seemed to help as well.

In his concluding chapter, he discussed how early on, he attempted to interest the medical community in a real trial, but he was unable to get funding or find an institution willing to test his hypothesis.

They shut him down.

He sacrificed so much, made himself a guinea pig, and they wouldn't even listen— dismissed him.

Just like me.

I'm in an exit row, and I want to pull the lever.

He has been objectified since he was in seventh grade.

Sexually exploited starting in eighth.

By tenth grade, he had a record and then an eighteen-month stint in juvie.

He needs partners like some of us need the pharmacy, so he never considered a relationship. The effect on a sustained partnership, the demands. The many partners who objectify him seem to serve his purposes best. Solo sexual acts helped when young but are no longer fully effective.

Then I realize *I* want to be his medicine.

I want him to be mine.

MINE.

FORTY-SIX

JUST ONE RICHARD

"Good morning, Bridget," Richard says when I walk into his office. I didn't even stop at Yvonne.

"Sorry I don't have an appointment."

"I would be shocked if you did. Where is my book?"

"Thank you."

"For what?"

"For everything. For picking me back up and sending me out the door with a mission, a plan. For sticking with me through everything. For all of it. Thank you."

"My pleasure," he says.

"We shall see."

He narrows his eyes.

I sit across from his desk.

"First, I think when a career author who has made untold dollars for everyone involved has an issue, their publisher should cut them some slack and help them out, rather than pile on the pressure. And I would like to assist said publisher in doing just that. I would like to suggest they push her book to fall, something that is done all the time—pushing a release date.

And publish our book in its stead in the spring. I'm asking you to fight for this book. I want the slot. I want the advance. I want the royalties. I want a career. And you and I both know this collaboration I have with Josh is astounding, miraculous, singular."

He lets out a breath and shakes his head.

"Much of what you say is true. Your work together is, frankly, stunning. And you have a point about my author. Trust me, I tried many things before this solution was presented. But it's done."

I brace myself for his shock.

"Before I say what I have to say, this is all my fault. If I had given you the information you needed, if I had talked to you about my offers and plans, we would not be here today. But, Richard, it's not too late. I have the manuscript, and I've made a decision. I won't publish the book without Josh on the byline."

"Bridget, you're under contract."

"I'll breach. Let them sue me. Let the world know it's not just women who are objectified in this world, that in romance it is the men, the beautiful men, that bring us to beautiful books. Readers love their cover models, no one more than Josh Silva. I wonder how they would feel to know he has been pushed out. Stolen from—"

Richard leans in. "Now, let's not—"

"Let's. Richard, I couldn't publish this book under someone else's name if I wanted to. It's not just my book anymore. The pacing—his. The spice—fucking his. The plot, the characters— we made them up together. And furthermore"—I take a deep breath—"I don't want to. I would rather it never see the light of day. I will not be that person. I will lose the house, lose the deal, lose it all before I am the kind of person who fucks over a friend. And I know you talked to Sable. Thanks for the heads-up."

"I'm your agent. She was making demands. I needed to protect you."

"From this, you can't. Those scenes—they are us. How could I ever hurt the man who gave me those moments? They gave me myself. I don't know how or why, but sex with Josh—physical intimacy on a level I never thought possible—gave me … me. And I don't give two shits who knows it."

I take a breath. How can I explain to him all that Josh has come to mean to me. I stand and point to the far wall. "Richard. All of my bottles. Every one of them, have his name on them."

"I see," he says softly.

"Do you? Do you really?"

"Oh, I see. Oh, I *see*." He reaches for the robin's-egg blue sticky notes that always sit on his desk and scribbles, one after another, until there are five, six, seven stuck to the desk and he is still writing. Clearly he has an idea, a plan. I hope it's a good one.

"I have to go. Call me if it works."

"It will work. You're brilliant!"

Now he is pacing, mumbling, calling out for Yvonne.

"Richard, you okay? I've got to go. I have to explain it to him. Just so you know, I am breaching my contract the moment I land. No more lies."

"Go. Go. Go get him. Yvonne!"

I roll my bag out, passing her in the hall. Hear Richard call, "I need publicity. I need marketing!"

FORTY-SEVEN

GRAND GESTURE PART 2

I t took another nine hours, but I find myself on the grounds of a film production. It is just like that scene in *Notting Hill* when Hugh Grant crashes the set where Julia Roberts is acting. But I am no Hugh Grant. There is no music building in the background, setting up the moment their eyes meet. There is even a guard at the gates.

"She's with me," Sable says from behind him.

"How did you know?"

"Someone calling themselves 'George' texted me. Told me to tell you," and she pulls out her phone to read from the screen. "Love makes fools of us all. It's natural, inevitable, and most often a little ridiculous. Go get your Richard." She looks back up to me. "I don't exactly know how I feel about this, but regardless you have to wait until they wrap."

"Where is he?"

She points.

I run.

"Bridget!" she calls out after me.

I see a person I assume is the director talking to the person I know is the star—seen him in half a dozen films—but that's not what has me running. It's who's standing with them. Who stops me in my tracks.

Josh is in period boots and a green-and-blue tartan kilt and nothing else. Scar on full display, holding a long sword, and he is the most beautiful fucking man who ever walked this earth. The midday sun shines down on him, his eyes stand out even at this distance, and he completely eclipses the star.

I take out my phone, find the song, and hit Play.

I hold my iPhone in the air, horizontal, with both hands, hoping he will understand.

I feel like a complete and total dork. The bloody men, even some dead ones on the ground, watch me as I walk through them.

My hands are shaking, but I'm committed. The director yells, "It won't work, you fool. He is the body, not the brains."

But the asshole is pointing to *my* body, to *my* person, and something snaps.

Just then Josh, hearing the music, turns my way.

———

I know the director is speaking to me, but I have no idea what he is saying, because a fair pixie, ethereal and wondrous, with sunrise hair and storm cloud eyes is walking toward me.

I must be dehydrated. Hallucinating. Because it's Bridget—with a phone over her head, playing the song. The midpoint song. The ride home song. The grand gesture song.

And then it dawns on me, Bridget is making the grand gesture. In Scotland. On a set. In front of hundreds. Someone is filming it.

I laugh.

I can't help it.

She's the most beautiful John Cusack anyone has ever seen.

By the time she reaches us, the director has noticed.

"Who ordered the fairy?" he yells out to no one in particular. "Listen, you …" she starts in.

Oh shit. "Bridget, no!"

But she puts her hand on my chest to stop me from getting in the way of what looks to be a rant coming on.

"You … you director person. If I *were* a fairy, I'd turn you into a newt. How do you get off talking to him that way? He is not just a body. And if anyone would know that, it's me. Shit, when I met Josh I was just looking for a dick. I mean, my agent thought I should go for an entire satchel of them, but then he became my person. Do you know what that is like? To have someone become your person? Nothing really happens until you tell them. Nowhere seems right until they are there. You long for them in a way that makes you think you have the flu, like, you are sick to your stomach when they are gone. Even when they should hate you and you don't know what to do, and when they build fences for dogs they don't even like—beautiful fences, but not half as beautiful as they are, and they are talented, you twat. So talented! They can plot so tight it seems like the next thing is a foregone conclusion and then come up with a twist that has you shaking your head and reading on, and our novel comes out this year from the biggest of the big five *and* he's on the cover. He is the whole package: a model, an actor, a novelist—even a brilliant screenwriter, something this place probably needs."

"And you are?" the director asks.

"Bridget Rose. Well, not yet, but soon to be." Then she turns to me. "And this is my co-author and my person. My Richard. I only need one."

As grand gestures, it's the best I've ever seen.

"Bridget Rose," I say. "You had me at STD."

She jumps. I catch, thanking god for nonsequential shooting, because if she had shown up yesterday, I would have had to drop my guts. And I would have. I will always catch this woman. Her legs are around my waist so tight I can barely breathe, her arms around my neck, squeezing like she is never letting go. Like I would let her.

"I love the hair," I whisper in her ear.

———

Clean sweat. Hard body. Soft words. My person. My Richard.

And all I want to know right now, surrounded by bloody strangers, is does he have anything on under that kilt.

And then some annoying person invades my bubble of bliss. Someone is tapping on my shoulder. I do not let go of Josh but turn my head.

"I like you. Not on this film, but I like you. We should talk. By the way, how did you get on my set?"

Josh pats my thigh, and I decide it might be embarrassing for him to wear me like a baby koala, so I slide down.

He clears his throat and places me in front of him. Blocking their view of him. I feel why and smile.

"I lied. Said I would wait until the end of filming to find him. His agent helped me," I say to the director.

"You lied for me?" I hear Josh ask from behind me.

I turn just my head because his arms are binding me to him and say, "I lied *to* you. For that I am so sorry. But yes I lied *for* you as well. I'm afraid there is no line I wouldn't cross for you."

"Good line," says the star, who so far has been quietly watching the scene unfold. "So you're a writer. We need one of those on this set."

"Enough already! That's a wrap. That's the fucking day." The director stomps off toward a trailer.

"Sorry. We've been arguing about the script for months. Seriously, I've tried, but it is not my forte."

"He's your writer," I say. "If I know him, he has already rewritten this scene in his head three times, and it will make you look better than even *you* can imagine."

Josh's hand grips mine, like he's telling me to stop.

I turn back to him. "You have, haven't you? And I bet it's breathtaking. I bet I'll cry. I bet it is the grandest of the grand gestures."

"Nothing will ever be grander than you, Bridge."

That nickname. What it does to me.

"You've rewritten the whole scene?" the star asks.

Josh nods, looking scared, a face I have never seen on him. I squeeze his hand.

"Make it work," is all the star says, holding out his script. "I'll deal with him"—he jerks his head in the direction the director went—"but help me, please."

Josh nods from behind me.

"You've got till morning." He hands Josh a pen. A Uniball. Nice clicker.

I step aside. Whatever Josh is experiencing has scared his Richard into submission. I look up at him.

He says, "I'm fine."

He takes the script and walks across the field to an open place with a big tree and no dying men on it, which is good, because all the fake blood and guts are making me a little sick.

"I'm fine. I'm fine. I'm fine."

He just keeps repeating it.

I hear myself, but I'm not in my body. I'm holding the pen, but I can think of only two words.

I keep saying them. Bridget is asking if I'm okay.

I tell her over and over I'm fine.

She seats me by a tree.

"I'm fine.

"I'm fine."

I have to find a way out. But I'm on autopilot.

"I'm fine.

"I'm fine."

Then she takes my face in her hands. Stares right into my eyes. I hold them. They are here. She is here.

"You are more than fine—you are mine. Do you hear me? I am right here. I'm going nowhere. You are fine, Joshua Anjo Silva. You are better than fine—you are real."

I blink.

"Mine."

I nod.

She sits back on her heels and asks, "Now what do you need? Earbuds, a song, silence, food, coffee, liquor?"

"Just you."

She sits behind me against the tree. I lean against her, her knee up to press the script against. But I'm blocked. I have been given the break of a lifetime, and I am completely blocked.

Then she reads the lines out loud. As she does, new lines come to me. I scratch them out. Then she reads the new lines and more come. More scratching. It goes like this, time nonexistent, only me and dying men and our chief acknowledging our sure death to come.

She starts to cry, but I can't stop scratching.

FORTY-EIGHT

INSATIABLE

I sit with him against that tree until dusk, which comes early and fast. The star brought us a blanket and a flashlight. Josh didn't even look up.

I was right. He's probably been rewriting this script since the first day he saw it, and now he is letting it flood out. He's moved from the battle scene, jumping around. I can't keep up.

He doesn't ask me any questions, doesn't bounce anything off me.

This is a solo project.

Then without preamble, he stands and pulls me with him until I'm being carried, the script against my spine, to a canvas tent on the edge of the dark and empty battlefield.

It's part of the set. The furniture is medieval, the pallet covered with actual furs. The brazier is still warm. He loads logs on top. Then turns to me.

I look up into his heart-stopping face, and he smiles like he has been blind and is seeing for the first time. It is overwhelming, his gaze. I let it wash over me. Then the script hits the wall. The flashlight hits the floor, and my feet are swept out from underneath me. My back on the fur.

He drops the kilt. And he's bare underneath. I smile, communicating, *Dedication*. His smile responds, *You have no idea*.

He strips me slowly by the light of the fallen flashlight. His bright eyes on mine. His hands everywhere. He touches me gently, like a work of art. Like he needs to test that all is well, there are no chips, and I go from cold to on-fire on top of those furs. Until like a switch, suddenly we're both ravenous for the taste of each other's skin.

I lose all sense of self, of propriety, even humanity. I scratch at him; he moans at me. I tug him where I want him. He growls; I cry out his name, again and again, and still, it's not enough. It will never be enough. We will die here, devouring each other in this place out of time.

When I finally succumb to sleep I'm stretched out on my belly, he's still inside me, pressing in again and again.

I dream of a fire blazing, a circle of beings dancing around it. Of joining them until my feet bleed. When I wake in the night, my head lays in his lap, the script in his hand. The sound of scribbling. But any movement from me and the script hits the wall and we begin all over again. Can one die from pleasure?

Scrambling from prone to wrap around his sitting form, rubbing myself against his cock that remains ever ready to thrust into me. I ride him wantonly—without shame or reservation. I discover all my wants and take them out on him. And he lets me until his wants pull me onto his face. His cock, his thigh, his abs. I come on every part of him. I drench him in me.

I had no idea anything could be this powerful. What need, what want, could surpass this?

Later, when distant voices join the continued noise of his scribbling, he goes to get us coffee.

I lie alone and realize all my secrets, all my wants, all my self —no matter how inscrutable, implacable, insatiable—all this is me.

And I am just fine with that.

Better than fine.

I think I might just be in love ... with myself.

FORTY-NINE

MAY DAY IN MANHATTAN

"Our next guests just came from a special event at the Flying Buttons Romance Bookstore to celebrate the release of *Scarred*—a best seller in preorder before even a single hardback could leave the shelves. Bridget Rose," I wave shyly. "And Josh Silva."

The clapping is loud. The hooting really loud.

We sit on the red couch, holding hands as the camera pans our way. This used to make me nervous, but we are midway through the whirlwind publicity tour spearheaded by Richard and Sable. Individually, those two are a force to be reckoned with; together they are The Force.

They said it was easy once the grand gesture in Scotland went viral, then dancing at La Candela hit the socials. But when me jumping Josh in the yellow dress at MIA dropped, well, everything went a little bonkers.

"Congratulations, Bridget and Josh! Honored to have you here on *Scarred*'s launch day, and what a launch!"

"Thank you. We're honored to be on the red couch," Josh says.

"So, Bridget, you took a pen name for this book. Can you tell us why?"

"No, Rose is my real name, the name I was born with. My prior novels were published under a former name."

"Well, Rose is certainly a romance author's name. And I hear your prior novels are running up the charts as well. You have an amazing breadth of work for one so young."

"Thank you. And I agree—about the name—but I didn't choose it as much as the internet wants me to have done so."

Josh squeezes my hand.

"Rose is my Sweetie's name—my grandmother—and my mother's maiden name. I am proud to own it."

"And even though I know you have answered this question many times, the audience is dying to know. Is it really you two in the book?" She whispers the last bit, like we should be ashamed. We are not.

"Yes. The sex is real. But, of course, we kept some for ourselves."

"Or for the sequel? Tell me there's a sequel."

"No, just for us. Some moments will always be just ours," Josh says.

"Well, that's a lot of exposure. And speaking of, Josh, that cover!"

I know they are showing it behind us because there is an involuntary gasp from the studio audience.

"You think that's breathtaking?" I wink to the crowd.

Nervous laughter erupts.

"So, Josh, what has it been like, not just being on the cover, but writing what's inside?"

He looks at me. "It's been amazing. A dream. Working with Bridget, with someone I love."

I can't help the surprise on my face. Not that he loves me—

he's been showing me every day since Scotland—but that he said it. Now. Here? He looks scared. I squeeze his hand.

"I'm sorry, Bridge. I shouldn't have. Not here," he whispers, but with the mike on his collar, everyone hears every word.

The host looks between us. "Wait? Is this the first time you've said those words to her?"

But he's speaking only to me.

"It just came out. But you've known. You must have known. Since at least midpoint. And it seemed more important to show you. But, yes, I love you so much. You've broken me—wide open."

Tears glisten in his eyes. The audience is so quiet, I can hear my breathing.

I smile at this extraordinarily beautiful-hearted man.

"I don't love you." I shake my head.

A gasp from the assembled audience, but my words are for an audience of one.

"It's too small a concept. I'm a writer, I know words, and those three can't encompass what I feel when I'm with you. I don't *need* you, either. I'm strong enough on my own. But you were the very first person to know me, maybe even before I knew myself. The very first person I could *be* myself with. And letting my body make the calls with you, trusting my feelings, my intuition, my drive, my *passion*, getting out of my oh-so-crowded head, you—somehow, you were the one safe place in this world where I allowed myself to discover who I am."

A smile breaks across his face. It's one I've never seen and by far my favorite because I put it there.

"Not just that I like sex—I do, I love sex with you! Slow burn be damned—we're wildfire, and I never want to stop burning."

"Bridge."

343

The heat in that one word. All the lights, the people, the world disappears.

"Let me finish. So, no, three words are not enough, because I love who I am when I'm with you. There is no room to worry about even one little thing when we are working together, being together, living together, because my life is so full of life there is no room for anything else. Joshua Anjo Silva, you enliven me. Like from the Latin root, 'in life,' I am *in life* with you."

He leans in, his forehead touching mine.

"That's the word," he whispers.

I nod.

"Yes. I do believe I enliven you too." He leans back, shaking his head, and smiles the you-have-no-idea-what's-coming-woman smile. "One touch, one look—that very look and a thousand others—you bring me to life."

He blinks. A tear falls. The crowd lets go of their collective breaths.

"I think that might have been the grandest of grand gestures," the host says, "and once again, it's being filmed live. Bridget and Josh, is there any part of your relationship that is still private?"

In one move, he stands and swoops me up.

"Sorry," I say, laughing nervously over his shoulder. "He likes to move me about sometimes. Which you'd know if you read the book," I shout out as I'm taken into the wings.

"Well. Okay," the host says behind us.

We barely make it to the dressing room.

When we finally emerge, no one is unhappy and "You enliven me" is trending.

We walk away from it all, onto the streets of Manhattan on the most glorious May Day that has ever existed. Josh is eighty feet tall in Times Square.

"That's one big scar," I say as we lean up against the building to take him all in. I'm not even the littlest bit jealous of the innumerable people that have seen Josh's special pointing-to-the-promised-land scar on this big screen or on the tiny e-book thumbprint.

What I feel is something very different.

Pride.

I did this.

I stood my ground, and no one, least of all the publisher, is complaining now. And I get to trace that scar with my tongue anytime I want—so let them look. Let them see. Let them dream. Because it turns out lust to love sells even when it's the co-authors' nonfiction story.

Although, Jess and Antonio's second-time-around romance is being well received, and not just for the light-your-pants-on-fire cover.

We kept the title, *Scarred*, kept Jess after shortening it, and Josh named our hero, Antonio, after his father. We realized in rewrites everyone is scarred.

Of course in the book, the HEA conquers all. But for the real Josh and Bridge, we're just RFHFN—really fucking happy for now—and riding the wave of not only a spectacular release but a movie deal in the works. They haven't determined the rating; Sable wants straight-to-streaming to avoid censorship.

Do I feel vulnerable now that everyone knows the sex in the book is real? Sure. But somewhere along the way, I decided I didn't care who knew my secrets, whether they be my sexuality or my wounds. Josh has always been comfortable in his skin, but putting out there his mental and physical health struggles has been courageous.

Of course, to get it done on time, we had to spend a lot of time together. So much so, Josh moved in. And our insatiable appetites evened out his testosterone. Or maybe it was something else. He is talking to his doctor about it—actually two doctors, as he's seeing a therapist now. As am I. But whatever it is, he's needing fewer and fewer shots.

So it turns out that Richard was right. All stories *are* love stories, even the stories about stories.

"It really is big," I say. "The enormity of it cannot be overstated. Seriously, up there it's like five-feet long."

"That might hurt."

I punch his side. "You know what I'm talking about. No more prevaricating. You promised. How did you get it?"

During edits, he refused to tell me, saying it would change my view of him *and* the story. I made him promise he would tell me on launch day, so it is time to fess up.

But suddenly I'm worried it might be something so traumatic that it is wrong to make him tell. I decide to give him an out.

He's leaning back, one foot against the theater wall, looking like an actual dream in low-slung jeans and a dried-to-within-an-inch-of-its-life black T-shirt—his uniform for appearances. I mentally pinch myself. Then take his soft five-o'clock shadow in hand and turn his face to me.

"You don't have to tell me. You don't have to tell anyone. Not if you don't want to."

He kisses my nose. "Trust me, I don't plan on putting it on a billboard."

I take Bridget by the hips and pull her bodily to me, pressing her against the subject she is dying of curiosity to know the origin of, amazed by this woman, amazed by her bravery and that she is mine, and prepare to tell her what everyone wants to know. Because if there's anyone I'm willing to tell, it's the fiery redhead in front of me. We're partners, after all.

———

From the look on his face, I think I'm about to get one of those kisses you see in the movies. The ones on busy streets that make you sigh, but he leans in and whispers what I thought I might never know.

When he's done, I look up at him. Ask his barely blue eyes, "Really?"

"Yep."

Then I laugh. I can't help it. I can't stop. It's too ridiculous.

"I'll never tell a soul," I say through laughter.

I can't stop until he gives me one of those kisses you see in the movies. The bending-backward kisses. The kind that strikes you with awe when you see someone else do it. The kind where you hang on for dear life when it's your turn. The kind that makes you realize this *is* life.

A deep sound moves through his body, turning mine molten. And unlike in the movies, there is no one to say cut. We have nowhere to go and nothing to do but live out our own fucking happy for right this fucking now.

Who knows where it will lead? what we will end up meaning to each other—as partners, lovers, co-creators—what we might create together. Where might we live? What might we do?

We don't talk about the future and family, not yet; we're too fucking happy to be in the present and have too much healing to do. But we also have no more secrets.

He pulls me up from the dip. Looks down at me, amused.

"Bridge. Your mind. So loud. You're distracting me from a *really* great kiss. Just stop."

"Make me."

A smile breaks across his face, so bright it could light this city for a year. And he swings me out, to music only we can hear, and in the middle of a busy Times Square—we dance.

ACKNOWLEDGMENTS

To the women writers of Atlanta who retreat with me—Mayra, Kimberly, Gilly, Lauren, Jessi, Rachael, Elizabeth, Jo, Carrie, Vania, Marie, and Mary Ann—thank you for years of writing retreats, even if I know I was only invited for my fire-starting skills and tarot readings :). Thank you for showing me the power of writing communities. A special nod to Vania for inventing the literary T-shirt swap, and to Mary Ann for the Shakespeare shirt that sparked *A Satchel of Richards*—this book wouldn't exist without you. I owe you a *really* nice satchel!

Marie Marquardt, my little sis and first reader—thank you for that all-caps "DEFINITELY" text exactly when I needed it. And for cheering me on that first morning in the mountains when all I had was Richard's quips and floating heads. I am deeply grateful for your love, support, and publishing expertise.

Allison Capps - Cover and interior book design extraordinaire. You have been game from the very start, when I was just figuring out my vision for Periwink Press. For collaborating in person on the cover, logo, and those silhouettes that somehow brought this story to life—for your impeccable design taste and for pushing back when needed, thank you!

Kate Orsini, book-to-film whisperer—you made this story sharper and braver, and our friendship has been one of the best surprises of this process.

Kimberly Hunt, developmental and line editor—your kindness, competence, guidance, and project management skills kept me sane.

Dayna Reidenouer, copyedit queen—you somehow made me a better person during the length of a copyedit. Thanks for always giving it to me straight!

To my niece, Bella, for making ASOR's Spanish cool, and one hell of a night in Little Havana!

Thanks to MindBuck Media—Jesse Glenn, Emily Keough, Deborah Jayne, Hannah Richards, and Bryn Kristi—for championing my tiny press with patience, creativity, and enthusiasm.

Special thanks to the Irish Wolfhound Association of the Mid-South for letting me meet their pups—one of whom inspired Sally Girl. (All Sally Girl's special needs are hers alone. To learn more about this extraordinary breed, reach out to the experts at the Irish Wolfhound Association of the Mid-South (donate if so moved) or the IWCA).

To my long-haul companions on this wild, ten-year writing/publishing journey:
  The Octapussies—Susan, Amy, Shelly, Kate, Katy, Kendra, and Gwen—thank you for always having my back!

To my mom, Elizabeth Friedmann, a talented writer and editor to emulate. Whose unwavering support kept me going no matter where my writing took me.

To my sister, Carroll Ann (Prashanti) Friedmann, a writer, editor, and evolutionary astrologer. For the unique support you gave me when *only you* could, thank you from the depths of my heart.

To my son, Jackson—thank you for agreeing to *never read my romances*! Love you so much.

Aaron—thank you for every hour. (Feel free to have a field day with this one ;)

And to my husband, Britt, thank you for bearing all the hours, so very many hours at the keyboard and conferences and retreats—for all the time I was away. I do love you so.

ABOUT THE AUTHOR

Having resisted the siren call longer than her writer siblings, Lee Taylor finally conceded and ten years ago wrote her first novel. It was not this one. As an Aries rising with a Virgo moon, this daughter of a writer and editor thought it only natural to start a small publishing house to share her work, and Periwink Press was born.

The literal path to her creative space has her stone-hopping a stream and winding through one of the most bewitching forests in the Appalachians. She can be found most mornings before daybreak in her "Yome Sweet Yome" (think "yurt" but so much better), loving all the tropes, particularly the ones she turns on their heads.

When not writing or hiking, Lee travels the country for a day job she loves and is always on the lookout for an indie bookstore. And if the store is romance only, all the better.

A Satchel of Richards is her debut novel.